This book is dedicated to myself for being able to thrive in the toughest year of my life.

TRY OVER

JILL BRASHEAR

PART I

Aloha

____

Chapter 1

____

Penny

SO MUCH FOR PARADISE.

Hawaii looked nothing like the pictures in the pamphlet. Penny had been expecting the airport to be a tiki-style structure with a welcoming line of women in grass skirts handing out leis, but it looked like any other airport Penny had seen.

There was nothing but black tarmac and a low, modern building in the distance. Hot, humid air pressed down on her, and the stench of jet fuel drifted along the tarmac.

She wasn't impressed. She'd spent the last six months saving for the plane ticket, and she couldn't help feeling disappointed. All those movies she hadn't gone to, all the canned soup she'd eaten, all the times she'd hand-washed her stockings to make them last instead of springing for a new pair... It suddenly didn't seem worth it.

"Oh, my gosh! It's beautiful!"

Penny turned to look at Lou, her roommate and best friend, who viewed the world through rose-colored glasses—and often from behind a camera lens.

"Put that thing away." Penny tugged on Lou's arm, dislodging the camera from her face. "We'll look like tourists."

"We are tourists."

"We don't have to look like them." Penny shrugged out of her jacket, sweat already beading on her brow. "What's there to take a picture of, anyway?"

Lou clicked the button a few times before lowering her camera. "Don't you see that palm tree over there?" She gestured toward the distance. "It looks sooo cool against the backdrop of the airport." Her forehead creased. "Mr. Tanaka was right about black-and-white film. Color might not do it justice."

Penny swept her gaze across the tarmac. Sure enough, a lone palm tree had sprouted next to the airport entrance. Penny squinted at the tree, trying to see it from Lou's perspective, but she wasn't a photographer. Neither was Lou, not officially. She worked as a bank teller, but no one would know it from the way she handled her camera like a professional.

A stiff breeze rolled across the tarmac, stirring the heavy air with the scent of sea salt. Excitement filled Penny's chest as she thought of the week ahead filled with sun and sandy beaches.

After months of picking up shifts waiting tables in addition to her job at the dance studio to afford a plane ticket to Hawaii, Penny was ready to relax. And maybe have an adventure.

Penny's cousin Henry, who lived in Hawaii and was picking them up from the airport, could always be counted on for a good time. They had stayed close after he moved to Hawaii to take a job as a stuntman on a television show. Even though she hadn't seen Henry in a few years, Penny knew they would pick up right where they'd left off.

She scanned the crowd for Henry, looking for his red hair that was nearly the same shade as hers, but her gaze skidded to a stop at a tall, powerfully built man towering above the others in the crowd. Her breath hitched as her gaze dropped over him. She'd never seen someone so incredibly masculine. His face had been sculpted by a master, with chiseled cheekbones, a straight, proud nose, and a wide mouth. He had bronzed skin, kissed by the sun, and dark hair that skimmed the tops of his mountainous shoulders. His biceps were nearly as big around as her waist.

Dark sunglasses covered his eyes, but she could feel his stare like a trace of fire across her skin. Goose bumps rippled down her arms.

"My, my," she said, catching her breath. "They don't make 'em like that in Seattle."

Lou lowered her camera and stared, open mouthed. "No, they don't."

"He's huge. I wonder…"

"Penny!" Lou laughed. "I can't take you anywhere."

The crowd shifted, and Penny noticed the man was holding a cardboard sign. She read the name printed in slanted block letters, and her heart dropped to her belly.

The name on the sign was hers.

Lou noticed it too. "Henry must have sent them."

Them? Penny shifted her gaze and noticed a man next to the giant specimen of pure masculinity. The shorter man was also quite tall—and devastatingly handsome. He was the kind of dreamboat she'd seen in the movies, with an intensely broody expression and thick, dark hair that framed his face in untamed waves. A bruise marred his cheek, giving him bad-boy vibrations, but when he smiled at something the big guy said, the effect was enough to make any girl's heart rate spike.

They made quite a striking pair. The taller one looked like he'd been ripped out of a history book on Hawaiian warriors. His serious expression and broad shoulders would have an enemy shaking in their boots. And the other guy had a graceful poise, like the descendant of a king.

Penny liked what she saw. They should have put those guys in the pamphlet.

The taller man pulled off his glasses and handed them to his friend. Time stilled as their gazes collided. There was something familiar about him, something that made her step falter and her knees weak. It wasn't just that he was gorgeous. It was more. She felt as if something was ripping through her.

Grandma Agatha had always said Penny had a touch of the old ways, which meant she had strange dreams that sometimes came true, and she could read people in an instant. Her instincts were telling her this guy was going to change her life.

"Do they look a little dangerous?" Lou's voice wavered halfway between concern and excitement.

"Yeah," Penny answered. "They do."

She'd never been so keenly aware of a man, and he wasn't even touching her. A thrill of anticipation raced down her spine.

They looked dangerous in the most delightful way.

Chapter 2

Bones

GROWING UP IN HAWAII, Bones had seen plenty of beautiful women. But nothing like the woman who was striding toward him across the tarmac.

Henry had warned him his cousin was a fox. He'd said she would knock his socks off, then had made a dumb joke about him not wearing any. Bones spent most of his time around Henry being mildly annoyed. The man was loud, obnoxious, and always trying to make everyone laugh. Henry wasn't on Bones's list of favorite people. Until today.

"Dibs on the redhead."

"Whatever, brah." Keoni pinched the bridge of his nose and pulled in a long breath.

Bones nudged his cousin in the ribs. "Try looking friendly, eh?"

"Watch it." Keoni groaned, and color drained from his face.

"You broke a couple of ribs," Bones said, not bothering to pull his gaze from the redhead in order to look at Keoni, who got black eyes and bruised ribs more often than anyone Bones knew. Except maybe Henry. Henry worked as a stuntman on a television show and was always marked up from a rough day on set.

"It was worth it. Am I right?" Satisfaction rang in Keoni's voice. He'd earned those bruises on some of the biggest waves the North Shore had ever seen. He'd made a name for himself as a big wave rider. Finally.

But it was dangerous as hell.

"You're nuts," Bones growled. "You're gonna get killed—"

"You were riding the same waves as me, cuz," Keoni said, cutting him off.

"I had no choice once I got out there. I had to get back to shore somehow." He gave his cousin the side-eye. He'd thought Keoni had been done for on those fifty-foot waves. He'd been lucky to make it out with a few broken ribs and a bruised-up eye. "You're gonna scare the shit out of these girls with that ugly mug o' yours." Bones took off his sunglasses and handed them to Keoni. "Here. Put these on."

Keoni put them on with a shrug. "Nice, brah. These ain't cheap."

"You're not keepin' 'em, hear?" He shaded his eyes with his hand and drank in the sight of the tall redhead. She had to be nearly six feet, and all legs. Thank God for friends like Henry. Even if he did bug the hell out of Bones most of the time, he had cousins who looked like *her*. "Don't blow this," Bones warned Keoni. "She's one looker."

"I hate tourists. Look at her with that camera. You'd think she never seen an airport before, eh?"

Bones had hardly noticed the other one. His gaze was glued to the redhead. "Shut your mouth. They're coming."

The women approached and stopped in front of him. Henry's cousin stood with her heels together, toes pointed out. He could tell from her perfect posture she was a dancer. He'd bet on it.

"That's me." She pointed at the sign. "I'm Penny. And this is my friend Lou."

Average women were a full foot shorter than Bones, and he was used to stooping. Not with Penny. A slight dip of his chin was all it took to gaze into her wide, expressive eyes. Her skin was incredible. Creamy pale and translucent, it looked like it would be soft as the fine sand at Waimanalo Bay.

Her brows pulled together in concern. "You're not my cousin Henry."

Even her mainland accent was cute. Bones tucked the sign with her name on it under his arm and held out his hand. "I'm Bones, and this ugly guy is my cousin Keoni."

Penny ignored Bones's outstretched hand and narrowed her eyes at him. Bones cocked his head, waiting for the usual questions. *How tall are you? Is Bones your real name?*

"Is Henry okay?" Her hand flew to her mouth, and her eyes widened. "He isn't hurt, is he?"

Bones had a sudden urge to take Penny into his arms and comfort her. He reminded himself he didn't know her, that she wasn't his to hold. "Henry's fine. He had to work."

Penny exhaled loudly. "Thank God. He's always getting hurt, you know? One of these days..." She trailed off, worrying her bottom lip between her teeth.

His heart softened at the sight of her distress. "Don't worry," he said. "Henry said his job is mostly illusion."

Penny flipped her hair over her shoulder, her expression annoyed. "Illusion didn't land him in the hospital with a broken leg a few months ago."

The quick change in her temper stirred Bones's blood. Penny may not be Hawaiian, but she had the spark of Pele in her soul. Her passionate nature flowed like molten lava.

He felt a shot of adrenaline speed through his veins. Penny was no ordinary tourist; she was someone special.

"I almost forgot." He reached for the lei draped across his forearm. "This is for you." In keeping with Hawaiian tradition, he kissed both her cheeks in welcome as he placed the lei around her neck.

She gazed up at him, her sapphire eyes colliding with his. "I think I'm gonna like it here."

For weeks, Bones had been feeling frustrated and edgy. His father had been pressuring him to find a career worthy of a Keakealani, and his mother and sisters never let up in trying to find him a suitable Hawaiian woman to settle down with.

Penny Longchamp was just the distraction he needed.

Bones adjusted the lei around her neck, fixing the soft petals of the flowers to frame her face. He was going to show this woman the time of her life. He'd never been more eager to share the true meaning of aloha.

Chapter 3

Penny

A TINY THRILL raced down Penny's spine as she watched Bones lift her giant pink Samsonite, as if it weighed no more than a grocery bag, and deposit it in the back of his station wagon.

"What should we do first?" Lou asked, nudging Penny with the Hawaiian brochure she'd grabbed from the airport.

Penny couldn't tear her attention away from Bones. His muscles flexed as he slammed the trunk shut, stretching the seams of his shirt across his biceps. He reached up to tug the rope holding the two surfboards in place on the roof of the station wagon, and his shirt lifted just enough to offer a glimpse of his tantalizing bronze skin above the waistband of his shorts.

"I wouldn't mind a snack, then we should unpack, and I need to make sure I've got enough film. Maybe they can recommend a good camera shop in town…"

Lou's voice sounded in Penny's ear, but she wasn't listening. She was too busy staring at the most gorgeous man who'd ever walked God's green earth. Bones was six and a half feet of raw masculinity. A work of art.

"I hope Henry's not working tomorrow," Lou said. "He was supposed to show us around."

Bones opened the passenger door for Penny. "We'd be glad to give you a tour of the real Hawaii." His white teeth flashed in a smile. "Ain't that right, Keoni?"

Keoni didn't answer. He was looking at something down the sidewalk. Even though his eyes were covered with sunglasses, Penny could feel the intensity of his stare.

She glanced down the sidewalk and saw a blond-haired man standing next to a white Rolls-Royce at the curb, staring straight at them with a concerned frown.

"Shit," Bones muttered quietly. His shoulders stiffened, and tension radiated off his body.

"Do you know that guy?" Penny asked.

"Yeah." Bones stalked to Keoni's side, forming a unified front as the man cautiously approached.

They stood just out of earshot, sizing each other up. Penny would hate to be the guy on the other end of Bones's intense stare. But the blond-haired man didn't shrink. He pulled off his sunglasses and eyed Keoni, saying something Penny couldn't hear.

Bones stiffened and glanced at Keoni. Something unspoken passed between them, and Bones took a step back, his shoulders relaxing.

"Who is that?" Lou asked. "He looks familiar."

Penny eyed the blond man as Keoni released him. He was shorter than Bones and Keoni, but so was just about everyone. His skin was golden brown, and his hair was bleached by the sun. His clothes were normal traveling clothes, worn by at least half the men in the airport—a pressed shirt, dark slacks, and shiny loafers—but there was something extraordinary about him. And Lou was right. He did look familiar.

Lou stepped closer to Penny and whispered, "I think he's famous."

He laughed, and the flash of his white teeth against his

tanned skin jolted a memory, and Penny knew where she'd seen him before. On the rag mags at Walgreens.

"Jeez Louise," Penny muttered, trying not to stare. He was some kind of celebrity. An actor? Singer? He was even better looking in person than he'd been on the cover of the magazine wearing a tuxedo. Their eyes met, and he gave her a smile that made her melt.

The men walked over to Lou and Penny, and Keoni made the introductions.

"This is Lou and Penny," Keoni said. "Declan Bishop."

Declan turned up the wattage of his smile and reached for Penny's hand. Instead of shaking it, he brought it to his lips and kissed it, giving her a wink as his lips brushed her hand. A lock of blond hair fell over his forehead, and he swept it aside with a practiced move. "What are a couple of lovely ladies like you doing with these chumps?"

Lou raised a brow at Penny. Keoni and Bones weren't the only ones who could communicate without words. This guy was handsome, well-dressed, and probably famous, but he so full of himself, he was brimming over.

Penny lifted her chin at Declan and met his ice-blue eyes. "They were kind enough to give us a ride."

Declan shot a knowing grin at Bones. "Gonna show dem da reel Ha-vhy-ee, yeah?"

Penny's stomach clenched. In his exaggerated Hawaiian accent, Declan's suggestion sounded eerily familiar.

Bones narrowed his gaze at Declan. "Watchu doin' home? Eh?"

Declan's smile dropped, and his posture stiffened. His eyes locked on Keoni, and something almost tangible passed between them. Tension filled the air. "You didn't hear?"

Keoni's eyes were covered by the dark lenses of his sunglasses, but Penny could feel the beam of his gaze burning a hole through Declan. "Hear what?"

Declan reached into his jacket pocket and pulled out an envelope. It was red and about the size of a wedding invitation.

Keoni's body went rigid when he saw it. "Congratulations."

After a long pause, Declan cleared his throat and slipped the envelope back into his pocket. "Yeah? Well, it shoulda been you."

Bones laughed a low, deep rumble that matched his size and made Penny feel all fizzy inside, as if a champagne cork had popped inside her.

"You're lucky Keoni isn't surfing in the Duke, brah," he said in his growly voice. "Or you would have no chance."

Declan lifted his chin at Bones, nodding. "Yeah. I know that's right."

"What's the Duke?" Lou asked, breaking the testosterone-laden tension in the air.

Bones shifted his gaze from Declan to Lou. "It's a surfing contest," he said. "Everyone will be there." He turned to look at Keoni. "Right?"

All eyes turned to Keoni, and Penny was beginning to understand the group dynamics. Although Bones was the biggest and Declan was famous, it was Keoni who was the center of gravity. It was Keoni who called the shots.

Keoni's shoulders lifted with a barely-there shrug, his expression never changing. "Sure. I'll be there." He dipped his chin at Declan, a small smile lifting the corner of his split lip. "I hope you win."

Declan's face paled, and he glanced down the sidewalk toward the Rolls-Royce idling at the curb. "Gotta scram. My ride's waiting."

When he was gone, Bones came back to the station wagon and opened the door for Penny. His face had lost all the hardness it had held while conversing with Declan. He was back to playing the charming tour guide. His smile was quietly soothing, his gaze intense on hers.

Penny could easily get lost in his chocolate-colored eyes,

darker than the midnight sky and just as endless. Even though his lips were set in a smile, the spark was missing. He was an incredibly handsome, less effervescent version of himself. Penny was dying to know the details behind the drama she'd just seen partially unfold. Who was Declan? What was the big deal about this surfing contest? And why did everyone bow to Keoni as if he were some sort of prince?

Penny loved drama. She lived for it. The twentieth-century version of a warrior holding the dinged car door open for her was drama. The way Bones looked at her made her heart pirouette.

She got in the car and exchanged a look with Lou while they waited for Bones and Keoni to walk around to the other side of the car. Lou was just as curious about the men as Penny. Keoni, with his bruised face, and Bones, with his effortless charm and masculine presence, were a hard duo to ignore.

Bones slid behind the wheel and started up the engine.

"So, how do you know Henry?" She wanted to know more about him, but she would start with the easy stuff.

His brows pulled together. "I'm not sure. Everyone knows Henry."

"Probably because he always picks up the bill," Penny replied. Henry didn't know how to be stingy with money. If he had it, he was spending it.

"I always see him at the beach. He's not bad at surfing." He tossed her a smile. "He's not great either. Eh? But he's fearless."

Henry didn't know the meaning of the word fear. As a result, he'd broken more bones in his body than she could count. "Did he say what time he was going to be home tonight?"

"Nah." Bones shook his head, pushing a lock of hair that had escaped his low ponytail behind his ear. "Might be late. It would be a shame for you to go to an empty house and sit around on your first day here."

A tingle of awareness shot through Penny's body. From the

confident half smile on his face to the way he steered one-handed, there was something effortlessly sexy about Bones.

"It would be a terrible shame," Penny said. "Maybe we could get started with that tour?"

"You hungry?"

Penny's heart raced. The thought of eating a meal with the sexiest man she'd ever laid eyes on made her mouth water. "I could eat," she said, hoping she could tear her eyes away from Bones long enough to choke down a meal. "And Lou is always hungry. She gets mean if she doesn't eat every few hours."

Lou piped up from the back seat. "I do not."

Penny didn't bother arguing. "What did you have in mind?"

"You like burgers?"

"Who doesn't?"

"I know the perfect spot."

____

Chapter 4

____

Bones

BONES GRABBED the bag of food and started back toward the car, where Penny and Lou were waiting. Penny was leaning against the car, her long legs crossed in front of her.

"I gotta get outta here," Keoni said.

Bones gave him an exasperated look. "You seemed to be hitting it off okay. For you."

Keoni rolled his eyes. He was the worst at picking up chicks, and everyone knew it. Probably because he never had to try. All Keoni had to do was look at a woman, and she fell at his feet. And if he picked up his guitar? The game was over. Panties were dropping.

Keoni stopped about fifty feet from the car and held his ground. "You know I hate tourists."

"Even a couple of lookers like them?"

Keoni couldn't argue with the truth. He pressed his lips together, clearly thinking of a way out. Bones could see his wheels turning. Ever since Keoni had been dumped by a tourist a few years ago, he'd wanted nothing to do with them.

"I've gotta work," he said. "Some people have regular jobs."

"You don't gotta be there till eleven." Bones checked his watch. "It's four thirty."

"I just remembered, Kimo is supposed to drop by my parents' place today. I better go."

Kimo was Keoni's younger brother. He'd enlisted in the army and was reporting for boot camp in a few days. "Kimo's around?"

"That's what I said."

"Cool. We can drop you off and stay for the party."

"What makes you say there's a party?"

Bones chuckled. "If Kimo's around, there's a party."

They went back to the car and passed out the burgers. When they were done eating, they loaded back into the car and headed to Keoni's parents' house. Bones had spent so much time there growing up, he thought of it as a second home.

Usually, Bones kept things straightforward with tourists. He took them to Waikiki or Diamond Head. He took them to their hotel rooms. But there was a big difference between his house, which was just walls and a roof, and the graveyard, which was home.

He didn't know why he wanted to take Penny to a place that was so special. Maybe it was because she was Henry's cousin. Henry had talked about Penny so much, Bones felt like he already knew her.

Plus, he was a sucker for redheads.

They turned off the main road onto a hilly street that weaved into the mountains. Bones tried to picture the scenery from Penny's perspective. He was used to seeing the lush jungle and the spiky crest of the mountains, but he never failed to appreciate the beauty surrounding him. Seeing it for the first time must be amazing.

Penny practically hung her head out the window as they drove farther into the valley. "I have to admit, I was a little disappointed at the airport," she said. "But this is more like it."

"The airport didn't impress you, eh?"

She gave him a saucy look, her gaze flicking down his body. "A few things did."

Bones laughed, his chest bubbling with a fizzy feeling. Penny was a woman who knew what she wanted. She was after a good time in Hawaii. He would happily give her something to write about in her journal.

They turned onto the long dirt road leading deeper into the valley. "I should warn you, Keoni's parents' place might not be what you're expecting."

"It's gotta beat the airport."

He grinned. "I can guarantee that."

When Bones turned at the sign for the cemetery, where Keoni's parents were caretakers of five hundred acres of burial grounds, Penny leaned out the window and gaped. They passed the red-roofed pagoda flanked by two giant stone statues of lions.

"That's Abbott and Costello." He gave the lions a friendly wave. "They're a couple of snobs. Never wave back."

When she flashed him a grin, his body reacted immediately. His chest felt tight, and his heart raced. "You're not scared, eh?"

"No way. I love graveyards. We had one near our family's farm when I was a kid. My cousins and I were always daring each other to do crazy things in the graveyard."

Bones caught Keoni's eyes in the rearview mirror, and they exchanged a look. They'd done the same. "Like what kinds of things?" he asked Penny.

"Like spend the night sleeping against a tombstone or dance over graves." Penny shrugged. "Seems disrespectful now that I think about it. But we were just kids."

They drove along the dirt road toward the Makai residence, winding between neat rows of tombstones, flowering trees, and stone statues until they were high in the lush green hills. Keoni's family took pride in keeping up the grounds of the graveyard. Bones had helped plenty, putting in hours of manual labor so

Keoni could join him surfing when the work was done. As a result, Bones knew the property like it was his home. A huge chunk of his childhood memories had been made there.

He pulled to a stop in front of the Makai house, where a half dozen cars were already parked. He was right about the party; it was already in progress.

They got out of the car, and Lou immediately wandered off with her camera.

"Is she always like this?" Bones asked.

"Always."

"I'll go with her," Keoni said with an exasperated sigh.

Bones wasn't surprised Keoni wanted to follow Lou. His cousin had a protective streak and couldn't stand to see anyone in danger. Lou seemed like a walking disaster, stumbling along with her camera glued to her face. Holding his arm out to Penny, Bones turned on the charm. "Come on, I'll show you around."

Her hand slid up his arm, shamelessly feeling his bicep, then rounded over his shoulder. "I have a confession to make," she said.

"What's that?" There was something bold but innocent about Penny that made every nerve in his body come alive.

"There was one dare…" Color rose to her cheeks, and she glanced away. "It was something the older kids did."

His mouth went dry. "What did the older kids do in the graveyard?"

She wet her lips, pink and inviting. "They French-kissed."

"French?" He laughed softly. "But we're in Hawaii. We have to kiss Hawaiian style."

"I could go for that."

The urge to prolong this moment, feel the pulse of heat between them as their first kiss hovered in the air, was too strong to resist. He ran his hand up her arm to cup her shoulder and felt the goose bumps break out on her skin. "You aren't scared to kiss in a graveyard?"

She smiled, a sinful combination of sex and sweetness. Her fingers curled around his bicep, and she squeezed. "I wouldn't be scared of anything as long as you're around."

He bent his head, closing the distance between them. Before he could touch his lips to hers, the front door banged shut, startling them. Bones took a step back and looked up at the house. When he saw the woman at the door, holding a baby on her hip and glaring at him, he winced, wishing he hadn't come to Keoni's.

Chapter 5

Penny

THE WOMAN STANDING in the doorway holding a toddler on her hip looked like she'd stepped straight out of a book of legends. Her skin was luminous, her face was flawless, and her neck was long and elegant. She wore a short tunic dress covered with bright flowers, and her feet were bare. Her nose tipped upward in the air, and she regarded Penny and Bones with the haughtiness of a queen.

The toddler was chubby, with cherub cheeks and a head full of dark curls. When she saw Bones, her dark eyes went round, and she reached for him. "Bozey!"

Bones jogged over and dropped a kiss on the woman's cheek before plucking the squirming toddler from her arms. He lifted the little girl over his head, making her squeal. "Howzit, Squirt?"

Something shifted in Penny's chest when the child's laughter drifted across the lawn. Penny had never given much thought to getting married and having babies, but as she watched Bones, the thought of herself as a mother invaded her mind. It wasn't that she didn't want children. She loved children. She'd just not consciously thought about having any of her own. Until now.

Penny blinked rapidly, pushing away the domestic images crowding her mind. She was in Hawaii for fun. For adventure. Not to plan her future beyond the next hour. Definitely not with the handsome tour guide who'd probably shown dozens of girls "the real Hawaii."

"You got so big," Bones told the little girl, tickling her round belly.

"She's been growing like a weed." The woman smoothed a curl from the baby's face. She shot a glance at Penny and then looked up at Bones. She was so much shorter than him that she had to crane her neck. "Where were you last night?"

A flush crept up Bones's neck. "Sorry, Myra. I forgot."

"You forgot, eh?" Myra threw her hair over her shoulder, doubling down on her glare. "What were you doing that was so important?"

Bones ignored the question, his attention focused on the baby girl. "Watchu been eatin', Squirt? You're gettin' too big too fast."

The little girl giggled and grabbed a handful of his hair, gazing at him with adoring brown eyes.

"Heh, Bones." Myra poked Bones in the chest. "I asked you a question."

"I heard you." He set the little girl down on her sturdy legs and squatted beside her as she took a few steps. "Let's talk about it later, 'kay?"

Myra snorted. "I swear to God, Bones. I am never setting you up with another girl again."

Bones squinted up at Myra. "Thanks, eh?"

The little girl tugged on her mother's skirt. "Puppies!"

Myra reached down and scooped up her daughter. "That's right, baby. Let's go see the new puppies." She jabbed a finger at Bones. "You should go inside and say good-bye to my little brother before he gets shipped off to war." She swiveled her head and focused her dark eyes on Penny. "And you, whoever you are, get as far away from my cousin as you can, you hear? He's good for nothing."

She marched off with her daughter on her hip, her braid swaying down her back.

When she was gone, Penny raised her brow at Bones. "What was that all about?"

"That was just Myra's way. She's always trying to set me up with women." He lifted his shoulders slightly, a tiny shrug nearly lost with his big body. "She thinks I should settle down."

Penny noticed the stiff way he held his jaw and the annoyed crease in his brow. "And you're not ready for that?"

Bones strode back to her side. "Hell no." He blew out a breath, and some of the tension drained from his face. "It's too fun being single."

Penny had just been warned off him, but she didn't want Bones for a boyfriend, and he definitely wasn't husband material. She wanted what he was clearly offering with no strings attached: an adventure.

Even if she tried thinking clearly, it was impossible with him so close. His scent was overpowering, scrambling her thoughts. Her heart pounded loudly in her ears, drowning out reason.

Bones took her hand and dipped his chin. A shiver of anticipation rushed through Penny's body as he lowered his head.

The door slammed again, and Bones froze. "What now?" he muttered, glancing toward the house.

"Bones! You bring Keoni?"

Impatience flickered in his dark eyes. "Sorry."

"It's okay." Penny glanced over Bones's shoulder at the young man standing at the door. He wore flared jeans and a faded T-shirt and held a guitar by its neck. Except for the buzzed haircut, he looked enough like Keoni to be his twin. He was obviously the younger brother going off to war.

"We want him to play a song."

"Keoni's here somewhere," Bones said.

"Cool." He strummed a few notes, glancing around expectantly. "You bring any other hot chicks?"

"Kimo." Bones's voice was a low growl. "Show some respect."

"What? I was being respectful. I called her a hot chick."

"This hot chick has a name," Bones snapped. "It's Penny."

Kimo smiled at Penny, his white teeth flashing against his bronze tan. "Hi, Penny. You get tired of this big grump, you can come hang with me, yeah?"

Penny laughed and looked up at Bones, whose mouth was set in a stern frown. "I don't mind grumpy." *She didn't mind big either, not one bit.*

Bones glared at Kimo. "I wouldn't be grumpy if you didn't go around interrupting people."

"Oh, sorry. Was I interrupting?" Kimo's smile stretched across his face. He didn't look sorry. "Since I ruined the moment, you mind helping me with Uncle Pete?"

"What did he do now?"

"He's passed out in his cups again, and we can't move him."

Bones smiled apologetically at Penny. "Might as well come in and meet the rest of the gang. Otherwise, they are gonna come out here one by one." He sneered at Kimo. "Too nosy for their own good. All of 'em."

They strode up the driveway toward the house, the interrupted moment still lingering between them like the fading scent of a rose, gone but not forgotten.

Bones stopped at the door and slipped off his shoes, then pointed at Penny's boots. "We don't wear shoes in the house."

Penny froze for a moment, glancing down at her boots. An embarrassed flush spread up her neck and stained her cheeks.

"Whatsthemattah? Eh?"

She laughed nervously, trying to be nonchalant. "I don't want to scare you off with my feet."

Bones raised a dark brow. "You got an extra toe or what?"

She shook her head, feeling the flush spread all the way to her ears. "No, but they're pretty ugly."

His lips curved in a sexy smile. "Nothing about you is ugly."

Penny bit her lip. "You haven't seen my feet yet."

Bones pointed at his own feet. "Take a look at these," he said. "They're a size sixteen."

Penny glanced down at Bones's feet and smiled. They were big, but far from ugly, while hers were hideous from years of dancing in pointe shoes. "I think your feet are cute," she said, looking at his sturdy feet.

He laughed. "No one's ever called these flippers cute before." He dropped to one knee and reached for the zipper of her boot. "Can I help you?"

Penny's mouth went dry. Seeing Bones on one knee gazing up at her did something funny to her belly. She licked her lips and nodded, knowing she couldn't hide her feet forever.

He tugged gently on the zipper, his eyes locked on hers. His fingers brushed her calf, spreading the boot open so she could step out of it.

She blushed furiously as he caressed her ankle then traced his fingers along the curve of her instep. No one had touched her feet before; she'd never allowed it. She braced herself for his reaction, staring at the top of his dark head as he bent over her feet.

He glanced up at her with a fierce expression, as if he wanted to harm whoever had bent her toes and torn off her toenails. The protective gleam in his eyes filled her with longing. She imagined Bones would do anything to protect the woman he loved. She wouldn't mind being that lucky woman.

"What happened?" he asked, brushing his fingers over the top of her foot.

She shivered at the gentle touch and gazed down at the warrior bent over her feet. "Dance," she said.

His expression cleared, and he nodded with approval. "It's

made you strong," he said, reaching for the zipper on her other boot.

She let her eyes shut as he helped her out of the boot, giving her left foot the same tender caress he'd given the right. He placed her boots next to the door with the other shoes, then rose to tower over her. In her bare feet, she had to lift her chin to look at him.

He smiled and opened the door, leading the way into the crowded house. The sound of music and laughter filled the air. A man played the ukulele, singing loudly over the buzz of conversation. As they walked past, Bones plucked the ukulele out of the man's hands and strummed a quick tune. Everyone cheered and demanded more, but Bones handed the instrument back and reached for Penny's hand.

"Come on, man!" Someone in the crowd called. "Give us another."

Bones shook his head. "Maybe later."

He took Penny's hand again and led her down the hall past surfboards leaning against the walls. In the kitchen, he helped himself to the refrigerator, grabbing two cans of beer.

"It ain't a Mai Tai, but it will get you the same result."

Penny wasn't much of a beer drinker, but she accepted the can he offered and popped the top. She took a sip and wrinkled her nose. "It needs a paper umbrella."

Bones tapped his can to hers and winked. "To interruptions. May they be far less frequent."

Penny drank, smiling as she swallowed the cold beer. The second sip wasn't nearly as bad as the first.

Bones led her back to the living room and introduced her to a few people, then found her a place to sit. The close-knit family reminded her of home—not her apartment in the city with Lou, but her grandparents' farmhouse, where so many family members gathered during holidays that the rooms seemed ready to burst at the seams.

"You sounded good on the ukulele," she said.

His brows drew together. "Nah. Not really."

"I thought you were great."

"It's not my thing. Keoni's the one who's good at music."

Penny stared at him, openly curious. "Is Keoni some sort of legend? Everyone seems to bow down to him."

His shoulders stiffened, and he took a long sip of beer before answering. "Keoni has rescued more people than all the life-guards at Waikiki put together. You should see him surf. He's not a legend, yet, but give him a few more years, and everyone in Hawaii will know his name. And when he plays the guitar, women fall in love with him."

Penny flashed a grin. "I prefer the ukulele."

A flush crept up his cheeks, and she realized she'd embarrassed him. It was cute to see a big, strong man have a shy streak.

"Can you play again for me?"

His expression clouded. "Maybe."

"Come on." She touched his shoulder. "You're really good."

He squinted at her, as if trying to decide whether to believe her. "You really think so?"

She realized he had no idea how talented he was. "I really do."

A slow smile spread across his face. "Thanks, eh?"

Penny suppressed a yawn. The beer had relaxed her, and she realized how tired she was after the long day of travel.

Bones checked his watch. "You must be exhausted."

She wasn't sure if she'd ever see Bones again, and she wasn't ready to say good-bye. "I'm okay."

The door banged shut, and Keoni and Lou walked in. Lou looked upset, and Keoni had his sunglasses on, even though they were inside the house. As soon as Keoni entered, the noise level in the room went up a notch as everyone greeted him.

Bones shifted closer. "You still like to dance?"

Dance had been a part of her life for as long as Penny could remember. She loved it more than just about anything. "Yes."

"I work security at Legends, the best nightclub on the island. You and Lou should come. Henry knows where it is, he can bring you."

Lou caught Penny's eye and frowned, gesturing at the door. Penny rose to her feet. "Looks like she's ready to go."

Bones pushed to his feet beside her, making her feel small as he towered over her. "Tomorrow night?" he asked.

She nodded, raising her chin to meet his gaze. The way he looked at her ignited a spark inside her, filling her with anticipation and desire. "I'd love it."

His luscious mouth curved in a smile. "I should go help with Uncle Pete, then I'll get you home."

Penny made her way across the room to Lou, who looked upset about something. Penny knew it wasn't going to be easy to convince Lou to meet Bones at a nightclub. Lou had two left feet and no rhythm, but Henry loved to dance as much as Penny did. It was two against one, and the odds were in her favor.

Chapter 6

Bones

LEGENDS ATTRACTED all sorts of people. The crowd was usually a mix of locals, tourists, and soldiers on leave. More often than not, somebody got the wise idea to start a fight or get too drunk. It was Bones's job to provide security, which meant he got to toss people out on their asses at will. He was perfectly suited for the job. Sometimes he had to get physical, but with his size and stern demeanor, it often only took one look to deal with aggressive behavior.

Bones was on door duty, sitting on a stool in front of the club. He surveyed the line of people spreading down the sidewalk, scrutinizing them for potential troublemakers. In his experience, it was easier to stop a fight before it started.

He crossed his arms over his chest and leaned his foot on the bottom rung of his stool, his posture deceptively relaxed although he was on full alert. It was ten o'clock, and there was still no sign of Penny. The minutes ticked by with no sight of her, and it felt like the slowest shift he'd ever worked.

Maybe she wasn't coming. He convinced himself he didn't care. Beautiful tourists were a daily occurrence in Hawaii. But there was something special about Penny. He hadn't even kissed her yet, but she pulled him like a magnetic force.

"Hey! You gonna let us in sometime tonight?" A man pushed to the front of the line. "We've been waiting out here forever."

Bones ignored the man, his gaze snagging on a tall redhead gliding down the sidewalk with a dancer's grace. His heart swelled, and a slow smile transformed his face.

Penny had arrived.

The noise around him faded into the background, and his pulse hammered so loudly in his ears, he could no longer hear the noise of the crowd.

She was even more gorgeous than he remembered. Between a short skirt and high heels, her legs looked endless. Her hair shimmered under the streetlights, a halo of reddish gold.

When Henry took her arm and said something to make her laugh, Bones felt a sharp stab of envy. He wanted to be the one making her laugh and feeling the soft skin of her arm under his fingers.

Penny swept her gaze across the crowd, and their eyes met. She flashed him a smile and a little wave that made his stomach flutter.

Their almost kiss in the graveyard weighed heavily on his mind. It was all he'd thought about since. He considered himself a patient man, but now that he'd seen her again, his patience was up.

Bones nodded at her, then crooked his finger for her to come closer. Penny strode past the long line of people, her gaze glued to him.

He didn't want to wait another minute to taste her lips. Public displays of affection weren't his thing, but he couldn't help himself. Penny tempted him too much.

Lowering his head, he closed the distance between them and

pressed his mouth to hers. The kiss was meant to be quick, something to get out of the way so he could go back to thinking clearly. But when their lips touched, Bones felt a shock from the roots of his hair to the soles of his feet, and he couldn't pull away.

Her fingers gripped his shoulders, and a small sigh escaped her lips.

Bones had never believed what his aunties had said about fated souls and destined lovers, but Penny's kiss bound him by an invisible thread.

It took all his strength to pull away. He was at work. He had a job to do. And he didn't do soul mates. He did one-night stands with tourists.

If only her lips weren't so soft and full and responsive against his. If only she didn't taste like ripe strawberries, and the promise of her tongue slick against his didn't make him instantly hard as steel.

He pulled away, his body throbbing with the need to do just the opposite.

She dropped her hands from his shoulders and stepped back, but her eyes held him captive. "Well, that was a nice hello."

"You came."

"I said I would." She checked her watch. "Even though it's one a.m. in Seattle. Past my bedtime."

The mention of bedtime was like a spark to the fire simmering inside him. Bones imagined the red silk of Penny's hair spread across his pillow, her body relaxed and warm under his sheets.

"I'll be done soon." Bones lifted the rope blocking the door to the club and nodded for Penny to step through. "I'll find you."

A blast of sultry music filled the air when Penny opened the door. "I'll be on the dance floor."

Anxiety swirled in the pit of his gut as Bones watched Penny disappear into the smoky haze of the nightclub. All his protective instincts came out, jabbing him under his skin like barbed wire.

He'd been crazy to ask Penny to come to Legends. She was too bright, too fresh for the gritty club on the wrong side of Honolulu. This wasn't Waikiki and the sparkling sands shown on the tourist brochures.

"What the hell, man?" Henry stepped into Bones's space, jutting his chin up at him.

Bones dragged his gaze away from the door. "What?"

Henry's eyes blazed. "I trusted you with her. She's my cousin."

Bones squared his shoulders, returning Henry's glare. "Nothing happened."

Henry jabbed a finger at him. "You just tried to suck her face off in front of everyone."

"Give me a break. It was nothing." It hadn't felt like nothing, but Bones wasn't ready to admit that, not even to himself.

"She's only here for a few days. Don't mess with her head."

Lou stepped up behind Henry. "Penny is a grown woman. She can make her own decisions." She glanced at Bones, her eyes slightly shy without a camera to hide behind. "Hi, Bones."

"Hi, Lou."

"Thanks for letting us in."

"No problem. Be careful, 'kay?"

Lou tilted her chin at him, and her hair fell over her shoulder in deep chestnut waves. "I've been to a nightclub before."

In her pale-pink dress, she was dressed for a beach party, not a nightclub, but he wasn't an expert on women's fashion. "Keep an eye on Penny, will you?"

She shrugged. "I'll try."

Bones turned his attention back to the line of people. A scuffle had broken out about halfway down the line. He closed off the rope entrance and stalked down the sidewalk. When he got within a few feet of the disruption, a fight broke out.

Bones flexed his fists, glad for a distraction from his intrusive thoughts of Penny.

———————————————

Chapter 7

———————————

Penny

AS A LITTLE GIRL, Penny had thought she'd dance on every stage in the world. She'd thought she'd be famous someday, that everyone in the dance world would know her name. It hadn't worked out that way, partly because of a knee injury and partly because Penny's body had betrayed her. It hadn't stopped growing. No male dancer wanted a partner taller than him.

She'd started losing the lead roles, and by the time she'd finished growing, she was five feet ten inches tall. Too tall for a ballerina. Too tall to dance on every stage in the world and have her name called from the rafters of the performance hall.

The band playing had a unique sound. They were part rock, part traditional Hawaiian, and part blues. The lead singer had a low, growly voice that made everything sound sexy.

Even though she still wasn't accustomed to the time change, and it was the middle of the night in Seattle, Penny felt energized by the music. It beat through her like a pulse, reviving her, filling her, and flowing through her until she had to move.

She swayed a little, feeling the music in her hips. It was a sultry beat, perfectly suited to the warm humid night. The singer's voice sent chills up her spine. He sang in a low, rumbling voice that made her feel liquid inside. The lyrics were in traditional Hawaiian, so she had no idea what he was saying, but she didn't care.

Someone bumped into her from behind, and she turned to see a young man with a buzzed haircut and sunburned cheeks standing too close. He smiled at her, his toothy grin making him look even younger.

"Wanna dance?"

Penny looked him over. He looked like he was still in high school, harmless. She was about to take him up on the offer when Henry put his arm around her shoulder.

"Get lost, Howdy Doody. She's with me."

The young man cocked his head at Henry as if he was about to challenge him, but then he thought better of it. Henry wasn't particularly tall or imposing, but what he lacked in size, he made up for in confidence. Henry had a swagger that was recognizable from across the room. He was lean and muscular and looked like what he was: a man who jumped out of helicopters for a living.

The young man glanced at Lou, who'd come up on the other side of Henry. "How's about you?"

Henry slung his arm around Lou's shoulders. "Forget about it. She's with me too."

The man's eyes went wide. "Both of 'em?"

"That's right." Henry's chest puffed up. He was enjoying the moment a little too much.

When the guy was gone, Penny slipped out from under Henry's arm. "I could have handled him," she said. "You don't need to protect me."

Henry took a step back, pinning her with his gaze. "It can get rough in here," he said. "What's with you and Bones, anyway?"

At the mention of Bones's name, Penny felt butterflies in her belly. The kiss he'd laid on her had awakened a desire so strong, she could still feel the sting. "None of your business," she told Henry.

"I thought you had a steady guy in Seattle," Henry shouted over the music. "What's his name?"

Penny waved her hand in the air. "That's done."

"Does Joe know that?" Lou asked, her brow furrowed.

Penny shook her head. She didn't want to talk about Joe. She didn't want to talk at all. The music seeped into her bones, and her patience with men had drained. "I want to dance."

Without waiting for Henry's response, Penny weaved her way through the round tables separating the bar from the dance floor. Henry was right behind her, tugging Lou along.

"I'm not much of a dancer," Lou shouted over the music. "Two left feet."

"You're in luck! I'm a great teacher." Henry tugged Lou's hand and spun her in a circle.

Lou laughed and caught Penny's hand, then drew her into their little trio. Soon, they were laughing and dancing together, and it was just like old times in the kitchen of Penny's grandparents' house. When she and Henry had been kids, they'd practiced all the latest dance moves to the scratchy music over the radio.

Lou was pretty horrible at dancing, but she was smiling and laughing as she stumbled through the motions, and Henry was a terrific sport.

Every few minutes, Penny looked toward the entrance hoping to see Bones, only to be disappointed when he wasn't there.

Her lips still tingled from the brief touch of his lips. His mouth was every bit as firm and commanding and devastating to her senses as she'd guessed it would be. She'd never been kissed with such intensity before, and she had the feeling that everything Bones did, he did with extreme care. If kissing him brought her so much pleasure, what would making love to him feel like? The slide of his smooth skin, the strength in his grip, the expressiveness of his dark eyes… She could only imagine how good he would make her feel—like she was the only woman in the world, and he wanted her.

Suddenly, the press of bodies on the dance floor and the grinding beat of the music made Penny feel overwhelmed.

"I'm getting a Mai Tai," she shouted to Henry. He gave her a look, but she stopped him before he could offer to come with her. "I'll be fine. Can I bring you anything?"

Lou shook her head. "I'm fine."

"I recommend sticking with beer here," Henry said.

The band struck up a Hawaiian version of "The Wah-Watusi," and Henry grabbed Lou's hand.

"I don't know this one," Lou said.

"Watch and learn!"

Penny pushed her way through the throng of dancers toward the bar, Lou's laugh trilling behind her as Henry began an elaborate lesson in the Watusi.

Henry had always been there for Penny. He was as solid as they came, even though he risked himself daily for his job as a stuntman. Henry had been the one who had taught her the dance steps to the Watusi, the Hully Gully, the Pony, and many more. Penny was an only child, and Henry had been more like a brother than a cousin.

She made her way to the bar and ordered her drink, fighting back tears. Watching Henry and Lou dance made Penny's chest tighten with emotion. She hadn't realized how much she'd missed her cousin.

"Hey, baby. Buy you a drink?"

Penny dragged her attention away from the dance floor and looked up at a man smiling at her. He was tall and attractive, with a wide smile.

"No, thanks."

The man pressed closer as the crowd surged around them. "One drink isn't gonna hurt."

"I just ordered one."

His smile grew. "Then join me at my table to drink it. There's plenty of room." He gestured at a table on the raised dais above the dance floor.

Penny knew better. "I don't think so."

"What?" he shouted, moving closer. "I can't hear you over the music."

"She said get lost, asshole." Bones was behind the man, glaring down at him.

The man turned and tipped his head back to look up at Bones. His eyes went wide when he registered the size of his opponent. "It's cool, man," he said, backing away. "I didn't know she was with you."

Penny's heart lodged in her throat, and a thrill ran down her spine. Bones was scary when he was in warrior mode, but he was also incredibly sexy. She swallowed roughly, both turned on and intimidated by him.

The bartender slid her beer across the counter, and Penny took a long sip. One look at Bones's mouth had her reliving their hot, brief kiss. The beer cooled her throat but did nothing to put out the fire in her chest.

"Put it on my tab," Bones said, raising his voice over the noise. "And grab me one too."

When Bones got his beer, they moved off to a less-crowded spot: a dark corner behind one of the tables. Penny had been to clubs in Seattle before—places where bands played, people danced, and smoke filled the air—but she'd never been to a club like Legends.

The mix of locals, tourists, and servicemen was unique to Honolulu. The locals clearly knew how to have a good time, and the tourists and servicemen were only too happy to join in.

There was something free about the place, something wild, and the music was impossible to resist. Couples danced with shocking intimacy, as if they were the only ones in the room, and the air pulsed with sexual tension—even more so since

Bones stood close enough to touch, his raw masculinity making every nerve in her body pulse with awareness.

"Henry's not so bad," Bones said, watching Henry dance with Lou.

Penny heard the reluctance in his voice and laughed. Lou was sweet and gorgeous, but she was the clumsiest person Penny had ever met. Lou could trip over her own feet, but Henry was good enough to make up for it. He could make anyone look good on the dance floor, even Lou. "Henry's great."

Bones grunted. "He's a pain in the ass."

Penny smiled, remembering the trouble Henry had got her into as a kid. He could be a bad influence, that was true.

The band launched into a rhythm-and-blues song, and couples formed on the dance floor. Penny felt the rhythm of the song flow through her body, and the urge to dance was too much to resist. She looked up at Bones, watching his throat work as he swallowed a sip of beer. Desire knotted her belly. "Wanna dance?"

In response, he finished his beer and set it on a nearby table, then offered her his hand. "Of course."

She put her bottle beside his and took his hand. An electric hum raced up her arm when they touched, and she remembered the feel of his mouth on hers. She suddenly felt like doing a lot more than dancing.

Bones led her to the dance floor, where there was just enough room for them.

"Do you like to dance?" she asked.

He wrapped his arm around her waist. When she was nestled tightly against his chest, he began to move, and she had her answer.

Electricity sizzled between them. They were two bodies moving in sync to the beat, lost to the pulse of the music.

His hips rolled against hers, and her body responded in an ancient rhythm. He spilled her backward in a low dip, then pulled her slowly back up and against his chest.

Bones danced like he did everything else, with power and grace and off-the-charts sensuality. Penny followed his lead. A good dancer was an extension of their partner. And Bones was more than a good dancer. He was everything she could ask for.

It was difficult to remind herself that he wasn't hers. And in no time at all, she would have to say good-bye.

Chapter 8

Bones

THEY DANCED until they were the last ones on the floor. Henry had taken Lou home an hour earlier, when she'd proclaimed she was too tired to stand, let alone dance. But Penny had wanted to stay, and Bones had offered to take her back to Henry's when she'd had her fill of dancing.

Bones was all too happy to stay on the dance floor as long as Penny wanted, prolonging their time together and dancing like no one was watching. She'd danced tirelessly, moving with sensuality and grace... seducing him with the swing of her hips. The sexy look in her eyes was an invitation he wanted to accept.

They didn't stop until the band quit playing and the bartender announced the last call for drinks. Even though she should have been exhausted—she was probably still on Seattle time—Penny was reluctant to stop.

Bones laughed at the pout on her pretty mouth. "I'll take you dancing again," he promised.

Her face lit up. "I'll hold you to that."

"We better get you home before you fall over. You must be worn out."

Penny shook her head, but he could see the lavender slashes of shadows under the bright blue of her gaze. He grabbed his keys from the break room and led her out of the club through the employee exit. His car was parked in a gravel lot, a block away from the street where rowdy drunks, evicted from the closed clubs, spilled onto the sidewalks, looking for their next adventure.

"You must be tired too," Penny said, settling into his ancient station wagon.

"Nah. I'm used to it."

Bones worked several jobs, piecing their earnings together to make a living. Sometimes the shifts overlapped so that he only caught a few hours of sleep at a time. But he didn't mind. He dictated his own schedule, taking time off whenever it suited him. It wasn't the life his father would have chosen for his only son, and he made that clear every time they saw each other, but it suited Bones.

He'd planned on putting in a full day at Waikiki, teaching surf lessons, taking tourists out on his outrigger canoe, and offering scuba lessons, but Penny had changed his mind. Thanks to the promise of a lucrative dive coming up, he wasn't worried about money. He could afford to take a few days off and spend them with Penny.

"What are you doing tomorrow?" he asked as he started the car.

"Henry has to work again, so I'm not sure. Probably hitting the beach and relaxing."

Bones seized the opportunity. "Would you like to spend the day with me? I could take you on a hike, show you one of my favorite spots." He often took tourists on a relatively easy hike. It ended at a waterfall and a shimmering pool perfect for a swim. It never failed to impress the mainlanders.

Penny sank back in the seat, stretching her long legs as far as she could in the cramped space. "I'd love that, but…"

Her hesitation made his heart squeeze, and he realized he'd been counting on her saying yes. He needed to see her again. "I get it," he said, clearing his throat when the words came out rougher than he'd intended. "You got plans, eh?"

"No." She sat up in the seat and turned toward him, tucking her legs under herself. "I'd love to go on a hike with you." Her voice was husky, making his blood turn to warm honey in his veins.

"Yeah?" Hope made pressure build in his chest. He'd only just met her. He didn't know her, but he wanted to. "So is that a yes?"

She frowned. "It's a Lou."

"What about her?"

"She's insistent that she doesn't want to spend any more time with Keoni."

His brows rose with surprise. It wasn't every day someone didn't like Keoni. He was the most beloved man on the island, a hero. "What's the matter with Keoni?"

"Nothing." Penny sighed and let her eyes drift shut. "That's the problem. Lou has a boyfriend back home, and she doesn't trust herself around Keoni. She likes him a little too much."

"Oh." That made sense. Bones was used to women liking Keoni too much. More than a few of his close women friends had an unrequited crush on Keoni. But he wasn't thinking about Keoni and his slew of admirers. Something else Penny had said snagged his thoughts. He shouldn't care, but he needed to know. "And you? Do you have a boyfriend back home? Someone special?"

Penny laughed shortly, an inelegant snort. "Yes, I have a boyfriend."

Bones tightened his fingers on the steering wheel, his heart plummeting to his stomach. It shouldn't matter if Penny had a boyfriend, but it did. The thought of her with another man made his chest ache.

He glanced away from the road and found her watching him with a small secretive smile. Her shoulders were turned toward him, her eyes bright in the darkened car. "But he's not special. And I realized something on the way here." She talked with her hands and her face, so animated it was hard to watch the road. Watching her was more fun. "I want to live in the moment from now on. No more hesitating to go after the things I want. It's 1968, you know?"

Nodding, he dragged his eyes back to the road. They'd left the darkened streets of Honolulu's business district behind and were heading toward Diamond Head Crater.

"I have more opportunities than my mother ever had. I don't have to get married. I can travel the world an independent woman. I could have gone to college. I probably should have, but I thought I was gonna be a ballerina. I had my heart set on dancing, not an education."

She paused for a breath, glancing out the window as they drove along the cliffside highway, and Bones smiled. He'd learned a lot about Penny in that short speech. She was a modern woman who wanted to make her own way in the world, but she was also a bit of a dreamer. The world only had so much room for ballerinas.

A comfortable silence filled the car as Penny gazed out the window. Bones concentrated on driving, trying not to be affected by her presence. She was a beautiful distraction, but the road was winding and hilly, and he needed to concentrate. After a while, her breathing fell into a slower pattern. He sensed she'd fallen asleep, and when he sneaked a look, he saw he was right. Her head rested against the window, and her hands were clasped lightly in her lap.

Bones drove the rest of the way to Henry's house, on the eastern side of the island, in contented silence. His own house was on the opposite side of the island, an hour's drive from Henry's, but he didn't mind. He was honored to be the one to see Penny home safely.

When they arrived at Henry's house, high on the ridge overlooking the back side of Diamond Head Crater and Black Point, Bones stopped the car and gently shook Penny awake.

Penny lifted her head, a serious expression on her face as she blinked. She stared at him in wonder. "Am I dreaming?"

"I'm real." He held out his arm when she looked at him skeptically. "Pinch me."

She gave his forearm a hard pinch, and he let out a sharp hiss. "Ow. Not so hard."

Penny grinned. "You're real."

"That hurt." He peered down at his arm as if she'd really hurt him, and her laugh echoed through the car.

"Come on, let's get you inside before you fall asleep again."

He got out of the car and went around to open her door and help her out. She took his hand, and together they walked down Henry's U-shaped driveway to his house. Henry's house was a small bungalow on a street of similar small houses. Bones could remember when there was only one house on the property, high on the top of the ridge. It had been an old Colonial-style mansion overlooking acres and acres of land. The owners had sold the house and the property, and not long after, dozens of small houses had sprung up along the ridge. They were an eyesore on top of a ridge, where there had been green hills for as far as the eye could see.

The houses were plain and ugly, but the view was still the same, still spectacular. The night was clear and cloudless with hundreds of bright stars. Shades darker than the midnight sky, the inky water lapped gently against the stark-white sand. In the distance, the fin-shaped slope of Diamond Head Crater descended into the sea.

"I think I could get used to this," Penny said, pausing to take in the view.

After a moment, they continued to the front door. "Let me know about tomorrow. Henry has my number."

Penny gazed up at him, and the corner of her lips turned

upward in a smile. "Why don't you come around eleven?"

Bones cocked his eyebrow. "What about Lou?"

"Leave Lou to me."

"You're sure?" The last thing he wanted to do was pressure Penny. He needed her to want to see him as badly as he wanted to see her.

Her gaze drifted over his face and settled on his lips. "I'm sure."

He wished they were at his house and he was taking Penny into his bedroom. He imagined her lying in his bed, her hair a burnished fire spread across her sheets. He leaned in close, his face hovering over hers.

Their gazes locked, and Bones's body reacted as if she'd touched him intimately. His muscles stiffened, and his heart raced. She placed a hand on his chest, and fire spread through him. Her hand trailed up to his collar bone, then wrapped around his neck. She reached up on her toes and pressed her mouth to his.

Her kiss was so soft, he was afraid to move, afraid to spoil the sweetness of the moment. The tip of her tongue licked against his lower lip, and a ripple of sensations tore through him. His hands locked around her, pulling her close against his chest. His mouth opened, and her tongue stroked against his. A splinter of desire pierced his chest and pulsed through him.

He walked her backward until she was pressed against the door, his hands coming up on either side of her face. Sweeping his tongue against hers, he deepened the kiss. She moaned into his mouth, a sound that made blood surge through him until he was hard as steel.

He thought of her on the dance floor, the way she'd moved with such sensuality and grace. She kissed the same way, with a passion that swept him away.

She stroked his tongue with hers, and he loved the way she took what she wanted. He knew his size was intimidating, a little scary, but Penny didn't seem scared. Even though she was pressed between his chest and the hard front door, she was the one in control, taking the lead.

A spark exploded between them, threatening to consume him. Thoughts of taking her right there against Henry's front door invaded his head, followed by a faint warning bell. This wasn't a regular hookup. It was different. Real.

Dammit, his aunties had gotten in his head. They'd planted that seed about the redheaded *Ehu* woman, the one they'd seen in his destiny, and because Penny happened to be a redhead, the seed sprouted. They'd said he'd feel it when he met her. He'd know immediately she was the one.

Bones thought back to his first impression of Penny at the airport. There had been a feeling that had washed over him. No, a knowing. He'd taken one look at Penny and he'd *known*.

She was the one. She pulled him like a magnet.

Her hands slid up his arms to cup his shoulders, then spread along his back. Her movements were smooth and fluid, feeling him, touching, soaking him in. He didn't think he'd ever been caressed like this before, by hands that seemed to know how he wanted to be touched.

Another warning bell went off, this one louder, almost like the sound of his voice calling his own name. The alarm rang sharp and clear, causing him to pull back and peer down at Penny.

He cautioned himself to slow down, play it cool. The last thing he wanted to do was spend forever with one woman, yet Penny enticed him. She sparkled without trying, reeling him in.

He framed her face with his hands, drinking in the fragile beauty of her face. Her eyes were heavy-lidded with desire, and her lips shined, plump from kissing. He ran his thumb along her lower lip, then released her. "I should let you get some sleep."

She came up on her toes and kissed his cheek, her lips a brief brush against his skin. "Thank you for a wonderful night."

Her hand was on the door, and although he wanted to stop her, to prolong the night a little longer, he let her go.

Chapter 9

Penny

PENNY FELT like she was a million miles away from the streets of downtown Seattle—a million miles from anything she'd ever known.

Bones hiked steadily in front of her, his broad back an easy target to follow through the lush jungle. It hadn't been easy talking Lou into spending the day with Bones and Keoni. Penny had tried talking to Lou about it, but in the end, she'd done what she'd needed to do to get Lou to agree. She'd lied.

Lou had objected to the very idea of Bones and Keoni, citing her and Penny's boyfriends back home as the main reason. Penny had tried to explain what was in her heart, what she'd realized when they'd landed on the island: Joe was ancient history. But it hadn't come out right. When she tried to put words behind her feelings, they made no sense. All she knew was that she felt free for the first time in ages, and Joe wasn't going to drag her down. That was why she'd lied to Lou and told her she'd cancelled with Bones and Keoni, when she'd never made the call.

Lou's laugh drifted up the trail, and Penny smiled. It sounded like Lou didn't begrudge her the lie.

Penny's arms and legs ached. Sweat trickled down her neck. Bones had said it would be an easy hike, and he was certainly making it look easy. He strode ahead with even, sure footsteps, while Penny huffed behind him, feeling the burn of every step she took up the steep slope.

She didn't mind the view of his strong shoulders and perfect backside. And the mountains weren't terrible either.

Bones stopped and waited for her, concern etched on his handsome features. "You okay?"

Penny wiped sweat from her forehead. "I'm great."

He pulled a canteen from his backpack and handed it to her. "Have a sip."

The water was fresh and cold, a soothing balm to her parched throat. She drank again, long and deep. Nothing had ever tasted half as good.

And no one had ever looked half as good in a T-shirt and shorts as Bones. His shirt strained across the bulges of his biceps, and his shorts hugged his muscular thighs. He'd pulled his hair back into a low ponytail at the nape of his neck, emphasizing the strong angles of his face. His cheekbones were high, his nose straight, and his jaw sharp. The gleam in his brown eyes invited her in.

Penny handed him back the canteen and watched his throat work as he swallowed. She stepped closer, eager to continue where they'd left off the night before at Henry's door. Her dreams had been filled with six feet and five inches of pure masculinity.

Bones replaced the canteen in his backpack and held a branch aside for her. "You should go first, so you can see without me blocking your view."

Penny looked at the overgrown trail, where a carpet of wild orchids and lush ferns bloomed, swallowing up the path. "What if I get lost?"

He laughed softly. "You won't get lost as long as I'm around."

Glancing up from the trail ahead, she met his deep-brown gaze. "What if I like the view of you in front of me?"

He laughed again, this time a sexy rumble that vibrated through her. "Trust me, you'll like this better."

She doubted it. Not much could beat the view of Bones's broad back, his tight buns, and his muscular legs.

"Go on," he said. "It's just up ahead."

Penny ducked under the branch he held for her, and she swept her gaze over the vibrant green hills. "Wow. Just wow."

"We're not there yet," Bones said. "Keep going."

"There are more wows?"

"Yeah. Way more." He placed his hand on the small of her back, urging her forward. "You wore your swimsuit, right?"

She nodded, thrilled by the touch of his hand on her back. His warmth pulsed through her, making her entire body throb with awareness. After a moment, he dropped his hand and fell into step behind her. His presence was a comfort. As long as Bones was around, she knew nothing could harm her.

They hiked deeper into the jungle, where tall trees blocked the bright sun and birdsong sounded from above. The smell of earth and wild ginger filled the air. The sound of rushing water grew louder until it filled Penny's ears.

She stepped around a large rock and saw the source of the water: a stream cascading from a tall peak. Water rushed down a sheer rock face, tumbling into a shimmering pool below.

This was what Penny had saved her money for. *This* was what she'd been longing for. It was the magic of the land, the wonder of a world she'd never known existed, and the promise that if something like this—something so pure and perfect— existed, then all her dreams were possible.

All her dreams could come true.

The rubber sole of her sneaker hit a patch of wet moss on the rocks, and she slipped.

Bones was there before she could fall. His arm cinched around her waist, and he pulled her against the solid wall of his chest. In his arms, Penny felt like nothing could harm her—except maybe her heart, which was racing at an alarming speed.

"You gotta watch your step." His voice was a sexy growl.

A spray from the waterfall blew across the pool, misting her heated skin. "Thank you for being there."

His dark gaze turned serious. "Always."

He dipped his chin just as she rose to meet his mouth. The kiss was soft, sweeter than she'd expected. Bones was big and intimidating, but he kissed so gently. It was an unanticipated delight. He seemed content to let her take the lead.

They broke apart when Lou's and Keoni's voices sounded close by.

Bones reached down to the hem of his shirt and peeled it off. "Let's have that swim."

Penny's jaw fell open as she watched Bones kick off his shoes. He looked like he'd been carved from stone. His body was perfectly sculpted. Muscles upon muscles rippled under his tanned skin. She couldn't tear her eyes away when he stepped to the edge of the rock and dived into the shimmering pool below.

A moment later, she undressed down to her swimsuit and followed.

PENNY AND BONES lingered at Henry's door saying good-bye, just like the night before. Penny should have been exhausted from traveling, dancing half the night, and hiking all morning, but she was the opposite. Her entire body hummed with antici-pation, as if it were begging to know what was next.

She hoped Bones was next. She could use another make-out session with him.

Lou was inside, getting ready for a nap, and Keoni was in the car, waiting for Bones. They finally had a moment alone.

Bones braced his hand against the door and dipped his head to kiss her. The kiss was long and lingering, and his mouth teased her softly, nibbling as if they had the rest of the day to say good-bye.

The car horn blared, then Keoni stuck his head out the window and yelled, "Sorry!"

Bones reluctantly lifted his head. "He's gotta work."

"So this is good-bye?" Penny sucked in a breath. They'd shared a few kisses and had a good time, and their chemistry was off the charts, but it didn't mean he wanted to see her again. Bones probably had his pick of women. Maybe he even had a girlfriend. He hadn't said anything when they'd talked about Joe earlier.

"Have dinner with me?" His hand slid into her damp hair, and he bent his neck to kiss her jaw.

Penny flattened her hand against his chest, delighting in the feel of his coiled muscles under her palm. She wanted to share more than a meal with him.

What would Lou say? Lou didn't approve of Bones. But neither had she approved of Keoni, and they'd spent the afternoon laughing together as if they were best friends.

As Bones's lips trailed up to her ear, Penny didn't care what her best friend thought anymore. "Yes."

Keoni honked again, two polite beeps followed by another apology.

Bones stepped back and flipped Keoni the bird before turning to Penny with a smile. "See you tomorrow." He kissed her firmly on the lips, sealing the date before he left.

Penny walked through Henry's small house as if on a cloud. Her skin still tingled from Bones's touch. She opened the door to Henry's room, which he'd graciously given up for their stay, and saw Lou stretched out on the bed, a dreamy smile on her face.

"What were you thinking about?" Penny asked in a teasing voice. "Keoni?"

Lou's cheeks reddened, and she sat up with a guilty start. "No."

Penny sat down on the bed next to her. "It's okay if you like him. That's why we're here—to have a good time."

Lou's brows drew together. "I couldn't do that to Paul."

Penny shrugged, figuring it was a good time to tell Lou about her dinner plans with Bones. "You mind if I venture out on my own tomorrow night?"

Lou raised a brow. "What are you doing?"

Penny stood up and stretched. Her muscles were filled with a pleasant ache she hadn't experienced since the days of daily dance practice. She bent to touch her toes, answering Lou from the bottom of her stretch. "Bones asked me to dinner."

"Penny!"

Penny peered at Lou from under the curtain of her hair. "What?"

"You can't be serious."

Penny rolled up to first position, placing one foot slightly in front of the other as she stretched her arms overhead. "Why not?" She leaned left and then right, feeling the pull of her muscles in her sides. It was easier to focus on her body than the emotions welling up in her chest. Guilt warred with excitement, and the pure pulse of lust won over. "What does it hurt to have a little fun?"

"You'll never see him again after we leave."

"So?" Penny refused to think about what happened when they returned to Seattle. The future was now.

"So? What about Joe?"

Penny sneered. "What about Joe?"

Penny had forgotten all about Joe. But now that she was thinking of him, she made the decision to break up with him as soon as they got home. No use carrying on with a man she didn't love, not when a man she'd just met had made her feel more than Joe ever had.

"I'm going to have the time of my life." She cocked her

head at Lou. A challenge. "You should do the same. Who knows when we'll get the chance again?"

"I can't."

"Why not?"

"Because of Paul."

"Screw Paul. He's a jerk."

Lou made a choking noise. "You like Paul."

Penny wrinkled her nose. "No one likes Paul."

"My parents adore him."

"Well, maybe your mother should marry him." She smiled mischievously when a crazy thought entered her mind. "And you should marry Keoni, and I'll marry Bones. We could live next door to each other on the beach instead of in Seward Park."

She was only partly joking.

$$\text{———————————————}$$

Chapter 10

$$\text{———————————————}$$

Bones

BONES'S MOTHER had taught him how to cook, and his father had taught him how to pull fresh fish from the ocean. Bones was a better fisherman than cook, but he managed all right in the kitchen.

He had enough skills to cook Penny an impressive dinner she wouldn't soon forget. He wanted to impress her, leave her with enough memories of Hawaii to make her want to come back again or, better yet, never leave. The thought surprised him. He'd never cooked for a woman before, and he'd never entertained a tourist at his home. He'd been in plenty of hotel rooms, but he'd never brought a woman back to his place. Why was Penny different?

The answer was obvious. Besides being gorgeous, Penny was special. There was something about her that drew him in. She made him want to be the best version of himself. He wanted to be charming and adventurous, as exciting and carefree as she was. It was unusual for him to care about impressing a woman, but he wanted to impress Penny. His lau lau dinner would do the trick.

An electric thrill raced through him as he knocked on Henry's door. He couldn't wait to see Penny again, to feel the sunny beam of her smile light him up.

Henry answered the door with a scowl. "You're taking Penny to dinner?"

Bones smoothed a hand down the front of his shirt. He'd dressed up in a button-down aloha style shirt in pastel colors and a pair of tan slacks. "You got beef with me or what?"

"Not if you treat her right." Henry crossed his arms over his chest, then nodded once at Bones. "You gonna treat her right?"

Bones had no intention of mistreating Penny. He eyed Henry from the vantage point of his superior height, and Henry glared right back, his eyes glittering fiercely. Bones thought Henry might want to argue with more than words, but Penny came to the door and defused the situation.

She was stunning in a pale-pink dress and high-heeled sandals. Her hair shone like red silk against her creamy skin.

She grabbed Henry's face and planted a kiss on his cheek. "Don't wait up."

Bones couldn't look away from Penny. There was something about her, something more than her fiery beauty that was capturing him. Her eyes danced with a thirst for adventure, and her smile beamed. In her heels, she was only a few inches shorter than him. He was used to stooping down with women, minimizing his height, but with Penny, he could stand up straight.

"You ready?" She grabbed his hand and pulled him down the driveway toward the car. "We should get outta here before Henry blows a gasket." Her laugh trilled in the balmy air. "Did you get a load of his face?"

Bones tugged Penny's hand, stopping her. "You're..." His voice caught on the words because beautiful wasn't the word he needed. Beautiful wasn't enough. "You look stunning."

She pressed a hand to the waist of her dress. "Is this all right? You didn't say where we were going."

Bones let his gaze travel over Penny. The dress was short, and he had a hard time dragging his attention away from her dancer's legs. "It's perfect." She was perfect.

"So where are we going?" Penny asked.

Bones stopped at the passenger door of his car. "I want to cook for you at my place."

She cocked her head to the side, her eyes narrowing. "Oh, I get it."

His skin felt tight, and an ache settled right over his heart. "What?"

She flashed a knowing smile. "I know your plan. You want to get me in bed."

Heat flared in his chest. Of course he wanted her in bed, but he also wanted to do something special for her, give her a memory of Hawaii she wouldn't forget that had nothing to do with his bedroom. "It's not like that," he said.

She lifted her brows. "So you don't want to get me in bed?"

His heart hammered. "I didn't say that."

She wound her arms around his neck, pressing her body against his. "You don't have to cook to impress me."

He wrapped his arms around her. She was as slim as a ti leaf, warm and pliant in his embrace. His hands spread up her back, pressing her against his chest. He might have a hard time keeping his hands off her long enough to cook, but he was determined to try.

"I'm an excellent cook. You'll see." *One taste of his food, and she'll fall in love.* The thought came out of nowhere, sticking in his mind like wet sand.

Penny pushed against his chest and stepped back. "Henry's glaring at us from the window," she said with a laugh. "Let's get outta here."

Once Penny was settled in the car, Bones shut the door and

walked around to his side, giving Henry a wave before he got behind the wheel.

"He wants to look out for you. My Pops was always sharpening his knives when boys came to pick my sisters up for dates."

"Henry and I were always close." Penny turned on the bench seat, her face alight with a smile. "We got into so much trouble together." Her eyes crinkled in the corners as the smile took over her face. "There was this dried-up creek bed on our grandparents' farm that we were supposed to stay away from. Our grandfather said it was too dangerous, so all the kids were warned to stay away. But Henry and I snuck out there and spent all day swinging across the creek on vines hanging from the trees." She covered her laugh with her hand. "We didn't realize until later that the vines were covered in poison ivy."

Bones smiled and forced his eyes back to the curving road ahead. Penny's story reminded him of the trouble he and Keoni had gotten into as kids. They were more than cousins; they were best friends.

"Henry took the blame," Penny said. "He told our grandfather he'd dared me to swing across the creek bed." Her voice was wistful, caught up in the memory. "He got poison ivy and a whipping."

They traded stories on the long drive to his house. Bones told Penny about helping Keoni with chores around the graveyard so they could go surfing and diving. Penny shared stories about how dance had consumed her life from a young age.

There was hardly a moment of silence between them the entire drive as they wound between the jagged cliffs and the blue Pacific. His house was in a quiet neighborhood on the beach. Most of the families had lived there for generations.

They passed his parents' sprawling house, built high in the mountains above his beachfront cottage. "That's where my folks live," he said.

Penny stared out the window at the impressive house in the

lush hills.

"Unless there's an emergency, I'm expected home for supper every Sunday night."

She pushed her hair off her face and smiled at him. "Even this Sunday? Aren't you going to the surfing contest to watch your friend?"

He shrugged. "My family will be at the contest, along with the rest of the island." The contest was the biggest event of the year. Bones would be going regardless of whether Declan was competing.

"Were you close growing up?"

Bones nodded. "Declan was a good friend. We had a few years when we did everything together…" Bones trailed off. Their story had a tragic ending. He hadn't seen Declan in two years, and he didn't want to ruin his night with Penny talking about it. "You're coming to watch the contest, yeah?"

"I wouldn't miss it."

He turned onto his street, and they drove in comfortable silence until they arrived at his small house near the end of the street. What his house lacked in size, it made up for in location. The backyard led straight to the beach, his own private oasis.

Bones gathered the groceries from the back seat and showed Penny into his house. He kicked off his shoes, and Penny did the same. Bones glanced down at her feet, and she attempted to hide her foot behind her ankle.

"They're hideous, aren't they?"

Penny had dancer's legs, but she also had dancer's feet. Her arches were high, and her toes were bent, the joints misshapen. Bones smiled at her reassuringly. "They're not hideous."

"You lie," she said, padding into the living room with a knowing smile. "But thank you for being sweet."

"They are well-used feet. I can respect that," he said, recognizing the work she must have put in wearing painful toe shoes to get damaged feet.

Penny glanced around. "Did you just move in?"

"Nah. Why?"

"You don't have any furniture." She turned to look at him, her hair swishing across her back.

"I'm not much for decorating." There was a plaid sofa, a sagging relic he'd inherited with the house, but little else in the way of furniture.

Penny shook her head and strode to the sliding glass doors. "I guess it doesn't matter what's inside when you have the beach as your backyard."

Bones deposited the grocery bags on the counter, then went to join her. "Are you much of a cook?"

She held up her thumb and first finger, pinching them an inch apart. "Not much."

"Good." He took her hand and pulled her toward the kitchen. "I'll teach you a few things."

He grabbed an apron from the wall by the refrigerator and handed it to her, then pulled another one from the pantry. His sisters thought it was cute to give him aprons for Christmas, and he had too many of them to count.

Penny read the words blazoned across the bib of his apron with a grin. "Kiss the cook?"

He shrugged. "It was a gift from one of my sisters."

She wound her arms around his neck and pulled him down so that their mouths were inches apart. "I like your sisters already."

Her lips were warm against his, and his appetite for food was replaced by a longing for her. But he didn't want to rush their time together. He ended the kiss and tied the apron around her waist, getting on with his plan to give her a memory she'd never forget.

They worked together to empty the grocery bags. Bones explained each ingredient that would go into making the dish. Sweet potato, carrots, and cod for the lau lau, as well as ti leaves and rice.

"What are these for?" Penny held up a bouquet of flowers

wrapped in wet newspaper.

"Those are for you." He pulled a large Mason jar from the cabinet and filled it with water. After taking the bouquet from her, he plucked out a single hibiscus flower, bright pink to match her dress. "Here." He tucked it behind her right ear. "You're taken for the night."

She touched the flower, and a sad expression crossed over her face. Bones knew she was feeling it too. That tinge of regret that their time together was so short.

"Would you like a glass of wine? Or beer?" Bones realized he didn't even know what she preferred. Even though he felt like he'd known her all his life, they were strangers.

"Wine," she said, nodding at the bottle of red on the counter.

Bones opened the wine and poured them each a glass, then set the Mason jar of flowers on the bar counter. His only dining furniture was two lawn chairs and a wicker table on the patio.

Penny raised her glass to his. "Here's to new adventures."

They drank to her toast, then started the preparations. He showed her how to cut everything into bite-sized cubes and how to de-stem the ti leaves they'd use to make neat packages for steaming. "Fish or pork?" he asked, brushing past her in the small kitchen.

"Both?"

He smiled and nodded. "Do you ever say no to anything?"

"Not if I can help it," she said. "I want to do everything."

Bones reached past Penny and added the fish to the tray. "You're not scared of anything, eh?"

Penny's blue eyes met his, shocking him with their intensity. "The way I figure it, my fate is already sealed. I might as well have some fun along the ride."

Bones stared at her for a long moment, his aunties' words lodging in his head. They'd promised him he'd meet a woman who was his destiny. His gut told him he'd just met her, and she was wearing his apron, cooking in his kitchen.

Chapter 11

Penny

THE SUN SANK toward the horizon as they sipped their wine. Penny leaned toward Bones, listening as he told stories of growing up on the beach and learning to fish, surf, and sail in the very ocean stretching in front of them.

"Tell me more about your famous surfer friend," she said.

Bones's shoulders edged up toward his ears. "What do you want to know?"

"Do you think he will win the surfing contest?"

Bones glared at the ocean. "He better."

Penny laughed at his unexpected response. "Why's that?"

"You should have seen him surf when we were growing up. There wasn't a wave he wouldn't ride. I think he used to wipe out for the fun of it." He shook his head. "Keoni's better on the big waves. He's stronger and braver. But Declan has finesse. He's quick and smooth. He can cut up a wave like nobody else." Bones stared off into the distance, his jaw set in his firm silence.

He had the profile of a warrior. His stern gaze and formidable features would scare off even the most determined enemy. Penny watched him for a long moment, wondering what he was thinking that had taken him so far away from their romantic dinner table.

She pushed her chair back and walked around to his side of the table, then settled herself on his lap. Winding her arms around his neck, she dipped her head to kiss his cheek. "Penny for your thoughts."

He turned his head and captured her lips in a slow kiss that made her bones melt. His mouth looked hard, but it was soft and sweet, tasting faintly of rich red wine.

"That doesn't seem fair." He trailed kisses along her jaw, his big hand spreading up her back. "I get all this, and you get nothing but the stray thoughts in my head."

Penny dipped her head and rested her forehead against his. "What happened?"

Bones lifted his shoulders in a shrug. "He and Keoni had a fight," he admitted.

Again with Keoni? Penny was starting to think nothing happened on the island that didn't involve Keoni. "What's Keoni got to do with you?"

Bones stiffened, the muscles in his shoulders flexing. "Keoni has got everything to do with me."

Penny didn't get it. What was so special about Keoni? In her opinion, Bones was the more impressive of the cousins.

She smoothed his hair back from his high forehead, letting her fingers trail through his luxurious waves. "Let me get this straight. You're not friends with Declan anymore because of Keoni?"

"There's more to it than that," he said. "A lot more. If I started telling you, it would take all night."

"I'm not going anywhere."

His eyes locked on hers. "Henry would kill me if I brought you home late."

There was nowhere she'd rather be than right there on

Bones's lap, feeling the press of his hard thighs under her legs. "I don't care about Henry."

"No?"

She shook her head. "Tell me the story. What happened with Declan?"

"If you really want to know, it's easier to show you."

Penny met his dark gaze. "I really want to know."

Bones stood from the chair and set Penny on her feet. Taking her hand, he led the way around the back of his house.

Flowers bloomed along the path, spreading over the small patch of grass that gave way to sand. They passed a window with the curtains open, and Penny snuck a peek inside. She caught a glimpse of a king-size bed and a nightstand before she hurried to catch up to Bones's long stride.

He stopped at a freestanding shed next to his house. It was painted green to match his house and had a roll-up door and two small windows. Bones rolled up the door, then flicked on the lights. Penny blinked, adjusting to the sudden brightness. Two long workbenches lined the walls, and a huge, tarp-covered object dominated the center aisle. The smell of sawdust and oil filled the air.

The shed reminded her of her grandfather's workshop on the farm, where he'd spent time tinkering with old machinery and hiding from her grandmother.

Bones walked to the shrouded object and put his hand on the tarp. His mouth thinned, and a pained expression came over his face. "This is what happened with Declan."

He pulled back the tarp, revealing a long, hollowed-out log. Penny narrowed her eyes at the huge hunk of shiny wood, not sure what she was looking at. Her gaze darted to Bones, questioning, but he was staring at the object with a glazed expression. Penny could feel the emotions radiating off him. Pain, sorrow, regret.

"It all started when Eddie died," Bones said, his voice a low rumble near her ear.

Pain filled her chest. She had no idea who Eddie was or what he meant to Bones, but her heart ached for his loss. "I'm sorry."

"He was too young to die. Gone too soon."

Penny placed her hands on his shoulders and massaged his rock-hard muscles, trying to soothe his tension. "Was he family?"

"No." Bones dipped his head and pressed his face into the crook of her neck. She felt him take a deep, shuddering breath. Against her skin. "He wasn't related. But he was our brother, you know?"

Penny felt that way about Lou. They weren't related by blood but by experience. By love.

"It was an accident," Bones said. "But Declan and Keoni both blamed themselves. They were there when it happened."

Penny smoothed a hand through his hair, pushing it off his face. "What happened?"

Bones tightened his arms around her waist and pulled her close. "The ocean stole him."

Penny had no idea what that meant. She waited for Bones to go on, stroking a hand along the silky strands of his hair while she waited for him to speak. She would stay all night, locked in his embrace, if it eased his pain.

After a long moment, he pulled away and rested his hand on the log. "Declan fell apart when Eddie died. He buried himself in a bottle of Jack and didn't come up for months. Then one day, he was gone. No good-bye, no explanation, no nothing. I didn't see him again until that day at the airport when I picked you up."

Penny nodded for him to continue. The story he spun didn't seem to have anything to do with the work shed, but she didn't want to rush him as he paced to the end of the shed and back, brushing his hand along the log as he walked.

"Have you seen an outrigger canoe?" Bones asked finally.

Penny shook her head. "I don't think so."

Bones stared at the piece of wood. "They start out with a single log from a koa tree. Only the koa tree is strong and supple enough to be used. There is a ritual to every part of the process. First the tree is cut, then it's hollowed out." He dipped his hand into the interior of the log, which was smoothed out and shiny. "It's faster now with modern equipment, but Declan and I wanted to do it the old-fashioned way." Bones lifted his gaze, smiling faintly. "We had this dream. We would build a canoe like the first Hawaiians, using the same materials, the same methods." He shrugged. "Some things had to be modified a bit, but we wanted to honor the first sailors."

Penny felt the emotions behind his story. She clasped her hands in front of her and tried to wait patiently as he told the story in fragmented pieces. Declan had designed the boat. Bones had provided the place to work. They met every weekend, spending long hours in the shed with the radio blasting as they sweat and toiled over carving out the canoe, then staining the hull. They'd weaved lashings to tie the sails out of coconut fibers, which had been soaked for weeks in seawater. It was a labor of love, and their plan was to launch the two-man canoe and sail to Maui using the same navigation tools as Bones's waterman ancestors: the stars.

But then Eddie had died, Declan had spiraled out of control and disappeared, and Bones had covered up the canoe and shut the door on his work shed.

"I didn't know if I'd ever see Declan again." He sighed heavily. "Then he shows up because he's surfing the Duke. Where's he been for two years? Eh? Then he doesn't say a word about this." He knocked his fist on the canoe, and the hollow sound echoed in the shed. His gaze narrowed, and his jaw flexed. "He apologized to Keoni, but I got nothing. Not a fucking word. For all I knew, he was dead."

His words, filled with pain, rang in the small space. Penny looked at the log and saw Bones's unfinished dreams, his failed legacy. She couldn't help thinking Declan was a jerk. He didn't deserve Bones. But, it was in her nature to look at the bright side. There was always a silver lining, even on the darkest clouds.

"What if you finish it yourself?" Penny asked, dipping a finger along the polished wood.

Bones scoffed. "It would take years."

Penny lifted her shoulder in a shrug. "So? Good things take time. Didn't your mother ever tell you that?"

Bones's brows drew together, and Penny could see the wheels turning in his head. "Maybe."

"You should listen to your mother."

That earned a hearty laugh. "My mother believes in the old gods. She thinks Pele is looking down on us from her volcano throne."

"Yeah?" Penny paused, considering. Her parents weren't overly religious, but they did believe a god was watching them from above. It wasn't so different. "What's wrong with that?"

Bones smiled. "She believes redheaded women are descendants of the volcano goddess, blessed with special powers."

Penny fluffed her hair. "I'm liking her more by the minute."

Bones eyed her thoughtfully. "It's too bad you can't come to the next Sunday supper. I think you two would get along great."

A fist closed around her heart. "Yeah, it's too bad." She remembered she'd never see Bones again after next week. She'd never sit down to Sunday supper. She'd never see the finished outrigger canoe that she had a feeling Bones would finish.

He crossed the room and took her hand. "You hungry? I think our dinner is probably ready."

They left the shed, and Bones insisted Penny sit at the table on the patio and let him serve her dinner. First he brought the Mason jar of flowers and set them on the table, then he returned with a fresh bottle of wine and silverware. He filled her glass and disappeared back inside to get the food.

Penny felt like a queen as she gazed out at the setting sun. She'd never seen anything half as beautiful. The golden orb of the sun sank into the horizon, leaving a splash of orange, peach, and lavender in its wake. The turquoise blue of the ocean seemed even more vibrant in the bold hues of the twilight. Even the heavy humidity seemed to know it was time to turn in for the day. A gentle breeze floated along the beach, bringing scents of wildflowers and sea salt. The tide caressing the shore and the rustle of palm fronds were the only sounds.

It was a far cry from the hustle of downtown Seattle, where Penny's view from her bedroom was the brick wall of the apartment building next door.

The door shut, and Bones came out on the patio with two plates of food. He'd tied his hair back at the nape of his neck, and part of her was sorry. Even though he looked very handsome with his hair off his face, showing off his chiseled features—his sharp jaw and broad cheekbones—she liked it down and flowing over his broad shoulders so she could run her fingers through it. He set a plate of food in front of her, and the delicious smell of spiced vegetables and meat made her mouth water. The ti leaves they'd used to tie up the packages of meat and vegetables had turned a deep green. Next to the ti leaf package was a rounded pile of rice topped with brown sauce. Penny's mouth watered.

Bones settled in the seat across from her. "You don't want to eat the outer leaves," he said, demonstrating as he untied the knot.

Penny untied the neat package of food. Steam wafted from the dish as the pork, fish, and vegetables spilled out. She forked a bite and blew on it before tasting. The heavenly flavors of buttery fish, spiced pork, and tangy vegetables hit her mouth like an explosion. She'd never considered herself a cook before, but she'd had a part in this deliciousness, and she was proud. She sighed as she chewed, savoring the taste, the atmosphere, and the man sitting across from her.

They ate the fruits of their labor and talked between bites. Bones told her how he'd inherited the house from his uncle.

Penny told him about her apartment in Seattle that she shared with Lou, which was furnished from her parents' castaways and thrift store finds.

When they were finished with dinner, they took their plates to the kitchen, where Bones said to leave them, and went to sit in the living room on the sagging sofa. It turned out to be surprisingly comfortable, especially when Bones settled in beside her.

Penny thought they would get to the part of the date she'd been looking forward to most. The sexual tension between them had been sizzling under the surface all night. Every brief touch or glance made Penny's body sizzle with awareness. Between the amazing food, the intimately shared stories, and the priceless ocean view, Penny felt like she'd been swept off her feet.

Spotting a ukulele on a chair in the corner of the room, she remembered he'd promised to play. "Play me a song?" she asked.

Bones shifted to his feet. "What do you want to hear?"

"Your favorite song."

"Awright," he said, picking up the ukulele. Such a big man with such a small instrument should have been comical, but it was somehow perfect.

When he began to strum, Penny felt tears prick behind her eyes. The music was poignantly reminiscent of an era gone by. She felt the itch to dance, something slow and wistful, an elegant expression. But the soft cushions of the sofa held her captive, and she felt too comfortable to move. Penny tucked her feet beneath her and let her eyes drift shut.

———————————

Chapter 12

———————————

Bones

THE DAY STARTED like every other morning of Bones's life. He woke early and dressed for his daily swim. The only thing different was Penny was in his bed.

He'd carried her to his room after she'd fallen asleep on his sofa while he'd played the ukulele. Bones wasn't offended that his playing had put her to sleep. He'd never claimed to be good at the ukulele.

After quietly closing the dresser drawer, he crept out of his bedroom so he wouldn't wake her. She was probably still exhausted from traveling and needed more rest. He paused at the door, looking at her in his bed. Last night hadn't gone as he'd expected. They hadn't done more than kiss, but somehow it had been perfect.

Showing Penny his unfinished canoe had rekindled his passion for the project. She was right—he should finish it on his own. He didn't need Declan or anyone else. It may take him a lot longer to do it without help, but he'd have all the glory. He might even sail it on his own. Why not?

He poured himself a glass of milk and ate a banana, rolling his shoulders as he walked out of the kitchen. His normal swim was two miles, but he might cut it short this morning. He didn't want Penny to wake up without him.

Deciding to leave her a note in case she woke up, he was searching for a pen when the phone rang. Bones checked the clock and saw it was early for a phone call. Not yet six a.m. He grabbed the phone off the wall, guessing it was one of his sisters. They knew he went for a swim every morning and was likely to be up.

"Hello?"

"What the hell, man?" It wasn't one of his sisters. It was Henry.

"Howzit, Henry?"

"*Howzit?*" His voice dripped with anger. "Is that all you have to say? Where's my cousin? She never came home last night."

"Relax, brother." Bones stretched the cord into the living room, still searching for a pen. "She fell asleep, and I didn't want to wake her."

Henry exhaled loudly "You coulda called me, man. I was worried."

"Sorry." Bones found a pen and started scribbling a note for Penny. "I'll have her call you when she wakes up."

"Don't bother. I gotta go to work. She and Lou were supposed to come with me to meet some of the actors."

"I can drop her off on set." Disappointment spread through his chest. He'd wanted to spend the day with Penny, but he wasn't the only one in Hawaii who wanted her time.

"Fine. I'll tell Lou."

"Thanks, eh?"

"And, Bones?"

Bones signed his name on the note and folded it in half. "Yeah?"

"Watch out for Penny. She's easy to love."

Bones had already figured that out. "Thanks for the warning."

"Don't say I never did nothing nice for you."

"We're still on for the dive Monday?" Henry was going to drive the boat on a diving excursion Bones had lined up.

"We're still on. Where's my fifty bucks?"

"I'm good for it."

They hung up, and Bones went back into his room to put the note on the nightstand where Penny was most likely to see it if she woke up and he was still gone. He reached over and smoothed a strand of hair off her face, and she stirred. A slow smile spread across her lips as she looked up and saw him.

"Go back to sleep," he said, brushing his hand along her hair. "It's early."

She shifted, turning to look at him. "Where are you going?"

"Gotta get my swim in. I'll be back before you know it."

She nodded and closed her eyes, snuggling under the covers. Something clenched in his chest as he watched her drift back to sleep. His sheets were going to smell like her, haunting him until laundry day. He'd slept on the sofa the night before, his feet hanging over the armrest. Sleep had eluded him, and he had to fight the urge to climb into his bed and wrap his arms around Penny.

Then he remembered the dive coming up on Monday. Skipping out on his swim wouldn't serve him well. Diving was dangerous business, and he had to be in top physical condition, ready for anything. He kept in shape with daily swims and training at his *hālau hula,* where they used ancient methods like carrying logs, climbing trees, and swimming with rocks to gain strength and flexibility.

His daily swim not only kept him fit but gave him time to think and plan. As his body cruised through the water, his mind dropped into deep thought. Bones had solved problems, planned adventures, and come up with genius plans while going through the repetitive motions of swimming.

The problem on his mind was the five feet and ten inches of warm, sexy woman occupying his bed. What was he supposed to do with Penny? Except fall in love with her?

Whoa.

Surprise put a hitch in his stroke. He jolted and sucked in a mouthful of water when he failed to lift his head before breathing. His body forgot what to do, and for a split second, he froze. Waves pushed against him, and he felt himself drifting away.

He wasn't in love with Penny. That was impossible.

He hardly knew her, and it wasn't like she would fit in with his lifestyle or family. He couldn't imagine what his father would say if he brought an outsider like Penny to Sunday supper. His family wanted him to marry a traditional Hawaiian girl, not a *haole* from the mainland.

Yet he could picture himself waking up to her in the mornings. Curling up with her at night. Spending long hours listening to her talk, watching her dance, and swallowing her sweet moans as he kissed her.

Picking up his pace, he sprinted through his swim and was back to the shoreline in record time. He strode out of the water, hoping to find Penny still curled up in his bed.

When he saw her sitting on one of his patio chairs, his mouth spread into a grin. Although he was slightly disappointed she wasn't still in bed, he didn't mind her sitting on his patio, wearing one of his aloha-style shirts.

She beamed when she saw him and rose to hand him the towel he'd left on the table. "Hello, gorgeous."

His heart stuttered. He'd been thinking the same about her. He reached for the towel, his eyes devouring her long, slender legs. The tops of her thighs were dusted with freckles, and he wanted to lick each one. His gaze grew hungry.

"I would have made coffee, but you didn't have any."

He dried his hair and then rubbed the towel against his chest. "I don't drink coffee."

Penny's jaw dropped in mock horror. "You don't drink coffee? It's the only thing that gets me up in the morning."

Bones could think of better ways to get Penny up in the morning.

"How far did you swim?" she asked, standing up to stretch.

Bones watched the shirt rise, exposing more creamy-pale skin of her thighs.

"A couple miles."

Her gaze dropped down his wet torso in appreciation. "Impressive."

"I have to stay in shape." He patted his stomach. "Or my teacher will punish me."

She cocked her head at him. "Teacher? Are you in school?"

"It's not book learning," he said. "It's hula."

Her smile beamed. "You're a dancer?" Her gaze dipped down him again. "I should have known."

Bones nodded. There was a big difference between someone who could dance and a dancer. Penny was a dancer. He was a dancer.

Penny swept her attention to the view of the white sand and gentle waves kissing the shore. "I can't believe this is your backyard. I've never seen a sunrise so beautiful."

He knew he was lucky to live in Hawaii. It was something he would never take for granted. The early morning was his favorite time of day. The sun lit the sky with a soft glow, and palm fronds rippled in the breeze. A balmy warmth hung in the air, fragrant with the scent of flowers.

In a few hours, the beach would be busy with locals, almost all of whom he knew by name, but for now, the sand was pristine.

He draped his towel over the back of the chair and took her hand. "Let's go for a walk. I want to show you the rest of my backyard."

"Am I dressed okay?" She ran a hand along the shirt.

"It's just down the beach. It's private."

He led her along the sand, his hand wrapped securely around hers in a protective grasp. The beach stretched before them, curving sharply to a point in the distance. Sand sparkled under the sunlight like thousands of tiny gems, and palm fronds swayed in the sea breeze.

"This land has been in my family for generations. The king gave it to my great-great-grandfather."

Penny turned her head to survey the view from the mountains to the sea. "That's quite a gift."

"I own the house I live in and the small plot of land around it, but I can't own any of this." His voice was thick with emotion as he gestured around at the formidable cliffs and the undulating sea. They stopped at the dead end, where the jagged mountains blocked the path. "This is the most western tip of the island," Bones said. "In Hawaii, we have a saying. When you die, you 'travel west.' The souls of the dead leap off here and find their way into the next life." He pointed at the rock face where the tide lashed the cliffs. "That splash is two soul mates reuniting." Bones slipped his arm around her waist and pulled her back against his front. "If two lovers witness the reuniting of souls, it blesses them with a long life together."

Penny leaned against him, her head resting on his chest. "Geez, you're handsome and romantic. I can't take much more."

They were quiet for a moment, watching the waves crash against the cliff. Bones dipped his head and inhaled the fruity scent of her shampoo. He knew he'd be smelling it on his pillow and missing her.

She turned her face up toward his. "Do you want to live here forever?"

He shrugged. There was nowhere else he'd rather be. "Sure. Why not?"

Penny stared up at him, her wide blue eyes curious. "Don't you want to see the world?"

Bones let his gaze drift over her face. At the moment, he

didn't care about anything but the woman in his arms. It didn't matter where they were, as long as he had a few more hours with her. "I never thought about it," he answered.

Penny smiled wistfully. "I want to see everything. Everywhere. Paris, London, Israel… the world."

Bones stayed silent. He didn't care to see the world, not when he had everything he needed in his own backyard. "Maybe after you see the world, you'll come back to Hawaii." *To him.*

"Maybe I will."

When they got back to his house, Penny pushed him into a chair and held him there with a hand to his chest.

"I'm going to make breakfast," she said.

He laughed, picturing his bare cupboards. "With what?"

"I'll find something. Stay here." She blew him a kiss and sauntered inside the house.

He sat back in the chair, a smile curving his lips. He wondered what Penny could do with Spam.

Chapter 13

Penny

PENNY WALKED into Bones's house, still feeling the tingle of his kiss. She'd expected last night to go very differently. Instead of sex, she'd gotten dinner, romance, and a piece of her heart stolen. She looked into the living room on her way to the kitchen and shook her head at the sad decor. Bones was a terrific cook—there was no way she could come close in the kitchen— but he was sorely lacking in the decorating department. His furniture—what little there was of it—looked ancient. The place really needed a woman's touch.

"Who the hell are you?"

Penny let out a surprised squeak and nearly jumped out of her skin. She spun around and found a woman standing at the counter in Bones's kitchen. The woman was tall, with long black hair twisted into a braid that hung over her shoulder. Even though she was scowling, she was stunningly beautiful.

Penny took a step back, her gaze sweeping across the kitchen. The woman had been in the middle of unloading groceries. Half of the cabinet doors were open, and a carton of milk sat on the counter. The gorgeous woman clearly knew her way around Bones's kitchen. Penny crossed her arms over her chest. "I'm Penny. Who are you?"

The woman dipped her chin to look Penny over from head to toe. Her dark eyes narrowed, and her lips pursed. "That's my brother's shirt."

Penny's shoulders sank with relief. She should have seen the resemblance immediately. Bones was tall and rugged, built like a warrior, and his sister was his equal. She was nearly six feet tall, and she carried herself like a queen. Her long neck, finely sculpted features, and high forehead were elegantly royal. She and Bones shared a wide, expressive mouth and dark, intense eyes.

"Where is he?" she demanded.

Penny tilted her head, indicating the patio, and Bones's sister immediately strode in that direction. She muttered something under her breath Penny couldn't understand as she brushed by her. Penny jumped at the sound of the door slamming. She heard the deep rumble of Bones's voice, then his sister's disgruntled answer. Penny listened intently as their voices rose in volume, but she couldn't understand a word they were saying. It was English, but not exactly, and their accents made everything harder to decipher.

The door flew open, and Bones's sister sailed through, her queenly nose in the air. Color stained her high cheekbones, and her dark eyes threw hot spears at Penny. "You're nothing to him, hear?"

"Kaliah!" Bones came into the house, his face as dark as a thundercloud. "Watch your mouth."

Kaliah spun on her brother. "You wanna kill Pops? Is that what you want, *Makoa?*" She spat his name as if it were a bad taste she didn't want in her mouth.

Bones lowered his chin and stared at his sister. "I want you to apologize to Penny and then I want you to leave."

Kaliah glared at Bones. "I'm gone," she said, stomping to the door and slamming it behind her.

After Kaliah was gone, Penny turned to look at Bones.

His dark eyes were already on her, narrowed in concern. "Sorry about that," he said. "My sister is a bit of a hothead."

Penny looked away. Kaliah's rejection stung, but she'd get over it. It wasn't like she'd ever see her again. Her eyes drifted back toward Bones. He was still shirtless, and his damp hair curled slightly at the ends, brushing the tops of his shoulders.

Forcing a smile, she shrugged lightly. "And they say redheads are feisty."

Bones strode over to Penny and cupped her shoulders. His big hands radiated heat through the thin cotton of her shirt. "I'm really sorry. Are you okay?"

Bones's tenderness made Penny's chest squeeze. For such a big guy, he was nothing but a teddy bear. "I'm fine."

He pulled in a deep breath. "It's none of her business who I date." His voice was a low growl. "Or who I love."

Penny's heart pounded so hard in her chest, she thought it might jump out. She cocked her head and stared at him, not sure what she'd just heard. "What?"

He shook his head. "Maybe I'm crazy, but I think I love you."

"But…" Her mind spun as she tried to make sense of what he was saying. "But you don't even know me."

He thumped his fist to his chest. "It feels like I do."

She searched for words. Was he really saying he loved her? They'd only just met. He couldn't possibly love her.

He tapped his knuckles to her chest. "Don't you feel it?"

A shiver ran down Penny's spine. If he was talking about the way she felt perfectly balanced when she was with him, as if something had been missing all her life but she'd never known, then *yeah*, she felt it. She felt it in her blood like a low hum, a steady beat. "It doesn't make sense," she said. "*We* don't make sense."

Bones shook his head, clearly puzzled. "I know. We have a belief that every person has a soul to match theirs." A soft laugh escaped his lips. "I never believed it before, but then I saw you… strutting down the sidewalk in those boots."

"I wasn't strutting."

Bones smiled. "You were the total package. I wanted you from the moment I saw you."

Penny gazed up at his handsome face. She'd thought the same. She'd wanted him more than she'd ever wanted any man. "I only wanted a vacation adventure," she said. "I didn't want this."

He laughed softly. "Believe me, I understand."

A spark of heat surged through her. She'd wanted a one-night stand with her sexy tour guide, but she'd gotten a whole lot more she hadn't asked for.

"I *did* wake up in your bed."

His mouth thinned. "Not exactly the way I pictured it."

She curled her hand around his neck and raised onto her tiptoes, then brushed her lips across his. "How did you picture it?"

"You naked." His voice was a low growl. His hands gripped her waist, and he dipped his head to hers, closing the distance between them. "Me inside you." His mouth devoured hers, kissing her breathless.

She kissed him back, arching against his chest as his hands splayed across her hips. Her hands explored the mountains of his shoulders. His skin was still warm from the sun, and he smelled like an ocean breeze. Salty and sweet and something incredibly masculine.

Her hands glided down his biceps and forearms, then back over his shoulders again. Everywhere she touched was rock solid and smooth. He was like a living, breathing sculpture.

He rocked against her, and she gasped. His thick erection pressed against her hip, throbbing with heat. Her body thrummed in answer. She'd never wanted a man like this before, like she wanted to climb him and devour him whole.

His tongue stroked into her mouth like a teasing invitation. For such a big man, he wasn't clumsy with his kisses. It was as if he knew exactly how she wanted to be kissed. How she liked to be touched.

As if they'd been touching and kissing for years.

His lips trailed to her ear. "What do you have on under my shirt?"

She reached up to its top button, her eyes on his as she undid it and spread it open.

Bones groaned when he saw the bare expanse of her skin. His head dipped, and he pressed a kiss to the top of her breast where she held the shirt open. With bated breath, she undid the next button and the next.

His mouth slid lower, his lips warm against her skin and his tongue a flash of pure heat.

Penny's body hummed with pleasure as his mouth trailed along her chest. Her greedy hands sought his skin, gliding over the rippling muscles of his back.

Bones finished the job of unbuttoning her shirt and spread the soft cotton until it hung open. His big hand wrapped around her waist, then trailed up to cup her breast. He squeezed softly, his fingers pinching the tip.

A spark of heat raced through her. His palm was rough, and the friction of his calloused fingers sliding over her nipple sent a surge of desire straight to her core.

She dragged her fingers up his back and buried them in his luxurious hair. It was still damp and smelled of the sea. Holding the back of his head in her hands filled her with a surge of power. He was big and strong, but when she urged his head to her breast, he yielded immediately, letting her lead.

He pulled her nipple into his warm mouth, and Penny went boneless, melting against him. His arm clasped around her back, supporting her as he teased and sucked her nipple. He kissed his way across her chest, pushing aside her shirt until it fell to the floor.

She arched against him when he took her other nipple in his mouth, pulling deep. Her fingers threaded through his hair, and she wrapped her leg around his hip.

He kissed a path up her chest to her neck. The smooth skin of his chest brushed against her naked breasts, making her nipples pucker.

Her hand glided down his chest and down his taut stomach, to where the thin line of hair disappeared under the waistband of his shorts. He groaned when she wrapped her hand around him and squeezed his hard flesh. The sound sent a jolt of pleasure through her. She stroked him again. He was hot and hard, bigger and thicker than she'd imagined. Desire sparked in her chest as he strained against her hand.

His lips found hers, and he kissed her deeply, his tongue thrusting into her mouth as she stroked him. He unbuttoned his shorts and pushed them down his hips, then kicked them off.

"Bedroom. Now." He walked her backward along the hall and pushed the door to his bedroom open with his free hand.

They fell onto the bed, Bones rolling so he didn't crush her with his weight. Penny pushed him flat on his back and hooked her leg over his hip, holding him in place with one hand planted on his broad chest.

"No. Don't move," she said when he tried to sit up and reach for her.

He lay back on the bed, looking up at her. "Do you want to stop?" His voice was pained.

"Absolutely not." Her gaze ran down his body, appreciating every detail. "I want to look first though." She'd never seen a man built like him before. He had warrior blood in his veins. Not an ounce of fat clung to his muscled frame, and his thick shaft was magnificent.

She pressed her lips to his chest, then kissed lower, tracing the line of hair down the middle of his sculpted abs. Her lips traced over his hip, then across the tops of his hair-roughened thighs. She kissed the swollen head of his cock, licking the salty bead of moisture leaking from the tip.

He groaned, his hips jerking off the mattress. "Penny… I need—" His voice cut off when she sucked him into her mouth.

She took as much of him as she could, savoring the taste of him, the feel of him throbbing against her tongue. He was too much to take all of him, so she wrapped her fist around the base, pumping as she sucked him as deep as she could.

"Penny," he warned.

But she didn't stop. She loved the way his body responded to her. He was losing control, and she loved every minute of it.

Suddenly, he pulled her off and up his chest. He rolled so he was on top of her, then kissed down her body, yanking aside her panties. Before she knew what was happening, his head was buried between her thighs, his mouth fastened on the swollen bud of her clit.

She rocked against him, his name tumbling from her mouth in a frantic plea. He pushed a long finger through her slick folds, stroking into her tight, wet sheath.

An orgasm snuck up on her, crashing over her in a sudden wave. Her body tensed all over, then she was shuddering and moaning, bucking her hips off the mattress.

She barely registered his weight shifting off her as she basked in the glow of pleasure. Then he was back, rolling a condom down his shaft. He pulled her on top of him so that she straddled his hips.

"Take it," he growled. "Take what you want."

She positioned herself over him and sank, lowering herself inch by inch until she was so full, she thought she would burst.

"You feel too good. I can't…" He gripped her hips, urging her to move.

She rocked against him, finding the rhythm she needed. He was big and powerful, but she was in charge. His body was hers to command. She planted her hands on his chest and pinned him to the bed, then took his mouth in a long, hard kiss. She feasted on his tongue, sucking it into her mouth and savoring him like a souvenir.

Then she fell apart again. Ecstasy exploded through her in a relentless wave. She cried out, and a moment later, he followed, shuddering as he spent his release.

It seemed like forever before he slid out from under her and rolled off the bed. When he was gone, she felt his absence like a physical pain. How was she ever going to say good-bye?

$$\rule{6cm}{0.4pt}$$

Chapter 14

$$\rule{6cm}{0.4pt}$$

Bones

BONES SLOWED to a stop at the gate that closed off the property where they filmed *A Long Road Home*. He leaned out the car window as a guard strode to his car. It was Alika, a cousin on his father's side who'd inherited the strong genes of the family. He was tall and broad shouldered, his muscles bulging under the black T-shirt he wore.

"Heh, cuz," Bones said, shaking hands with him through the open window.

"Howzit, Bones?" He leaned down and peered in the window, nodding at Penny. "Champ's cousin?"

Henry's coworkers all called him Champ on set. It was short for Longchamp, but it was also because of his dangerous job as a stuntman. "Yeah, that's right," Bones said. "This is Penny."

"Howzit?" Alika smiled at Penny. "This gate is new," Alika said. "They stuck me out here until they get someone permanent. It's on account of that movie star who just got here. Claudia Montgomery, you heard of her?"

"She was in *Jezebel*," Penny said. "I saw it three times."

Bones had seen it too. He remembered Claudia in a bikini for most of the movie, but not much else about the plot or story.

"She's one big deal. Her own all-pink trailer and everything." Alika pushed the button for the guardrail to lift so Bones could pass. "See you at The Duke tomorrow?"

Bones nodded. "See you there."

He drove under the railing and along the dirt road leading to the property where they filmed several television shows. Bones parked in a grassy lot filled with equipment trucks and trailers. The jungle framed an outdoor set depicting the old West, and dozens of people scurried around wearing period costumes or western gear. Bones had watched *A Long Road Home* plenty of times. His mother was a big fan, and it aired on Sunday nights, which was one reason Sunday supper with the family was early. If everyone wasn't gone by 7:55 p.m., Bones's mother was showing them the door.

"Do you want to hang out for a little while?" Penny turned toward him, leaning into the space between them. "You can meet the hotshot movie stars."

"Nah." Bones shook his head. He had too many other things to do. Since Penny had been in town, he'd been neglecting everything. His big dive was coming up, and he had many things to do to get ready. "Maybe another time."

Penny winced at his poor choice of words and looked down at her lap. "Yeah, maybe."

He reached for her hand, drawing it out of her lap. He swallowed roughly before finding the courage to say the words in his heart. "I wish you could stay."

Penny met his eyes. "This is crazy." But she was smiling. "What if I did stay? I mean, maybe not forever, but just another week or so." Her gaze drifted down his face. "I'm not ready to say good-bye. Are you?"

Bones leaned forward and kissed her, staking his claim on her mouth. He wasn't even close to being ready to say good-bye to her. He'd take another day, another week, whatever she was willing to give him.

She curled her fingers in his shirt and pulled him close when he backed away. "One more." She kissed him hard, her tongue boldly sweeping into his mouth.

When she released him, he chased her lips with his mouth, needing more. They kissed again, more heated this time. Bones thought they could sit there in the parking lot all day making out, but a knock sounded loudly on his roof and pulled them apart.

It was Henry, scowling at them through the window. "You decided to show up, huh?"

Penny leaned forward and waved at Henry. "Hi, Henry!"

"Hello, Penny. Good to see you." He glared at Bones, then nodded tersely. "Let's go. I've only got a few minutes before I have to be in makeup."

Penny slid out of Bones's arms. "I guess I'll see you tomorrow at The Duke along with everyone else on the island?"

"You bet."

Penny reached for the door, giving him one last smile before she got out of the car. He watched her walk away until he couldn't see her anymore, then he drove off, feeling a lightness in his chest that was almost like floating.

BONES HAD BEEN neglecting everything in his life since Penny came to the island. He had the most important dive of his life coming up in a few days, and he wasn't ready.

He had a long list of items to check off before an early morning at Sunset Beach, where he'd volunteered to help set up the judges' stage for the Duke Championship.

First, he drove to No'ono'o Jewels in Honolulu and met with the owner, who was advancing him three hundred dollars in order to rent the dive boat and equipment he'd need for the coral dive. In a few days, he'd have enough rare coral worth triple the loan amount.

"I will see you on Tuesday morning," Bones said, shoving the envelope of money in his pocket.

"Bright and early." Mr. Taki smiled, showing off his perfect dentures. "This is going to be the beginning of big business for us." His eyes narrowed. "Don't disappoint me."

Bones assured him he wouldn't.

His next stop was the marina, where he gave Clyde the envelope of money in exchange for renting the dive boat.

Bones had known Clyde his whole life, but he hadn't confided in him the reason he was renting the boat. He didn't want word spreading around that he was diving for coral in dangerously deep waters. It was bound to get back to someone who loved him and would put a stop to it. After stopping at the marina and checking to see everything was ready for the dive, he headed to the farm on the east side of the island, where he pitched in when they needed hard labor or an extra hand in shearing the alpacas.

He drove along the winding highway, thinking of the woman he loved. His mouth spread into a smile, which was still there when he got out of his car and headed toward the barns, where the alpacas were being prepared for shearing.

The farmhands were glad for another body and immediately put him to work. Bones was contented with the physical labor. It was simple work that demanded little from him and allowed his mind to wander. He thought of Penny and their future. They would make a home of his uncle's house he'd inherited. They would be in love. He would finish his canoe and sail to Maui. Maybe she would come with him. And if she didn't, she'd be waiting there when he got home.

Fingers snapped under his nose. "Hey! Bones! You in there?"

Bones found Keoni's mother hovering over him. He smiled up at her. "Heh, Auntie Lele. I didn't see you there."

She scoffed. "You wouldn't see a bulldozer coming at you. Where's your head, boy?"

Bones straightened from the stool, where he'd been staring at the ground, lost in thought.

"Sorry, I was thinking about something else."

"Were you now?" She cocked her head and studied him. "Wouldn't happen to be a tall, skinny redhead on your mind?"

Bones narrowed his eyes. "She's not skinny."

Auntie Lele laughed. "You like her."

He joined his aunt. "I more than like her," he said.

"Ah. Young love, so sweet. I remember when I met your uncle." She smiled fondly. "He was skinny too."

They headed away from the stable toward the long shed set up with tables, where groups of people sat making leis. It was an orderly process. They stripped the stems, cut the leaves, and passed them down the tables to be woven into leis for the Duke Championship.

Bones slowed his steps as they neared the others. Auntie Lele was kind and wise. She'd raised five children, and she was like a second mom to Bones. "I asked her to stay," Bones confided. "I had this feeling. You know?"

Bones thought if anyone knew, it would be his Auntie Lele. She believed in the old ways and had been telling him for years he had a soul mate waiting for him.

"Do you think this is her?" Her eyes were wide, her mouth stretching into a smile.

"I don't know. Maybe I'm crazy."

Lele stopped short and looked at him. "You need to talk to Hanani. She will know."

Auntie Hanani was a wise woman who lived in the woods in the central part of the island between the two large mountain ranges. People sought her out for her advice from every island. She was said to be a descendant of the old gods, with one foot already in the heavenly realm. She knew things no one else did and could communicate with both the living and the dead.

Bones had known Hanani since he was a child. His grandmother used to take him with her when she visited Hanani. She'd always given him freshly baked cookies and sat him in a comfortable chair with a book while she consulted with his grandmother.

He hadn't seen her in years, but if anyone could erase his doubts about Penny, it was Hanani.

When he was finished with the heavy labor at the farm, he went straight to Hanani's house in the woods.

Flowers spilled onto the stone path that led to her front door. A swing hung from the rafters of the porch, swaying gently in the mountain breeze.

Bones climbed the stairs, thinking it looked exactly as it had when he'd been a child of seven. He was standing in front of the door, his hand poised to knock, when it swung open.

Hanani stood at the door, smiling at him. She hadn't aged a day in almost twenty years. She'd been ancient then, and she was ancient still, her brow a crease of wrinkles and her eyes filmy with age.

The smell of chocolate chip cookies wafted out of her kitchen.

"Welcome, Makoa." Her smile stretched, revealing remarkably solid teeth for a woman of her undetermined age. "I've been expecting you. Come in and have some cookies."

Chapter 15

Penny

THE MORNING of the Duke Kahanamoku Surfing Championship, Lou and Penny got up early and were on the road before sunrise. Henry had been called in to work to help train his new famous co-star, so Penny and Lou had borrowed his car. He'd drawn them a map to the North Shore, which cut through the interior of the island, and warned them the road was pretty rough.

They'd been driving for about an hour, passing through a valley between the mountain ranges filled with rows and rows of pineapples, when Penny told Lou she was going to stay in Hawaii with Bones.

"You've got to be kidding me," Lou said, taking her eyes off the road to stare at Penny.

"Watch the road!" Penny pointed at the long stretch of dirt in front of them. It barely qualified as a road. She'd seen better-maintained roads on her grandparents' farm in the country.

"You don't even know him." Lou stared ahead, her fingers tight on the wheel.

"It doesn't matter." She leaned her head out the window. Even in the middle of the island, she could smell the ocean. "I love him. He loves me. We are meant to be together."

"What about Joe?"

Penny shook her head. "Joe is history." She glanced at Lou. "What about you and Keoni? You could move out here with me. We could find a little place on the beach—"

"Penny! You're out of your mind. We can't just root up our lives because we fell for two charming men. It's nothing but a fling. Isn't that what you wanted?"

Penny was quiet for a while, and Lou concentrated on driving as the road climbed into the mountains and toward the coast. The smell of the sea grew stronger, and a breeze filled the air.

"It's so beautiful here," Penny said. The islands and the man had enchanted her.

"The Penny I know would never want to be stuck on an island, even if it is paradise. The Penny I know wants to see the world." Lou nudged Penny's leg. "What happened to seeing Paris, London, Milan?"

Penny shrugged. She hadn't given it much thought, but she knew it would work out. Her decision had been made on a gut feeling. She knew it was right to be with Bones. "I can still see those places," she said.

Lou shot her a surprised glance. "You're serious, aren't you?"

Penny nodded.

"Does this mean I need to get a new roommate?"

Penny hesitated. She was leaving her home, her family, her best friend. Fear tightened her belly. Doubt filled her mind. But her heart was leading this train, and her heart knew she was making the right decision. "Yes," Penny said. "You need to find a new roommate."

Lou turned toward her with tears shining in her eyes. "I'm

gonna miss you. But if this is what you want, you have my blessing."

Penny felt the prick of tears behind her eyes, but she managed a smile. "Thanks, sweetie. I appreciate that. I'll make sure to write."

They held hands across the seats.

"You better."

THE CONTEST DIDN'T START for another hour, but the entire island had shown up to see the show. The road leading up to Sunset Beach had become a parking lot, and the beach was crawling with spectators.

The waves looked bigger than any Penny had seen, and the word in the crowd was it was going to be an exciting day. Penny had never seen a surfing contest, and it seemed more like a party than a championship event. Families sat on the roofs of their cars, eating lunch or playing cards. Music blared from speakers, and anticipation was in the air.

Penny searched the crowd for Bones. He was tall enough to stand out, so it didn't take her long to spot him. He was on top of the stage, hanging a speaker to a column. She watched him work for a long moment, admiring the fluid grace of his movements. He didn't move like a big man, slow and lumbering; he moved like a dancer.

He was deeply involved in his work, and he didn't notice Penny watching him.

Lou tugged on Penny's arm. "Look! There's Keoni!"

Penny shifted her gaze toward the ocean, where Keoni zipped through the waves on a bright-red surfboard. His hair flowed back from his face, and his bronze skin gleamed like armor. The ocean rippled and crashed under him, but he rode it like he commanded its every move. Penny couldn't take her eyes off him. Neither could the rest of the people on the beach. Keoni's name echoed down the shore as a chant rose.

Lou's cheeks flushed as red as Keoni's surfboard as she watched him. It was obvious to Penny that Lou wanted Keoni. She only denied her desire because she had a boyfriend. Paul Sullivan, King of Jerks. If anyone deserved to be cheated on, it was Lou's boyfriend, Paul. Penny was tired of seeing Paul treat Lou like dirt.

"You should go for him," Penny said, nodding at Keoni as he strode out of the water with his long surfboard under his arm. "You deserve to have some fun."

"But he hates tourists." Lou raised her voice as the crowd chanted Keoni's name loud enough to be heard in the pineapple fields.

"He doesn't hate you." Penny had seen the way Keoni looked at Lou. "It's your last night here. Are you gonna waste it? Or go after what you want?"

A smile curved one corner of Lou's mouth. "You're right."

The crowd engulfed Keoni with hugs and kisses. "Everyone loves him," Penny said, her gaze straying to the stage, where Bones labored to put up the judges' table. Penny wondered how it had been for Bones growing up in Keoni's shadow. Did he resent his handsome cousin who'd captured the heart of the island?

As if he sensed her watching him, Bones straightened and met her gaze across the crowd of people. Penny raised her hand and waved. Bones nodded and flashed the shaka sign— three fingers tucked to his palm and his pinky and thumb extended—the Hawaiian version of waving hello. Penny tried to signal that she was going to come to him, but he'd already resumed working. The crew scrambled to get everything ready as helicopters hovered overhead and new crews took their positions.

A loud cheer went up from the beach, causing Penny to turn her attention to the ocean. A surfer glided over the calmer section of the waves with an adorable white dog on the front of his surfboard.

"That's the guy from the airport," Lou said. "Keoni and Bones's friend."

Penny narrowed her eyes at the surfer and recognized his wheat-blond hair and the flash of his smile against his deep tan. "Declan Bishop."

"Keoni says he's gonna win."

Penny watched Declan slide effortlessly over the waves with the dog balanced on his board. She didn't know whose smile was broader, Declan's or the dog's.

The crowd went wild as Declan rode the wave to shore and allowed the dog to hop off before he jumped off and grabbed his board. As soon as they were out of the water, a voice came over the speaker, announcing the start to the all-female talent exhibition.

"You want to see if we can get closer?" Lou asked.

Penny's gaze strayed to the stage again, but Bones was no longer there. She grabbed onto Lou's hand before they could get separated in the crowd, and they pushed their way to the front row.

The female surfers tore up the waves, dazzling the crowd with their skills. Penny got caught up in the excitement, cheering at the top of her lungs for her favorite: the woman wearing jersey number six. She was a petite woman, much smaller than the other competitors, but her power and skill were incomparable.

Number six was announced as the winner and given a trophy, and still Penny hadn't seen Bones. A strange feeling twisted her stomach. She couldn't help but think he was avoiding her.

When he'd flashed her the shaka sign earlier, it had seemed overly casual, almost impersonal. Given what they'd shared over the last week, Penny felt entitled to more than just a hand gesture.

The horn sounded, announcing the start of the championship. The first heat of surfers, including Declan Bishop, raced into the water. A buzz of excitement hummed through the crowd as the waves crashed against the shore. The ocean seemed angry. Waves lashed against the sand in unpredictable sets, crushing the competitors in a show of pure power.

Penny gasped as a surfer's board was ripped from under him and tossed into the air. The helicopter dipped low, capturing everything for a live audience on the mainland.

Keoni fought his way through the crowd and stood next to Lou, giving her a commentary on the contest. They were so into each other that they didn't notice Penny slip away. She wanted to find Bones. A gnawing feeling of unease spread through her belly.

When she finally spotted him again, he was bent toward a much shorter woman. They seemed to be having a serious conversation despite the commotion around them. Penny stared as the woman wound her arms around Bones's neck and pressed her lips to his.

It was like watching a car wreck. Penny couldn't look away.

Bones raised his head and said something to the woman, and she stared up at him. Penny knew the feeling of being over-whelmed by Bones's dark, mesmerizing eyes.

The woman finally sauntered away, and Bones glanced up, spotting Penny staring from a few feet away. They made eye contact for a long moment, Penny's heart beating uncontrollably in her chest.

Anger and confusion warred within her. Tears burned behind her eyes. She tore her gaze away from Bones and hurried back into the crowd, where it was easy to disappear.

Chapter 16

Bones

BONES KNEW Kaliah was a pain in the ass, but he'd never known she was cruel. Setting poor Mary up to kiss him was plain cruel—both to Mary and Penny, who had unfortunately seen the whole thing.

Mary had kissed him because Kaliah had fed her lies. She'd told her friend Bones was interested in her but too shy to let on.

He'd made it clear to Mary that there would be no more kisses. He wasn't interested. Mary was like family to him. One of his sister's best friends, she'd been around forever. Bones couldn't think of her as a potential girlfriend. He couldn't think of her as anything but the best friend of his pain-in-the-ass sister.

Bones pushed through the crowd, ignoring his friends and family as he searched for Penny. He'd been intentionally ignoring her all day. He knew he'd have to talk to her eventually, to let her down as gently as he could and make her get on the plane to Seattle to leave him. It ripped his heart out, but he had to do it. After what Hanani had told him, it was the only way.

Maybe Mary's kiss had been a good thing. Penny might be so angry with him, she would break up with him before he had to do it. It would save him the trouble, if not the heartbreak.

He spotted her bright-red hair in the crowd and shoved aside the people in his way to get to her. By the time he reached her, she was on the outskirts of the crowd, hurrying toward the main road.

"Penny!" His shout echoed over the noise of the crowd.

She froze and turned to face him, a look of confused outrage on her face. He wanted to kiss the pout right off her lips, but that was out of the question.

She straightened her shoulders and tossed her hair, looking like Pele herself descending from her volcanic throne. "What do you want?"

It was on the tip of his tongue to deny what she'd seen, to justify the kiss and blame his meddling sister, but he knew what he had to do. "We need to talk," he said.

She cocked her head to the side, her eyebrows lifting. "So talk."

Bones cleared his throat. His shoulders sagged with the weight of unspoken words. "I made a mistake."

Penny's face softened, and she blinked back tears. "So that kiss wasn't what I thought?" Her voice cracked, and she leaned into him, her eyes pleading.

They were close enough to touch, and he desperately wanted to shift closer… press his mouth to hers. His heart ached, but he told himself to stop stalling and get it over with. "I shouldn't have asked you to stay."

Penny exhaled sharply, her breath stirring his cheek. "What do you mean?"

Bones swallowed roughly. His eyes dropped down over her face, lingering on her lips until he dragged his gaze away. "It's for the best."

Penny's eyes shot daggers at him. "Can you explain that kiss or not?"

"No." He raked a hand through his hair. "I can't."

"I know there's an explanation. You wouldn't just kiss another woman right in front of me. Something's going on." Penny put a hand on his chest, over his heart. "Let's leave and go back to your place where we can talk. Work this out."

Bones shook his head. "I've got an early dive tomorrow morning. I need to get some rest. And you need to go home tomorrow."

Penny pushed his chest, hard enough to have him reeling. "Why?"

He found his footing and glared down at her. "We can't be together."

Penny pushed him again, her palm warm through his shirt. "Why not? What changed?"

Bones took a step back. Standing so close to Penny was dangerous. He felt himself on the verge of breaking and pulling her into his arms.

"Go home," he said. "You don't belong here."

Penny's eyes turned to blue glass. "I was nothing to you from the beginning. Just another dumb tourist."

He wanted to argue, but there was no point. "And I was just an exotic adventure to you." He threw the words in her face, unable to contain his bitterness. It wasn't fair. He'd finally found love, but he had to send her off. Hanani had promised it was the only way. Penny needed to get on that plane tomorrow.

Sending her away was the last thing he wanted to do, and when she looped her arms around his neck and pressed her mouth to his, he thought he might cave and beg her to stay. Her lips were warm and soft, the kiss brief.

"Good-bye, Makoa."

Her words were made more final by the use of his real name. It was the first time she'd called him that, and maybe the last.

She stared up at him for a long beat as if giving him a final chance. When he said nothing, she spun on her heel and hurried toward the beach. After a moment, he lost sight of her when she disappeared in the crowd.

Chapter 17

Penny

PENNY FAKED ENTHUSIASM for Lou when she told her she was going home with Keoni that night. She wouldn't rain on Lou's parade, not when she'd been the one to encourage her to take a chance on Keoni in the first place.

She drove back to Henry's house alone, managing to get lost only twice. By the time she got back to his house, it was long after midnight, and Henry was already stretched out on the sofa asleep. She tiptoed past him and went to the bedroom, where she and Lou had been sleeping since they'd arrived.

She went through the motions of washing her face, brushing her hair, and changing into her pajamas. When she curled up under the covers, she was ready for the tears to come.

There was an awful, hollow ache in her chest, growing with every breath she took, and she craved the relief of tears.

But they wouldn't come.

She closed her eyes and pictured Bones's face, but still they wouldn't come. She felt nothing, and it was the coldest, emptiest feeling she'd ever known.

She lay awake, staring at the dark ceiling, her mind replaying the scene with Bones over and over. At some point she must have slept, because she woke to the sound of Henry moving around in the kitchen.

He was annoyingly cheerful, a morning person, and he was singing as he prepared his breakfast. The smell of frying meat and strong coffee wafted down the hall.

"Good morning, sunshine," Henry said, flipping a thick slice of Spam in the skillet.

Penny poured herself a cup of coffee and slid onto a stool at the counter.

"How was the contest yesterday?" Henry asked, popping two slices of bread in the toaster.

"Fine."

Henry gestured at the newspaper lying on the counter. "Looks better than fine."

The picture on the front page showed Declan Bishop holding a bottle of champagne in one hand and a trophy in the other. Penny sipped her coffee. "It was all right, I guess."

Henry turned his back on the stove and gave her a sympathetic smile. "It's hard to leave, isn't it?"

Penny shrugged. She was glad she hadn't shared her plans to stay in Hawaii with Henry. It was one less problem to deal with.

"You can always come back," Henry said, slapping the fried Spam between the bread. He took a big bite, talking as he chewed. "I'll give up my bedroom for my favorite cousin anytime."

Penny sighed and rubbed her aching head. "Why are you so cheerful this morning?"

Henry took another big bite. "Someone woke up on the wrong side of the bed."

Penny glared at him over the rim of her mug before taking another long sip. "And why are you up so damn early?"

The sun wasn't even up, yet Henry was freshly showered and shaved, eating a hearty breakfast of canned meat and bread.

Henry checked his watch and grimaced. "Shit, I'm gonna be late. Bones is gonna kill me if I'm late."

Penny's chest tightened at the mention of his name. "Where are you going?"

Henry stuffed the last of the sandwich in his mouth. "Didn't he tell you?"

"Tell me what?" Penny followed Henry into the living room. There was a lot Bones hadn't mentioned. A lot he'd lied about.

"The big dive is this morning." Henry shoved his feet into his shoes. "Don't worry, I'll be back in plenty of time to see you before your flight." He crossed the room and gave her a big hug. "Sorry I've had to work so much. Next time you come out will be different, I promise."

Penny leaned into Henry's embrace. Her arms went around his waist, and she clung to him for a long beat. She had no intentions of coming back to Hawaii.

"It's still early," Henry said, stepping away from her. "You can catch the sunrise."

After Henry left, Penny went outside on the deck and sat on a flimsy lawn chair. Henry's house was built high on a ridge overlooking the eastern coast of the island. The view stretched for miles, blue ocean as far as she could see.

The sun poked up from the horizon, spreading golden bars across the space between sea and sky like an unfinished painting.

Penny stretched out in the chair and closed her eyes. She couldn't stand to watch the beautiful sunrise. It only reminded her of what she'd be missing when she got back home in Seattle. She drifted off to sleep and woke hours later with a terrible headache. Her nap had been plagued by unsettling dreams, and a tight ball of worry filled her chest.

She tried to tell herself it was just anger and unshed tears that made her feel antsy, but as the day wore on, her feeling of unease grew. She showered and packed, placing her suitcase next to Lou's, and all the while, she couldn't shake the feeling that something was desperately wrong.

A chill ran down Penny's spine as she checked her watch. Henry should have been back, and where the hell was Lou? Their flight back to Seattle was mere hours away.

By the time Lou finally showed up with Keoni, Penny had worn a path from the deck to the front door from pacing. "Where have you been?"

"We were at the beach." Lou narrowed her eyes at Penny. "What's wrong?"

Penny laughed tersely. For a moment, she thought the tears might finally come, but they didn't. "Bones dumped me."

Lou reached for Penny's hand. "I'm so sorry."

Penny shrugged. It still didn't feel real. "Looks like I'll be going home with you." She sighed. "We might need a ride to the airport if Henry doesn't get back soon."

"He's not back yet?" Keoni frowned and checked his watch. "I'll call the marina."

When Keoni was gone, Lou led Penny out to the deck. "Are you okay?"

"Not really." She'd never see Bones again. Never feel his arms around her. Never watch a sunrise with him again. The nevers were stacking up.

The sound of a car pulling into the driveway was followed by a slamming door. Henry rushed onto the deck, his face pale and worry etched into his features.

As soon as Penny saw his face, an icy chill raced down her spine.

She hurried to meet him. "What happened?"

Henry clenched his jaw. He darted a look at Keoni, then back at Penny. "Bones dove, but he never came back up." He swallowed hard, his Adam's apple bobbing. "He's missing."

A sob caught in Penny's throat, and the tears that had been at bay since Bones had broken up with her finally started, cascading down her cheeks in an unstoppable torrent.

PART II

A Hui Hou

Chapter 18

Penny

EARLY MORNING WAS Penny's favorite time of day in Manhattan. A gold shimmer stained the empty sidewalks, and a thin bright line of sunlight shined between the tall silver buildings. Cabs were few and far between, and most of the city was asleep.

Penny had been up all night. She hadn't even gotten started until midnight. She'd spent the night traveling from one party to the next. Dancers, showgirls, and musicians knew how to find a party and when to leave one, at the first sign of dullness.

They had traveled in a pack, a kaleidoscope of butterflies flitting from one party to the next.

She'd started off the night standing in line for cheap tickets to a Broadway show and capped it off in a swanky Madison Avenue apartment owned by someone's cousin. When she left just before dawn, the party was still going.

No one realized she'd slipped away. They wouldn't miss her when they did. Penny's friends in New York were good fun, but they weren't deep.

Not like Lou.

Penny missed her long talks with Lou, which she had taken for granted when they'd lived together. About the same time Penny had relocated to the East Coast, Lou had moved to Hawaii to be with Keoni. Now that they were thousands of miles apart and the phone calls were limited to once a month or emergencies, she missed Lou like a hole in her heart.

Sadness swept over her. Thinking of Lou made Penny think of someone else she missed. Her heart squeezed in memory of six feet and five inches of muscular man she'd never see again and never forget.

As always, she pushed thoughts of Bones away. She'd moved to New York to start over, and Bones was in the past.

Drawn by the line that had formed outside a bakery that had just opened its doors, Penny splurged on a cup of coffee and a freshly baked croissant. It meant she would be eating leftover soup for lunch for the rest of the week, but the flaky, melt-in-your-mouth, buttery goodness was worth the sacrifice. Her salary at the dance studio didn't cover luxuries like fresh croissants, but at least it was a steady income.

Penny strolled down the sidewalk, sipping her hot coffee and glancing in the shop windows. The only store open was Woolworth's. Everything else was still shuttered from the night before. There was a feeling of anticipation in the air, as the day was about to begin and the bustle of locals and tourists would soon fill the streets.

She slowed to a stop in front of an elaborate display of jewelry in the Tiffany's window.

Penny and Lou had seen *Breakfast at Tiffany's* a dozen times in the theater. They could quote entire scenes. Lou had thought George Peppard was the cat's meow, but Penny had been more impressed with Holly Golightly.

She stopped in front of the window and nibbled her croissant, wondering if Audrey Hepburn had stood in the same spot while filming the movie.

Lou was going to be so jealous when Penny told her she'd recreated the iconic scene in front of Tiffany's.

She would love to call her once she got home, but Penny didn't have a phone. She didn't want to waste the money it cost to have a line. She used the phone at the studio when she needed it, and she relied on letters back home to her parents.

A black town car slowed to a stop at the curb, and the driver got out to open the back door. A black high-heeled shoe hit the pavement, followed quickly by another. An older woman with auburn hair in an elegant pantsuit climbed out of the car carrying a paper bag and a to-go coffee cup.

Penny smiled a greeting as the woman strolled across the sidewalk to join her at the window. "Looks like we had the same idea."

The woman nodded, her expression hidden behind a large pair of sunglasses. Everything about her, from her car to her perfume, screamed old money. "Who are you wearing?"

Penny raised her eyebrows. "What?"

The woman shifted her coffee cup to the same hand that held the paper bag and tipped her sunglasses to look at Penny over the rim. Her gaze dropped to Penny's shoes and back up again. "Your ensemble. Who designed it?"

Penny plucked at the hem of the men's T-shirt she wore. Someone had spilled red wine on her dress, and the host of the party had given her a plain white T-shirt to wear. She'd tied a striped necktie around her waist and shoved her dress into her purse, hoping to scrub the stain out later.

"It's a Penelope Longchamp original," she said.

"Hmm." The woman inspected Penny more closely. "What's that style called?"

Penny took a bite of her pastry and chewed thoughtfully. "Disaster couture."

"Very modern." Her boldly painted lips turned upward in approval.

They walked to the next window together and sipped their

coffees in silence as they peered at the sparkling display. The jolt of caffeine revived Penny from the long night with no sleep. She could nap for an hour or two before her first class of the day, a group of three-year-olds who loved to hang on the bar more than learn ballet.

"You're a dancer?" the woman asked.

Penny smiled. "Used to be."

"I knew it, with legs like those."

"That's the pot calling the kettle…" Penny glanced down at the woman's legs.

She shrugged, smiling fondly. "A lifetime ago."

"You still got it."

"Thanks."

Penny polished off her croissant. "Gotta go catch a train." Sharing an apartment with three girls meant she had to fight for bathroom time. If she didn't hurry, her roommates would be up and hogging the facilities. "Nice having breakfast with you."

"Wait." The easy way the command fell off her tongue told Penny the woman was used to giving orders and having them obeyed. "Have you ever done any modeling?"

Penny shrugged. "Not really."

The woman snapped at her driver and called for her purse. She rummaged inside and pulled out a business card. "I'm in fashion," she said, writing something on the back of the card and handing it over.

Penny read the card. Hilary Vandermusen. *Look* magazine. "Nice to meet you." Penny held out her hand.

They shook hands, and Hilary headed back to her car. "I'll be expecting your call."

Penny watched the car drive away. She could always use another gig, but modeling wasn't her bag. Too old to compete with teenagers ten years younger than her for a job, she'd be better off teaching them dance instead.

On her way to the train, Penny saw a billboard advertising a new hotel in Hawaii. The white sand beaches sparkled under the golden sun, and Diamond Head Crater loomed large in the backdrop behind a canopy of lush palms.

Her chest tightened at the familiar sight of the most recognizable beach in Hawaii. The billboard was just the reminder she needed to keep her head on straight. Taking a risk didn't always work out. Penny had a steady job, a group of friends she could count on for a good time, and at least a few more years of youth before she hit the dreaded thirty.

A risk wasn't what she needed in her life.

Hilary's card went into the trash receptacle along with the remains of her breakfast.

Chapter 18

Bones

NIGHTS WERE THE WORST. During the day, Bones kept busy. He took tourists on dives, he taught surfing lessons, and he trained at his hālau. But at night, his thoughts crept back to the woman he loved, the tourist he'd fallen for and could never get over. He'd tried filling the hole in his heart with other women, booze, and partying, but nothing worked. As soon as he got into bed, all he could think about was Penny, the flame of her hair against his sheets, her soft skin so pale against the bronze of his tan, and her lips and tongue, so sweet yet so demanding. He'd done everything Hanani had told him to do. He'd sent Penny away, knowing she was the only woman he'd ever love, and he was still waiting for her to come back to him as Hanani had promised.

It had been almost two years. Sometimes he thought about giving up, but then he would remember Hanani's grave prediction. Penny would be his, but not yet.

Everywhere he went, there were reminders of Penny, as if she were determined to haunt him. Even while working at

Legends, a club full of the best-looking women on the island, who were dressed in crochet dresses that left nothing to the imagination and hip hugger jeans that showed off their curves, Bones thought of Penny.

He sat on the stool at the front door, watching the line of people waiting to get into the club, but his mind was on the night Penny had come to Legends years earlier. He still remembered the minidress she'd worn and her long dancer's legs. She'd kissed him in front of everyone, and Bones had loved every second. If Penny came back—*when* Penny came back—he wasn't letting her leave again. No matter what Hanani had warned, he wouldn't let her go. He'd followed all of Hanani's instructions, and he'd nearly died. He'd been swept away to sea, and his family had thought he was dead. By the time he'd gotten back to Oahu, all he'd wanted was the safety of Penny's arms. But she had been gone. Hanani had been wrong.

"You're gonna burn a hole through somebody, glaring like that."

Bones snapped out of his fantasy at the voice of a cocktail waitress who was standing next to him. Lani was wearing the shiny gold tube top and tight black shorts required for all the waitresses. Like the other women who worked at the club, she was one looker. Her long hair was pulled back in a ponytail, and her full lips were painted bright red. She was tiny, barely five feet tall. Even though he was sitting on a stool, he still towered over her.

"I thought you might be thirsty," Lani said, offering him a glass of water.

"Thanks, eh?" He took a long swallow and rested the glass on his knee, returning his attention to the crowd. If he was burning a hole in them, so be it. He had a job to do. He'd already busted up two fights that night. One of the bastards had sucker-punched him in the jaw, and soreness was starting to set in.

He sighed and flexed his bruised jaw. It was going to be a

long night at the club, but anything was better than lying awake in his bed, dreaming of the woman who'd left him.

"What time do you get off tonight?" Lani asked.

Bones checked his watch. Three more hours of breaking up fights and tossing drunks out of the club. Then he would go home, struggle with sleep, and wake up the next morning to do it again. He'd start the day with a grueling three-mile swim, train at the hālau, and check in at Makamaka Farms to see if they needed his labor, all the while going through the motions, hoping his soul mate would come back to him and make his life worth living again.

"Midnight," he said to Lani, who was waiting patiently for his answer.

"Right on," she said, taking his empty glass. "I'm having some people over tonight. You should come."

He grunted a response that was neither yes nor no. Making plans took too much energy. He'd see how he felt at the end of the night.

Lani was undeterred. She squeezed his bicep and gave him a flirtatious smile. "You know where I live," she said.

Indeed he did. It had been a year since he'd visited her place near Waikiki in the Silver Sands condominiums. The building was across the street from the beach, a twenty-story monstrosity looming over the smaller, older stores and hotels. Construction cranes were more common than seagulls at Waikiki now, and soon he expected there would only be a tiny patch of sky visible from the crowded sidewalks.

He and Lani had gotten together once, and Bones didn't plan on a repeat performance. Not that it had been horrible… just the opposite. It had been forgettable. Bones couldn't remember any of the details. Meanwhile, his vivid memories of Penny kept him up at night.

A few tipsy patrons exited the club, and Bones lifted the red rope, allowing the same number of people to enter. His job, if going smoothly, was all about numbers. Three people left, three more entered. There would be a line of people waiting to get into the popular club until it closed. During peak hours, the line stretched all the way down the sidewalk and around the corner of the block.

When his shift was finally over, Bones went inside Legends to collect his pay. The club vibrated with loud music and reeked of beer, cigarettes, and sweat. He pushed his way through the crowd and walked down the darkened hall to the manager's office.

Troy was behind the desk, eating noodles from a takeaway carton and reading a detective novel. When Bones walked in, he looked up and reached in his pocket for his keys. "You wanna work again tomorrow night? Sal's got the clap."

Bones grimaced and shook his head. "I'm busy." He was diving on Sunday, so he needed a cool head and a full night's sleep.

Troy handed him a wad of cash, and Bones left the office, heading down the hall toward the back entrance to the club.

Muffled voices from the shadows caught his attention, stopping him before he reached the employee exit. He listened carefully, recognizing distress in the high pitch of a woman's voice.

"Get off me! You're drunk!"

Something inside him snapped, and he immediately strode toward the voices. In a darkened corner, a man had a woman trapped against the wall. It was Lani and a lank-haired hippie wearing bell-bottom jeans and a bandana tied around his head.

"You heard her." Bones's voice boomed over the music drifting from the dance floor.

The man didn't bother turning around. "Get lost, asshole."

Bones put his hand on the man's neck and squeezed. "You want beef?"

Color drained from the man's face as he sized up Bones. "It's cool, man. We was just getting to know each other."

Bones glanced at Lani, whose flimsy top was torn and

hanging around her waist. Her arms were crisscrossed over her chest, hiding her breasts.

A storm of anger raged through Bones, and he tossed the man to the floor. He stood over him, his fists clenched. "Get outta here before you can't walk."

The man scrambled to his feet and hurried down the hall toward the club, muttering curses.

"And if I see you in here again, you're gonna be eating your lunch through a straw! Hear?"

Bones was tempted to follow him and carry through with his threat, but he turned his attention to Lani instead.

"You okay?"

She straightened from the wall, teetering on her high heels. "I'm okay." She tried to pull up her top, but it was damaged beyond repair. Her cheeks blazed with embarrassment.

Bones yanked off his shirt, a fitted black tee with the Legends logo emblazoned across the front, and handed it to Lani. "Here. Take this."

"Chee, Bones." Lani took the shirt and clutched it to her chest. "You're such a sweetheart."

Bones nodded tersely. "You shouldn't have to put up with that bullshit."

She smiled at him, her eyes hungrily devouring his bare chest. "I owe you one, big guy."

He turned around to give her privacy while she pulled the shirt over her head. "I was just doing my job."

"Now you have to come over tonight," Lani said. "So you can get your shirt back."

Bones laughed. "I have plenty of shirts."

Lani touched his bare shoulder. "I'm still a little shaken up. You think I can get one ride?"

His blood heated, and he felt a stirring he hadn't felt in a long time. Suddenly his king-size bed seemed like a lonely place to spend the night.

Chapter 19

Penny

AS SOON AS her class was over, Penny hurried down the hall to the studio's tiny office. Her boss had said she could use the phone anytime she wanted. The long-distance call to Hawaii was going to cost a fortune and come out of her paycheck, but Penny had to do it. Lou's last letter had begged her to call the first chance she got. She had news she didn't want to share in a letter.

Penny dialed Lou's number and waited for her best friend to pick up.

"Hello?" Lou's voice sounded small and tinny. Thousands of miles away.

"Lou? It's Penny."

"Penny!"

Lou's scream was so loud, Penny had to pull the phone away from her ear.

"I was just writing you a letter! I didn't think you'd ever call."

"I called as soon as I could." Besides the fact that it cost a fortune, there was the time difference to consider. It was after eight at night in New York, and in Hawaii it was mid-afternoon. "I just finished teaching, and Miss Donna is letting me use the phone at the studio. I can't talk long. What's so urgent?"

"I have some news."

Lou's voice wavered, and Penny's stomach dropped. "Is it John?"

Lou's younger brother was in Vietnam. And the news from that part of the world was worse every day. Penny clutched the edge of the desk, her heart pounding painfully as she waited for Lou to continue.

"No," Lou said. "It's not John."

Penny's grip on the desk relaxed. "That's good, I guess."

"No news is good news," Lou said.

"So…"

"Keoni asked me to marry him!"

"Congratulations." Penny's voice came out a little flat, the bitterness clear in her tone. She swallowed hard and tried again. "You're getting married!" Her forced cheer was worse, and she winced at the sound.

But Lou didn't notice Penny's lackluster reaction. She gushed on about the lavish plans already in the making. Keoni had saved a rich businessman's granddaughter from drowning at the North Shore, and the man was so grateful, he'd offered them the use of his brand-new luxury resort for their wedding festivities.

Penny had known it was only a matter of time before Lou and Keoni got married. Settling down and starting a life together was the natural next step. Penny had thought it would be her moving to the islands and marrying a local Hawaiian, but it hadn't worked out that way.

"That's amazing!" Penny tried to sound happy, but it was hard to pretend. The thought of Lou living in Hawaii for good caused a sharp pain in her chest. She and Lou would never live on the same continent again. They'd never go to the movies on a rainy Saturday afternoon or get drunk on cheap wine while playing cards.

"I want you to be my maid of honor," Lou said.

"Oh!" Penny lost her breath. "Are you sure?"

"Don't be silly. It has to be you." Lou sighed. "I know it's expensive to come out here. Maybe I can split the plane ticket with you. I've got some money saved up."

Heat flooded Penny's cheeks. Her gaze strayed to the clock on the wall. This phone call was already costing her hard-earned money that Miss Donna would take out of her paycheck. A plane ticket to Hawaii was going to cost her a fortune. But she would die before admitting she couldn't afford it to Lou.

"The money's no problem," she said. She'd take a second job waiting tables if she had to. "Of course I'll be there. I'm thrilled."

"Thanks, Penny. I couldn't do it without both you *and* John."

"Has there been any word from him?"

"Not since Christmas."

"Hopefully he's okay."

"Me too. I can't believe I'll be getting married without my baby brother at the wedding." She sighed. "I told Keoni maybe we should wait."

"No. Don't do that."

"Keoni said the same thing. Even though it means Kimo won't be there either."

Keoni's brother, the same age as John, was in Vietnam too.

"When's the wedding?"

"September twenty-fifth," she said. "I hope you don't have other plans."

"As if anything would keep me from being there."

"One more thing." Lou paused. "You might want to sit down for this."

"What?"

"Are you sitting?"

"Spill it, Lou."

"Okay." There was another long pause, and Penny heard Lou pull in a breath. "Keoni is going to ask Bones to be the best man."

A wave of dizziness washed over Penny, and her mouth went dry. Tears pricked the backs of her eyes.

"Penny? Are you there?"

"I'm here."

"I'm sorry. I told you to sit down."

As if sitting would relieve the severe pain in her chest at the mention of Bones. "It's fine."

"I thought I should warn you."

Penny's heart pounded so loudly in her ears, she couldn't think straight. She and Bones hadn't spoken since he'd broken up with her and sent her home. He hadn't even had the decency to call and let her know he was alive after he'd gone missing at sea.

She'd spent almost twenty hours paralyzed with fear, thinking he was dead. It had been the worst day of her life. Nightmares of him lost at sea still plagued her two years later. She could hardly look at a body of water without having chest palpitations.

Fresh anger pulsed to life as she thought of all the pain he'd caused her. He'd lied to her, used her... thrown her away.

When she saw him again, she might punch him in the belly. Then again, that might break her hand. Bones was built like a brick wall. Without warning, her mind tripped down memory lane. She pictured his broad shoulders, wide chest, trim waist...

She forced herself to let the image go. With any luck, Bones had gotten fat.

"You know, he's still in love with you," Lou said. "Maybe you can have a second chance."

A buzzing noise filled Penny's head. "Over my dead body."

"But you two were so perfect together."

She glanced at the clock again and sighed. Time was money. She needed to cut the call short. "Forget about it."

"Okay, but—"

Penny cut Lou off, determined to put an end to the subject. "I'm seeing someone."

"Oh! That's fantastic! Maybe you can bring him to the wedding!"

"That's an idea." *A terrible one.*

"Who is he? I want to know everything!"

Guilt pricked Penny's chest. She was a horrible liar. Good thing Lou couldn't see her face from all the way in Hawaii. She would know in an instant Penny wasn't telling the truth.

"It's new," she said.

"I'm so happy for you, Penny. I was worried you'd never date again after what happened with Bones."

What happened with Bones. That was one way to put it. Losing her heart, her head, and her hope was another. Penny laid her head on the desk as memories washed over her, fresh as if they'd happened yesterday. Bones had been the love of her life. There was no doubt about it. No man could compare to him. He'd made her feel sexy, desirable, alive. He'd made her think being in a relationship was a possibility. She missed everything about him—his reluctant smile, his powerful calming presence, even his mediocre ukulele playing.

A knock on the door startled her, and she picked her head up. A man stood at the open door. Penny recognized him as the father of one of her dancers, Bianca Lennox. Mr. Lennox stood out in a sea of governesses and mothers as one of the only men who dropped off and picked up their daughter.

Half the dance teachers had a crush on him. He was tall with thick blond hair and broad shoulders. His suits were tailor made and probably cost more than Penny made in a year, and his features were usually arranged in a bored, tolerant expression Penny associated with the obscenely wealthy class of New Yorkers.

"Lou, I've got to go."

"Okay. We'll talk again soon. I love you."

Mr. Lennox crossed his arms over his chest, his eyebrow lifting as he studied her.

"I love you too," Penny said into the phone. "Talk to you soon."

Penny hung up and took a breath, forcing her attention away from Hawaii and back to New York. Mr. Lennox was staring at her, his expression no longer bored.

"Boyfriend?" he asked.

"Excuse me?"

His gaze darted to her left hand. "You're not married, so that must have been your boyfriend. Lou?"

Penny suppressed a flicker of annoyance. Everyone assumed Lou was a man. "How can I help you Mr. Lennox?"

"May I come in?"

Penny pushed back her chair and prepared to stand. "You're probably looking for Miss Donna."

"No. I'm looking for you."

Mr. Lennox had a direct stare that was discomforting. His attempt at a smile was too calculated, too cold. It didn't reach his ice-blue eyes.

Penny assumed he wanted to complain about his daughter, who hadn't made the cut to move up with the other girls her age. She was used to dealing with overinvolved parents who thought they knew better than the teacher.

"I'm actually late for an appointment." Her shoulders sagged just thinking of the job she needed to apply for in order to afford a trip to Hawaii. Waitressing was a good way to make money, but it wasn't easy, and her feet were already killing her from teaching all day.

Mr. Lennox stepped into the office without being invited. "I only need a minute of your time."

Penny checked her watch with a deliberate flick of her wrist Mr. Lennox couldn't miss. "Fire away."

"I'm concerned about Bianca," he said. "She isn't moving up."

Penny smiled with an equal mix of sympathy and relief. Since she didn't make the decisions for advancement, the meeting was going to be over before it started. "You'll need to speak with Miss Donna," she said.

He took a step closer to the desk, and Penny fought the urge to stand to level out their equality. Mr. Lennox wasn't a particularly tall or broad man, but he exuded power. Penny assumed a man of his wealth and class didn't often hear the word no.

"I've spoken to Miss Donna. She told me to talk to you."

Penny's brow raised. Miss Donna ruled the studio with an iron fist. She never deferred to her junior staff. But, since she had, Penny didn't mind being the one to tell Mr. Lennox no.

"I'm sorry," she said. "There's really nothing I can do."

His careful mask slipped, and Penny glimpsed the desperation on his face before he carefully schooled his features into a smile. "Of course there is," he said. "You're her teacher."

Penny checked her watch again, conveying the message loud and clear: meeting over. "Bianca can try again next season," she said, pushing back her chair to stand.

Mr. Lennox frowned. "Next season isn't going to cut it. It's crucial she move up now."

Penny studied him for a moment. His cheeks were flushed, and his pale-blue eyes blazed with intensity. Why was he so desperate for his daughter to advance? If Bianca showed half the passion her father did during lessons, she would have already moved up.

"She'll move up when she's ready," Penny said with an air of finality, picking up her bag and placing it on her shoulder.

Mr. Lennox moved to stand in front of her, so close Penny could smell the subtle scent of his cologne. "You don't understand what this means to Bianca. If she doesn't move up—" He shook his head, the lines deepening around his mouth as he frowned. "It will be devastating."

Penny got the impression that Bianca was more interested in gossip and fashion than ballet. Her father had shown more interest in dance in the last few minutes than Bianca had all season. Penny tilted her chin and met his gaze. "Devastating for whom?"

His posture stiffened, and his jaw clenched. "Miss Donna mentioned private lessons," he said. "If you'd be willing to work with Bianca, she can reaudition at the end of the summer."

"I've never given private lessons before," she said.

His shoulders relaxed and a smile replaced his frown. "That's okay."

Penny shook her head. "I don't have access to a studio, and Miss Donna's is fully booked with classes."

He waved his hand as if sweeping aside her protests. "I've got that covered."

Penny felt a headache building. "I'm gonna shoot straight with you Mr. Lennox," she said. "I don't think Bianca's heart is in dancing."

He drew in a breath and released it slowly. "She's going through a rough time. Her mother and I are divorced. It's hard for a teenage girl to be without her mom."

His demeanor changed with the admittance, his features softening with vulnerability. Penny's heart went out to both him and his daughter. She couldn't imagine what it would have been like growing up without her mom, who was like a best friend to her. Penny's dad was great, but they didn't share the same kind of relationship she shared with her mom.

Even though Penny felt sorry for Bianca, there wasn't much she could do to help the girl if she didn't have passion for dancing. Penny had been dealing with dissatisfied parents for years. Everyone thought their child was the next big star. Unfortunately, not every girl had talent.

"I don't know," she began, careful to choose the right words.

"I understand your reservations." He reached into the pocket of his immaculate suit jacket and pulled out his wallet. "How about you give her four lessons?" He plucked four bills from his wallet and offered them to Penny.

Her heart stopped when she recognized Benjamin Franklin's face on the bills. It would take her nearly a month working at Miss Donna's to make four hundred dollars.

He pressed the money into her hand. "If she hasn't improved after four lessons, then you can quit."

Penny lifted her gaze from the money and met his ice-blue eyes. "When would you like to start?"

Chapter 20

Bones

WEIGHED DOWN BY A SIXTY-POUND SLEDGEHAMMER, an axe, and a single tank of air, Bones sank under the surface of the water. A moment later, Keoni plunged in behind him, and together they made their way to the bottom of the ocean.

A school of silver fish swam by in a flash of brightness, and Bones started with a jolt. Keoni laughed, the tinny sound echoing in the waves. Bones made a rude gesture at Keoni, which only made him laugh harder.

Bones ignored him and focused on the task at hand. Even though they were experienced divers, it was still dangerous. Anything could go wrong under water. Every minute was crucial.

They dived with one tank of air because less equipment made it easier to swim back to the surface. One tank was enough to make the dive, harvest the coral, and return to the surface, but it was pushing it. If anything went wrong, there wouldn't be enough time to decompress, which added another deadly element.

They had to be efficient and smart, always keeping in mind the threat of narcosis. Diving one hundred feet was the equivalent of drinking two strong martinis. They were diving twice that depth. Bones was already feeling drunk.

It was a different world so deep underwater. Darkness surrounded them, and every move they made took longer than it should have.

When they finally reached the bottom of the deep ocean where it was so dark, they had to strain to see, Bones signaled to Keoni that he was going left. Keoni signaled back, pointing right. They would meet up in exactly eight minutes to swim back to the surface together.

Bones kept safety in the forefront of his mind as he harvested the largest, most profitable coral trees. He dug quickly, using his axe and sledgehammer to pry the trees from the sand by their roots. Jewelry stores paid top dollar for the rare coral trees. Their black skeletons were cut and polished, then fashioned into jewelry. Bones wore a necklace made of black coral beads whenever he dived. It brought him luck. After the disastrous dive when he'd been swept away by the current and nearly lost at sea, he took every precaution he could, even if it seemed ridiculous to others.

Time was ticking down when Bones spotted a giant tree. It would provide a huge payoff, maybe even enough for the down payment on the boat he'd been eyeing.

He tried to keep calm and conserve his energy as he swam back to meet Keoni. Pointing at his watch, he gestured for more time. Keoni shook his head and nodded at his float bag, which he'd already inflated. The trees Keoni had harvested were tied to the rope and rising to the surface, their bright-red fronds undulating in the waves. In a flash, it would be too late for Keoni to grab on. He had to go.

Bones was insistent that he needed a few more minutes. Rubbing his fingers together in the universal sign for money, he jabbed his hand toward the large tree in the distance.

Instead of inflating his bag and rising with Keoni, Bones swam back for the treasure. He knew his cousin would give him a piece of his mind when he joined him at the surface, but the tree would be worth getting an earful. It would bring in a thousand bucks or maybe more, and Bones wasn't the only one who needed money. Keoni was newly engaged, and weddings weren't cheap.

He approached the tree and said a silent prayer of thanks. Bones's ancestors had been making their living off the ocean for generations, and he had been taught to honor the creatures who gave their lives for human benefit. The tree would die, but it would be made into something beautiful, and it would provide for Bones. It would make it possible for him to do less dangerous diving and concentrate on a new business venture he had in mind: giving dive lessons to rich tourists. He wouldn't have to rob the ocean of precious black coral, and he would still be fulfilling his legacy as a Keakealani waterman. He needed the tree.

Aiming for the root ball, he struck hard with his axe and buried it deep. The pressure of two hundred fifty feet of water made every movement infinitely harder than it was on land. Bones pounded the axe with his sledgehammer. His grunts of exertion accompanied the echoing *tink, tink, tink* of metal hitting metal.

He was nearly finished when he felt a shift in the water. Icy fingers of dread ran up his spine, and he knew he was no longer alone. Glancing up, he saw the sleek underbelly of an enormous shark. The ringing of his sledgehammer against the axe had called the predator like a dinner bell. About thirteen feet long and eight feet around, the shark was striped with distinctive silver markings like a tiger.

With one eye on the tiger shark cruising the water above, Bones ripped the coral tree from the mound and tied it to his rope. His heartbeat slammed in his ears, drowning his thoughts.

He had no choice but to wait out the shark, hoping it would give up on him in pursuit of a more appealing meal.

Each second that ticked by could be his last. There was only about ten minutes of air left in his tank, and he had to allow time for decompression.

The shark continued to circle, as if it were playing a game with its dinner.

Finally, Bones needed to act. If he did nothing, he would die. He had to take a risk. Sharks were the spirit animal of his family. Their purpose was to guide and inspire, not harm.

Trusting his instincts, Bones lifted his mouthpiece from his lips and inflated his float bag with air. As it rose to the surface, he grabbed the rope attached to it. Even though his pulse was racing with fear, he forced himself to rise slowly, allowing time for decompression.

He inched up from the bottom of the ocean, right into the path of the shark. He'd been close to sharks before but never a tiger shark, and never one so big.

Unfortunately, he'd seen the damage sharks could do to a human body. He shuddered, remembering the body he'd seen. It had washed up on shore missing its torso. The top half of the body had been ripped off in one clean bite, leaving its spine sticking straight out of its shorts.

The shark circled him slowly as he stopped to decompress. Bones would have laughed if he hadn't been so afraid. The hunter was taunting him. Playing with his food.

When Bones was about twenty feet from the surface with the boat in sight, the shark closed in on him. With each pass, the shark locked eyes with Bones, sizing him up. The shark's pupils were cold and dark, reflecting Bones's terrified face behind his mask.

The boat was so close, yet so far away. If the shark didn't eat him, he would be out of air in a matter of minutes. He would die either way.

His life flashed before his eyes. He remembered learning to

surf with Keoni at Queen's Beach, his first kiss, meeting Penny at the airport two years ago, and Hanani's prediction that had made him send her away.

He'd never believed people when they said their lives flashed before their eyes when they thought they were dying, but now he knew it was true. When he'd been lost at sea two years ago, he'd been afraid, but he'd never actually feared for his life. Bones saw his family and friends as clearly as if they were swimming beside him.

He saw his father's stern face, his mother's patient eyes, and his sisters' smiles. If Bones died, the family name died along with him. His father would be pissed at him for not carrying on the line. His mother would be devastated he'd never given her grandchildren. And his sisters would cry at his grave.

Would Penny miss him? Would she mourn his untimely death?

Did she still think about him as much as he thought of her? Bones had tried everything to get her off his mind, but nothing worked, and there he was, thinking of her as he pulled in what was surely the last breath of air in his tank.

Something splashed into the water nearby. A huge marlin sank through the waves, leaving behind a bright stain of blood. The shark whipped in the direction of the fish, its tail slashing the water inches from Bones's face as it sped off toward the bait.

As soon as the shark took off, a rope dropped into the water beside Bones. He reached out and grabbed it, hanging on for dear life as he was yanked toward the boat. With a jerk that ricocheted through his entire body, Bones was pulled to the surface.

Henry grabbed him under the arms and hauled him up and onto the boat. Bones collapsed on the deck and yanked off his mouthpiece, dragging in great gulps of air. He'd never been so glad to see Henry in his life.

"You owe me a fish," Henry said.

His heart raced, and he couldn't catch his breath. "I'll give you all the fish you want, brah."

Keoni pulled in Bones's float bag with the trees attached, giving him the stink eye the whole time. "Next time come up when you're supposed to."

"Yeah, yeah, yeah." Bones waved him off like it was no big deal. He would never admit how scared he'd been, but at least he was alive. At least there was still a chance Hanani's prediction about his soul mate might come true.

WHEN BONES WENT in to deliver the coral trees he and Keoni had harvested, the store owner, Mr. Taki, spotted him and held up a hand. "Aloha. I'll be right with you, my friend."

Bones nodded and walked to the corner of the store where the black coral jewelry was on display. It was surreal to see the finished pieces of jewelry made from the coral he'd pulled from the depths of the ocean. Polished black beads carved from the rare coral had been made into earrings, bracelets, and rings. Bones's stomach clenched when he saw the prices. If one small pair of earrings sold for fifty dollars, he needed to rethink his prices. Next time he would ask for double. He risked his life to dig the coral from the ocean, and the jeweler was making a fortune from it.

But he couldn't complain. This payoff would earn him enough money for the boat he wanted to buy. He could start the business he'd been planning, providing dive tours for wealthy tourists off the coast of Oahu, and give up the odd jobs he'd been working to piece together a living.

With a business of his own, he'd show his father he was worthy of the Keakealani legacy.

While Mr. Taki finished up with his customer, Bones wandered through the store. He checked out the elaborate displays, noting pieces of jewelry that reminded him of his mother and sisters. Other than the black coral necklace he wore for luck, Bones didn't wear jewelry, but the women in his family loved it. He could remember his father saving up for months to get his mother a pearl ring for their anniversary.

Bones paused at the engagement ring selection. A sparkling diamond ring in an antique setting winked at him from under the bright lights. It was a spellbinding ring with an intricately carved band and a large marquis cut center stone surrounded by a double halo of small round diamonds.

"Something catch your eye?"

Bones looked up and saw a salesclerk hovering over the case. "Nah." He glanced back at the ring, mesmerized by its unique beauty. A sharp pain pierced his chest as he imagined slipping it onto the finger of the woman he loved. He shook his head slightly, clearing his mind. "I'm waiting on Mr. Taki."

The clerk cocked his head and smiled. "I can show you something while you wait."

Bones's gaze locked again on the diamond engagement ring. "I'm not interested, brah."

"Mr. Taki is almost finished. No harm in looking." He unlocked the case and reached inside. His fingers stopped on a ring in the back row. "This one?"

Bones grunted. "Two over."

"Ah." The clerk plucked the ring from the velvet box. "This one is one of my favorites."

An ache settled in Bones's chest, a dull, thudding pain that made him feel hollow inside. Maybe there was harm in looking. His heart squeezed, reminding him of what he'd lost.

The clerk took the ring from the case and held it up to the light. It sparkled brilliantly, prisms of light reflecting in fascinating patterns. The diamonds enchanted him, promising a future that could never exist.

"Only a very special woman can wear this ring," the clerk said, offering it to Bones for a closer inspection.

A reel of memories starring Penny played through his mind —from the first moment he'd seen her at the airport to their final good-bye at the surf contest. He'd been waiting his whole life to meet a woman like her. Someone who wasn't intimidated by him or afraid to speak her mind. Someone he could trust and protect and love.

The ring would be perfect on Penny's finger. He was a traditional guy, and he wanted his wife to wear the best diamond money could buy. He imagined getting down on one knee and slipping it on Penny's finger.

"Heh, cuz. What's taking so long, eh?"

Bones tore his gaze from the ring and looked up to see Keoni standing a few feet away, eyeing him curiously.

"You were supposed to wait at the truck."

Keoni raised a brow at the ring in the clerk's hand. "You doing some shopping or what?"

"Nah." He turned toward the clerk. "Can you tell Mr. T to wrap it up? I ain't got all day."

The clerk put the ring away and quietly disappeared behind the counter. Bones strode across the floor to his cousin, forcing the ring from his mind. "What gives, brah? You're supposed to be waiting outside."

"It's about to rain." He cleared his throat and lowered his voice. "I thought we should bring the merchandise inside."

Bones resisted rolling his eyes at Keoni's dramatics. "It's fine. Go back outside."

Keoni was focused on something behind Bones's shoulder. "Those engagement rings you were looking at?"

A muscle ticked in Bones's jaw. "Nah. The clerk was trying to make a sale."

Sympathy flashed in Keoni's dark gaze. "You know she's coming out for the wedding."

Bones played dumb. "Who?"

Keoni stepped toward the jewelry case housing the engagement rings and looked inside. "Penny."

Every muscle in Bones's body tightened. The sound of her name plucked at the taut strings binding his broken heart. Every success he'd achieved was nothing compared to the loss of her.

"This might be your chance to get her back. If you two are meant to be, this might be it."

Bones scoffed. "If we were meant to be, she wouldn't have left."

"You asked her to leave. You fucked up, cuz. But you're getting a second chance to make things right. Don't blow it."

Heat rose up Bones's neck to flush his cheeks. He glanced at the jewelry case and felt a rush of hope fill his chest. In his wildest dreams, he pictured himself on one knee, offering Penny that ring. And if his dreams came true, she was saying yes.

Chapter 21

Penny

BIANCA LEAPED into the air and landed gracefully. Penny burst into spontaneous applause. "Wonderful Bianca!"

Bianca had worked hard over the last two months, improving more than Penny thought possible. Penny understood why her father had been so adamant about Bianca taking private lessons—she was more talented than she let on. With a little encouragement and attention, she'd blossomed into a wonderful dancer. Penny was confident Bianca would ace her audition and that Miss Donna would approve her advancement.

"Was it really okay?" Bianca leaned against the barre for support, catching her breath.

"No, it wasn't okay." Penny moved to Bianca's side and locked eyes with her in the mirror. "It was amazing." She grinned. "Your dad was right."

Bianca blinked, looking down at her slippers. "What did he say?"

Penny put her hand atop Bianca's. "He said you didn't belong in my class."

Bianca flinched, pulling her hand away. "I don't belong anywhere."

Leaning against the barre, Penny crossed her arms over her chest and dipped her chin at Bianca. "I only meant you've improved enough to advance. You belong with the best group in the studio."

Bianca's piercing blue eyes were arresting, so much darker and bluer than her father's, whose pale, grayish-blue eyes reminded her of iridescent feathers.

While her eyes weren't the same blue as her father's, they shared a similar intensity. It was impossible to have a casual conversation with Heath Lennox. He was always inquiring, pushing, probing her with his curious gaze.

Since the dance studio was on the second floor of the Lennox's grand home, Penny sometimes shared a few post-lesson dinners with them. Bianca's original four lessons had been doubled. Penny had worked with Bianca twice a week to prepare her for her audition, and the girl was more than ready.

Penny had gotten to know both father and daughter better over the course of the lessons.

At first Penny had been reluctant to stay for dinner, but she wasn't in a position to say no to a home-cooked meal. She loathed cooking and often ate cereal for dinner before going out with friends. The Lennox's housekeeper made the same hearty meals Penny's mom had cooked growing up—casseroles, puddings, and meat pies.

She often stayed for dinner, not only for the food but for the company.

Bianca pinned her with her direct gaze. "Did my dad tell you about my mom?"

Penny bit her lip, not sure how to respond. "He mentioned they're divorced."

Bianca raised a dark brow. "That's it?"

Penny crossed the room to take the record from the player and place it back in the sleeve. "Pretty much."

"He didn't tell you who my mother is?"

Penny shook her head, aware the conversation was heading into dangerous territory. She could hear the hurt and anger dripping from Bianca's voice. "He said she was overseas."

Bianca took off her slippers and patted her feet with a dry towel. She had the abused toes of a dancer, bruised and misshapen like knotty twigs. Bloodstained tape was wrapped around several of her toes, and Penny would bet that water-filled blisters sat on the balls of her feet.

"My mother is Nadia Stanisky," she said, unwinding the tape.

Penny's eyebrows shot upward. Nadia Stanisky was a famous ballerina. She'd graced stages all over the world. Penny had idolized her as a teen. Nadia had been all the rage, but about fifteen years ago, she'd dropped off the circuit. Penny guessed that had something to do with the fourteen-year-old girl staring up at her.

"My dad wants me to be just like my mom," Bianca said, "But I'll never be as good as her."

Penny swallowed hard. No one could be as good as Nadia; she was one of a kind. Penny's heart went out to the teenager who had shoes too big to fill.

"My grandmother wants me to quit dancing and focus on school, go to college like she did." Bianca pulled her knees to her chest and hung her head. "Maybe I should listen to her."

Penny knew she had to tread carefully. Bianca was young and impressionable. Penny was twice her age and still hadn't figured life out, and she wasn't one to give advice. She took a breath and planned out her words.

"You're a talented dancer. Very talented." Penny had been talented too, but her world had been ripped away when her body had betrayed her with its insistence on height. Everything she'd worked so hard for had crumbled when she'd reached nearly six feet. "But it's not a bad idea to have a backup plan."

Bianca raised her face from her knees. "So my grandmother is right?"

Penny nodded. "But so is your dad. If you really want to dance, don't give up on your dreams."

Bianca huffed in annoyance. "Watch out for my dad."

Penny fidgeted with her dance bag, avoiding Bianca's sharp gaze. "What do you mean?"

Bianca stretched forward to touch her toes. "My dad does this all the time. He can't help it. It's just the way he is."

"I'm not sure I understand," Penny said, although that wasn't quite the truth. She'd seen the way Heath Lennox looked at her across the table at dinner. He was interested in her for more than what she could teach his daughter. But Penny knew better than to fall for a man over a few home-cooked dinners. She'd learned her lesson in Hawaii.

Bianca widened her legs and folded her torso to the ground between them. Propping herself up on her elbows, she looked at Penny directly. "My dad is handsome. Women fall for him."

Penny raised her chin. "Not this woman."

Bianca smiled, looking much wiser than most fourteen-year-old girls. "I like you, Miss Penny."

Penny smiled back. "I like you too, Bianca."

"But you're not very smart."

Penny's mouth dropped open. Bianca's rebuke had caught her off guard. "You're being very rude."

"I'm sorry if it seems that way, but I'm just looking out for you. I don't want you to get hurt."

Penny didn't need a teenager's help in managing her love life. She was perfectly capable of screwing it up on her own. "I'll see you on Thursday at the audition." She picked up her dance bag and slung it over her shoulder.

"Wait." Bianca hurried to the door. Her big blue eyes filled with tears. "Don't be mad at me."

Penny's chest tightened. It would be cruel to hold a grudge against the girl when she was only trying to protect her. "I'm not mad."

Bianca's chin quivered. "I'm sorry if I hurt your feelings."

Penny softened. She didn't want to make the girl cry. "You aren't the first person to call me stupid," she said, opening the door. "This is New York. Someone called me dumb on the train this morning."

Bianca's nostrils flared. "You ride the train?"

Penny winked. "You should try it sometime."

Bianca's eyes widened. "Why would I ever do that?"

Penny laughed at the horror on Bianca's face. "It's really not that bad."

"I've heard it reeks and there are rats."

Penny nodded. "Bigger than cats, some of them. And it does stink of old socks and pee, but you get used to it."

"My grandmother would faint if I rode the train." Bianca smiled mischievously and tapped her bottom lip with her fingernail. "Maybe I should try it."

"I wouldn't want to kill your grandmother."

"My grandmother is too mean to kill." A high-pitched giggle escaped the girl's mouth. "She only has to look at a man and make him wish he'd never been born."

"I need to meet this woman."

Bianca let her gaze drop over Penny approvingly. "She'd like you. She's a redhead too."

"We witches need to stick together."

Bianca giggled again, and a moment later, Penny joined in. She'd been so stressed over her upcoming trip to Hawaii, she hadn't had many reasons to laugh lately.

"I like the sound of that."

Penny looked up at the sound of a masculine voice. Heath stood in the hallway, looking handsome in a tailored suit with wide lapels and a bold-colored tie. His hair was perfectly combed and parted on the side, and his smile was worthy of a toothpaste commercial.

"Can Miss Penny stay for dinner?"

Penny shot Bianca a warning look. Hadn't the girl just been warning her off her father? Bianca smiled sweetly and rose up on tiptoe to give her father a kiss on the cheek.

"Of course. She's welcome to stay. Mrs. Johnson is making your favorite, and there's always plenty."

"Chicken casserole?" Bianca asked.

As if on cue, Penny's stomach growled. Unless she ate here, she hadn't been eating regular meals. She'd been socking away every cent for her ticket to Hawaii. Chicken casserole sounded heavenly.

"Yes, love. Chicken casserole, garlic bread... and cheesecake for dessert."

"I'll go change," Bianca said.

"Don't forget, your grandmother is joining us tonight."

"You can meet the witch," Bianca said.

"Bianca!" Heath narrowed his eyes at her daughter in reprimand.

"Sorry, Daddy," she said. "I didn't mean it like that. Miss Penny said redheads were witches."

Penny shrugged. "Everyone knows it's true."

Bianca hurried out of the room before her father could say anything else. When she was gone, Heath turned to Penny. "A witch, huh?" He stepped closer, his expression intense. "Should I be afraid?"

Bianca's warning echoed in Penny's head. Women fell for Heath, but Penny wasn't a green young thing. She'd been brokenhearted before, and she'd been guarding herself ever since. It would take more than a rich, handsome man to change her mind.

Penny adjusted the bag on her shoulder, avoiding the bright beam of his gaze. "Are you afraid of your mother?"

"Yes," Heath admitted, taking a step closer. "That's why you should stay for dinner. I need your protection."

His masculine scent filled her nose. Cedar and spice. Power and money. She hadn't had feelings for a man since Bones, but she had to admit, she wasn't immune to Heath's charms.

"I don't have any other clothes." Penny gestured at her leotard and ballet skirt.

"It's casual." He pulled off his tie and stuck it in the pocket of his suit as if to prove it.

"I don't want to intrude on a family dinner," she said.

"Please stay."

A SHIVER RAN down Penny's spine as she looked into Heath's blue-gray eyes. It was impossible not to be affected by his charm. "Okay."

He smiled and slid a finger under the strap of her bag, lifting it off her shoulder.

"My mother can be a real bore, but your company will make the meal bearable."

They stepped into the hall, and Penny glanced at the paintings adorning the walls. They were starkly modern, a bold contrast to the antique furniture. The hall opened up to the grand staircase, where a crystal chandelier hung from the high ceiling. Heath was tight-lipped about what he did for a living to have such a fancy house with priceless art, a full staff, and a ballet studio. Whatever he did, it was lucrative.

She'd earned enough money teaching Bianca lessons to pay for her trip to Hawaii.

Penny stopped at the top of the stairs, where a large chandelier hung from the ceiling, casting slivers of light down to the foyer below. "You were right about Bianca," she said. "She's very talented."

Heath's smile widened. He was obviously enamored by his daughter. He gazed down at Penny, his expression turning serious. "I knew you would be perfect for her."

A tingle of awareness sent goosebumps down her arms. She could do worse than a man like Heath Lennox. After two years of closing herself off, maybe it was time to open up again.

"Your mother is here," Mason, one of the staff members

Heath employed, stared up at them from the bottom of the stairs.

Heath didn't take his eyes from Penny's face. "Did you fix her a drink?"

"Of course," Mason said. "She's waiting in the sitting room."

Heath sighed. "She hates to be kept waiting. Would you like wine?" he asked.

It was what she usually drank when she stayed for dinner, but Penny thought she might need something stronger to deal with Heath's mother. "I'll have what you're having."

Heath told Mason to make two martinis, and placed his hand on her elbow, guiding her to the stairs. "Mason makes an excellent martini. He should have been a bartender."

Mason cleared his throat loudly before exiting the foyer, and Penny fought a smile. Heath and Mason had a funny relationship. Mason acted like he barely tolerated Heath, and Heath took every opportunity to tease the older man.

Heath's fingers rested on her lower back as he steered her toward the sitting room. "Thank you for staying," he said in a low voice as they neared the sitting room.

"I can't say no to chicken casserole and an excellent martini."

Heath chuckled softly. "What about the company?" he asked.

Penny didn't have time to answer before they entered the room, and a woman turned to greet them.

She wore a silk pantsuit in bright fuchsia that set off the deep auburn of her shoulder-length hair. Something about the woman was familiar, but Penny couldn't quite place her.

"Mother, I have someone I'd like you to meet."

Heath's mother's eyes blazed, and she crossed the room in long strides. Taking Penny by both hands she beamed at her. "I've been searching all over the city for you. I've gone back to Tiffany's a dozen times, but you never showed up again."

Penny suddenly remembered where she'd met Heath's mother—at the window of Tiffany's.

Heath glanced from his mother to Penny with concern. "Mother, this is Penny Longchamp, Bianca's dance teacher."

Heath's mother let her gaze drift over Penny. "That explains the outfit."

Penny laughed and searched her memory for the woman's name. After a moment, it came to mind as clearly as if she were reading it off the card. "Hilary?"

Hilary's face transformed with delight. "Yes! I'm so glad to have found you." She glanced at Heath, accusation in her bright-blue gaze. "This is the woman I've been telling you about. Why have you been hiding her?"

Heath's brows furrowed, and he cocked his head at Penny. "Penny is the face you want for the new campaign? My Penny?"

Penny's heart squeezed at the endearment, then annoyance flashed. She wasn't *anyone's* Penny. No one but her own. "It's nice to meet you again, Hilary. But like I told you before, I'm no model."

Hilary smiled and nodded as if Penny hadn't just told her no. "You don't have to be a model for me to make you famous. You just have to be you." She raised an elegant eyebrow at Penny. "Do you want to be famous?"

It was a question Penny had never expected to hear. Once upon a time, she'd thought about being famous. She'd pictured herself on stage, dancing before a rapt audience, but she'd packed away her dreams when she'd reached a height of five foot ten. Hilary's confident expression ignited a spark of curiosity inside Penny.

Maybe it was time to unpack.

Chapter 22

Bones

THE CHRISTENING of his own boat should have been one of the most exciting days of his life, but Bones could hardly enjoy it. He felt like there was something missing.

Someone missing.

All of his friends and family were gathered at the marina. They welcomed him with cheers of congratulations, engulfing him in tight hugs and kissing his cheeks. He smiled and returned their gestures of affection, all the while searching the crowd for a face he knew he wouldn't see.

One by one, his loved ones came up to offer him words of advice and congratulations.

"Try smiling," Keoni said. "It's your big day."

Bones looked across the dock at his boat. Decorated with ti garlands in preparation for the christening, it sparkled under the high sun. Pride filled his chest, and a smile tugged at his lips.

"That's better." Keoni slapped him on the back.

"I'm gonna make a lotta dough with this boat. You're crazy not to go in with me."

"I ain't got anything extra. Not with the wedding coming up and all." Keoni fidgeted with the medallion he wore around his neck, a sure sign he was nervous.

Bones stared at Keoni. "What's wrong with you?"

Keoni cleared his throat. "I got something to ask you."

"Yeah?" Even though they didn't always see eye to eye, Bones would do anything for his cousin. "You need money, or what?"

Keoni shook his head. "Nah. I need a best man."

Bones suddenly felt like he was on top of the world. His heart swelled, and his chest felt tight. "For real?"

Keoni shrugged like it was no big deal. "For real, brah."

"What about your dad?"

"He's too busy. I can't ask him to add one more thing to his plate."

"And Tau?" Keoni's older brother was the oldest of the cousins. The most respected and dependable.

"Nah, brah." Keoni's voice was flat. "It wouldn't be right. Because of Kimo."

It had been months since anyone had heard from Kimo in Vietnam. Kimo had thought his warrior blood made him invincible, that he'd make a difference in the war. But it turned out he was just another dispensable soldier.

"It's gotta be you, eh?" Keoni gazed out at the turquoise water, his profile stony. "I want it to be you."

Keoni was more than a cousin to Bones; he was his best friend. They'd been inseparable since middle school, when Keoni had stood up for Bones against the bigger guys. When Bones finally hit his growth spurt and filled out, no one messed with him anymore, but he'd never forgotten Keoni's loyalty.

Now was his chance to repay him. "Don't sweat it." Bones clapped Keoni on the back too hard, making him stumble forward a step to regain his balance. "I'm your man."

Keoni grinned and pulled Bones into a hug. "Thanks, eh?"

"Yeah, yeah, yeah." Bones brushed Keoni off.

"I gotta wear a monkey suit or what?"

"Yeah. I'm thinking of white tuxedos instead of black. What do you think?"

"I look good in white."

Keoni laughed. "No one's gonna be looking at you." His laugh died as he stared at the top of the dock. "What's she doing here?"

Ryla Aikau walked down from the parking lot, wearing a pair of short shorts and a halter top that showed off her full figure. Ryla was like a kid sister to Bones. When he looked at her, he didn't see the sexy starlet she'd become when her singing career had taken off. He saw the pigtailed kid she'd been at ten.

"Whattaya think?" Bones asked. "She's here to sing."

"You shoulda warned me she was coming." Keoni's voice was tense.

"Next time, I'll give you the guest list for approval." Bones may have been immune to Ryla's charms, but Keoni and Ryla had a different history. "Chill out, brah. You're gonna see Ryla all the time, she's basically family. You might as well get used to it."

Keoni gave Bones the stink eye. "Don't think that's possible."

"Heh, at least Henry and Claudia couldn't make it." Bones laughed gruffly. "I can't handle all your ex-girlfriend drama."

"Ryla is not my ex. That was a onetime thing, and you know it." Keoni shook his head in disgust. "A mistake."

"Does Ryla know that?" There was no mistaking the way Ryla looked at Keoni, as if he'd hung the moon.

"I can't even talk to her."

"That ain't right, cuz."

Across the dock, Ryla lifted her hand to wave at Bones. He waved back, but her gaze had already drifted toward Keoni. Her expression was a mix of adoration and regret.

"Shit." Keoni saw the look too. "What am I supposed to do now?"

"Be cool, man." Bones elbowed Keoni in the ribs. "She knows your ass is as good as married."

"You won't be looking so smug in a few months at the wedding," Keoni warned.

"What? Why?"

"When you see Penny again, you're gonna lose your shit, brah."

His thoughts drifted back to Penny. He'd done what he had to do. He'd sent her away for her own good, and he was hoping Hanani's prediction would come true and she would find her way back to him.

He forced his attention back to the present. Now that Ryla had arrived, it was time to get started with the ceremony. He cleared his throat and called for everyone's attention.

"Thank you all for coming today to celebrate with me." He cut the garland of shiny leaves hanging over the gangway and stepped onto his boat. "May this boat be blessed with love," he said, dipping a ti leaf into a bowl and sprinkling fresh water over the deck. "May it be blessed with power, success, and safe returns."

He gestured at Ryla, inviting her on board. She kicked off her shoes and joined him. When she sang, silence fell over the group. Ryla's voice enchanted everyone within earshot.

Bones put a hand on the polished silver railing. Pride filled his chest, and a thrill ran through him. This boat, built for speed with a powerful engine and stainless-steel twin propellors, was going to be the key to his future, but he'd named it for the past: *A Hui Hou.* Translated into English, it meant "until we meet again."

Chapter 23

Penny

PENNY WAS on her way to the Lennox residence for a lesson with Bianca, who'd moved up but wanted to continue private lessons, when a dress in a shop window caught her eye. She stopped and stared at it, debating on whether she should splurge on a new dress for her upcoming trip to Hawaii.

Thanks to her lessons with Bianca, she had enough money to buy her ticket to Hawaii, *and* a new outfit for the trip. The cash in her purse was begging to be spent, but she had to be smart. She couldn't blow it all in a dress shop, not when she needed to save money for the wages she was missing while she was in Hawaii.

However, the dress was her favorite color—bright fuchsia. Despite what they said about redheads not wearing pink, fuchsia looked amazing against Penny's fair skin. The short hemline of the dress would show off her legs, and the fitted bodice would hug her waist. A smile curved her lips as she imagined Bones's reaction to seeing her in it, and her decision was made.

She walked to the door with a determined expression. Bones

had broken her heart, but he hadn't killed her spirit. She was going to enjoy seeing him squirm when he got a load of her in the pink dress. She reached for the door and felt a sudden sharp pull on her arm. There was a loud snap, and then she was being pushed to the ground.

By the time she got to her feet, the man who'd grabbed her purse was halfway down the block almost to the corner.

Adrenaline shot through her veins, and she took off after him.

She pumped her arms and legs, dodging men in business suits and nannies pushing baby carriages, but the streets were too crowded. The thief was making off with her hard-earned money and her favorite purse.

"He stole my purse!" She raised her voice, but it was swallowed up in the noise of the city.

The thief used the crowded sidewalk to his advantage. He ducked behind a tall man and slipped in front of a couple holding hands. In a few moments, he would be gone.

Penny waved her arms over her head, trying to get the attention of the people coming in the opposite direction. "Grab him! He took my purse!"

Tears sprang to Penny's eyes as she realized the futility of her chase. Just when she was about to give up, she recognized a man in a suit. Heath Lennox was only a few feet from the thief.

"Heath!" she cried. "Stop him! He took my purse!"

Heath's expression went from surprise to determination in the blink of an eye. He sprang into action, blocking the sidewalk as the thief tried to run by. A struggle ensued. The crowd parted around them, giving Penny a view of Heath wrestling the thief to the ground. Her heart hammered as she raced across the sidewalk. Before she could reach them, the thief broke loose of Heath's hold and hurried off. Penny's heart sank as he rounded a corner, swallowed up by the crowd.

Meanwhile, Heath was slumped on the ground. One arm was flung over his head, and the other was crumpled beneath his body. His suit jacket was rumpled, and his neck was red with scratch marks.

Penny's muscles tightened as she sank to the concrete next to Heath. Her mind skipped ahead to the possible consequences of Heath's bravery. Pain filled her chest as she realized he could be injured.

"Are you okay?" she asked.

Heath lifted his head and grimaced. "Sorry I didn't catch him, but I got this." He raised his hand triumphantly, clutching Penny's purse in his hand.

Penny grabbed his cheeks and planted a kiss on his mouth. "You're my hero!"

One corner of his mouth quirked up in a smile. "I'd have wrestled a purse thief sooner if I'd have known it would get me a kiss."

Penny rocked back on her heels, a blush staining her cheeks. "You could have been killed, you know. It was stupid of you to do that."

Heath's brows pulled together. "You told me to do it."

She took her purse and helped Heath to his feet. "I'm glad you did. Thanks."

It was the first time Penny had seen Heath disheveled. A lock of thick, sandy hair fell over his forehead, and his tie was askew. He looked less intimidating, more normal than she'd ever seen him.

Penny unzipped her purse and checked for her money. Relief spread through her when she saw the stack of twenties. She grabbed the money and stuffed it down her bra, where she should have put it to begin with. "Thieves have a sixth sense for payday." Penny's hand fluttered to his shoulder and smoothed the fit of his suit jacket. Heath always looked so unflappable, it was kind of cute to see him slightly off-kilter. "You saved the day."

Heath straightened his tie. "Are you okay?"

"I'm a little shook up, but it's nothing." She patted her chest where the money was secured against her breast. "I'll be more careful next time."

The flow of foot traffic surged around them, and Heath stepped closer, wiping his brow with the back of his hand. "I could use a drink. How about you?"

Penny pressed her lips together. "I have a job to do, remember?"

Heath checked his watch. "You're early." He winked. "And I won't tell your boss."

They walked to Heath's house, and he unlocked the door, then ushered her inside. His house was cool and filled with light. There were fresh flowers on the marble-topped console in the foyer, and the smell of lemon furniture polish filled the air.

"Where's your faithful sidekick?" Penny asked, looking for the older gentleman who always seemed to be lurking around with a stare.

Heath took off his jacket and hung it over a chair in the sitting room. "Mason? He's probably upstairs ironing my sheets."

She lifted a brow. "You iron your sheets?"

"No. Mason does." Heath walked across the room to a fully loaded bar cart. "What's your poison?"

Penny sat on one of the chintz-covered love seats. Still a little shaken by the encounter, she guessed a drink before Bianca's lesson wouldn't hurt. "I'll have whatever you're having."

"I don't make a martini as good as Mason, but I can pour whiskey." He splashed liquid in two glasses and crossed the room to hand her one.

Penny took a sip and grimaced.

"You don't like it?" Heath asked, his expression concerned. "I can have Mason make you something else."

"It's fine." She sipped again and swallowed roughly.

Heath took a seat in the chair next to the love seat. "I wish I would have caught the bastard."

Penny shuddered, remembering the sharp tug she'd felt

when her purse had been yanked off her arm. "You got my purse." *And her money.* "That's all that matters."

Heath leaned forward, and his knee brushed hers. A jolt of awareness rushed through her from the brief contact. It had been a long time since a man had touched her, and even longer since a man had looked at her the way Heath did.

"Can I ask you a question?" Heath's voice was low and tender, but his eyes were intense. He was more disheveled than she'd ever seen him. His hair was mussed, his tie was crooked, and his cheeks were flushed.

"Go ahead," she said, choking down another sip of whiskey.

"Are you in some kind of trouble?"

Penny smiled and shook her head. "No."

"If you need money, I'm here for you."

Emotion swelled in her chest at his generosity.

"You've done enough. Thanks to you, I've got enough money for..." She paused, not wanting spill her problems in his lap.

"For what?" He set his drink on the table and took her hand. "Let me help you."

She shook her head; Heath couldn't help her with a broken heart. He couldn't help her face the man who'd broken it.

A sob caught in Penny's throat. Seeing Bones was only part of her worries. She'd also lied to her best friend. There was no boyfriend, no date coming with her to Hawaii. "Money won't fix my problems," she said.

Heath nodded sympathetically. "You'd be surprised."

She gulped the whiskey and felt some of her troubles melt away and her tongue loosen. It had been so long since she'd had anyone to talk to, and Heath was looking at her with an open expression, inviting her to share.

"My best friend is getting married, and I have to go to Hawaii for the wedding. Her fiancé is a hero on the island. He saved a kid from drowning, and the father offered them exclusive use of his fancy resort on the North Shore of Oahu." Penny rose and crossed the room, unable to keep still. "All the guests will be there for the entire week, enjoying the luxurious accommodations and island charm."

Heath cocked his head and sipped his drink. "My, my, that does sound terrible."

"You don't get it. My best friend thinks I have this wonderful life in New York."

Heath turned to look at her, a curious smile on his face. "Don't you?"

Penny stared into the amber liquid in her glass, swirling it gently. "Not really. I lied to Lou."

Heath's eyes narrowed for a moment, then his expression cleared. "Lou is your friend? The one getting married?" His mouth turned up at the corners. "Not your boyfriend?"

Penny remembered the first time they'd met in Miss Donna's office, when Heath had heard her tell Lou she loved her before hanging up the phone. "I don't have a boyfriend. That's the problem. I lied to Lou, and she's expecting me to show up with a date."

"Why did you lie?"

"I don't want anyone to know I'm alone."

Heath stood up and crossed the room. "You aren't alone." He smiled down at her. "I'll go with you."

Penny's heart skipped. "What?"

"I'll be your date."

Her heart rushed, pumping blood so fast, it made her dizzy. "I can't ask you to do that."

His gaze never wavered. "I'm offering."

Penny pressed her hand to her forehead, feeling faint. "You'd do that for me?"

"I'm not that noble." Heath took her hand and tugged it away from her face with a gentle squeeze. "I'm dying to see Hawaii. I've never been, and this luxurious resort sounds fascinating."

Penny stared down at their clasped hands. Maybe it was the

mugging, maybe it was the whiskey, or maybe it was Heath's warm hand cradling hers, but she felt unable to contain the rush of emotions filling her. The words fell out of her mouth before she could stop them. "There's more," she said. "A man who broke my heart will be the best man in the wedding."

Heath squeezed her fingers. "Are you still in love with him?"

Penny's cheeks flushed. "No. I hate him. I wish I could make him suffer the way he made me suffer."

Heath frowned. "You don't want me to beat him up, do you? Fighting's not my forte."

The image of Heath taking on Bones made Penny cringe. Heath wouldn't stand a chance. "No. Of course not."

"How about we make him jealous? Purely fictional, of course. I could pretend to be your boyfriend." Heath gestured at the mirror hanging over an antique console. "We look pretty good together."

Penny studied their image. They did look swell together. His aristocratic good looks complemented her fine-boned features. And he was tall, over six feet. It might work.

She would save face in front of Lou and get revenge on Bones, but what about Heath? "What's in it for you?" she asked.

"I've never been to Hawaii," he said, still gazing at their reflection in the mirror. "And I could really use a vacation."

Penny met his eyes in the mirror. Heath was rich, polished, and handsome. With him by her side, what could possibly go wrong?

PART III

Mahalo

Chapter 24

Penny

DÉJÀ VU WASHED OVER PENNY. The Honolulu Airport looked exactly as she remembered. It was hard to believe it had been more than two years since the first time she'd landed in Hawaii. She remembered being filled with hope and anticipation.

Now all she felt was dread. Her stomach was in knots, her nerves were frayed, and her muscles were stiff from sitting on the plane for so long. The noise of laughter and conversation grated on her ears. The sense of excitement in the air annoyed her, and the smell of flowers tickled her nose like a sneeze coming.

Penny wished she shared the joy of the other visitors, but paradise had been ruined for her. All she could think of was Bones. The thought of seeing him again, being trapped with him at a luxury resort, made her break out in a nervous sweat.

Heath came up beside her. "Relax," he said. "Everything is going to be fine."

His promise did nothing to loosen the knot in her stomach. "You have no idea if that's true."

"Maybe this will help." He presented her with a tall glass filled to the brim with a pink beverage. A paper umbrella topped the frothy concoction.

Penny's mouth watered. "Where'd you get that?"

He gestured at a man behind a table. "The guy over there is selling them." Pressing the drink into her hand, he looked over her shoulder at the luggage ramp. "I'm going to collect our bags. Don't go anywhere. I don't want to lose you."

Penny drew in a long sip of the pink drink. It was cold, fruity, and definitely alcoholic. Some of her nervousness eased once she swallowed. "Do you want help?"

Heath pulled a folded bill from his pocket and smiled. "That's what this is for."

He went off to take care of the luggage, and Penny took another long sip. The fruity drink helped calm her nerves, but her body ached from the long day of traveling and the tightness of nerves. She bent and touched her toes, stretching her tight back and legs. Rolling up to stand, she took another long sip of the drink and scanned the crowd for Lou. She was about to lie to her best friend, and she wasn't sure if she could pull it off. Lou knew her better than anyone. She'd take one look at Penny and Heath and know they were a sham.

Her gaze skipped over the well-dressed crowd and came to an abrupt halt like a needle dragging on a record when she saw a tall, dark-haired man who stood head and shoulders above those around him.

The air rushed out of her lungs, and a wave of dizziness crashed over her.

Bones Keakealani.

He stood just inside the glass doors. With his feet set wide apart and his chin raised, he scanned the crowd from his superior height. He looked like a replica of his warrior chief ancestors, dressed in twentieth-century clothing. His powerful build made every other man in the vicinity look like an underdeveloped boy.

Penny froze, forcing foot traffic to part around her as if she were a stone in a river. Her heart seized and throbbed to life again, pounding loudly in her ears.

A man grunted, pushing past her. "Watch it, lady."

Penny's gaze fixed on Bones as he pulled off his sunglasses and swept his dark gaze around the airport. He was dressed more casually than the other travelers, in an aloha-style shirt and a pair of surf shorts. A lei of flowers, like the one he'd given her when they'd first met, hung around his neck.

Excitement buzzed through Penny. The loathing she'd felt for him for nearly two years was replaced by an intense longing. She had the urge to run to him and launch herself into his arms.

Her plans for revenge no longer mattered, not when he was there in the flesh, looking more handsome than she'd allowed herself to remember.

His long dark hair was pulled back in a ponytail at the nape of his neck, and his jaw was cleanly shaved. He exuded masculine power and strength. Vitality radiated off him like a thunderbolt.

When he looked her way, Penny panicked and ducked behind a group of tourists. Doubt crept into her mind, and suddenly she couldn't breathe. She hadn't planned on seeing him so soon. She wasn't prepared.

Tears gathered behind her eyes, and her stomach heaved. She was going to throw up or faint. Maybe both.

She dropped her drink and fled, rushing through the crowd to the restrooms. Tears blinded her vision as she ducked in and hurried into a stall. After slamming the door, she locked it and tried to force air into her lungs.

Why was Bones at the airport? And why did he have to look so damned gorgeous? She'd managed to forget his luxurious dark hair, his generous mouth, and his enchanting eyes. Did he still smell the same, like sunshine after a rainstorm?

A knock on the other side of the door startled her.

She jumped and grabbed a handful of tissue, swiping at her cheeks. "Occupied."

There was a muffled thump against the door. "Penny? You okay in there or what?"

The sound of Bones's deep voice sent goose bumps down her spine. She hadn't heard his voice in two years, but it sounded exactly like she remembered: rough and gravelly, as if he'd just rolled out of bed. Her thoughts scattered, and heat spread through her like a wildfire.

He knocked again. "Heh. I know you're in there. You gotta come out, you hear me?"

She heard him, all right. Every cell in her body reacted to the sexy rumble of his voice.

"You can't be in here." She glared at the door between them. "This is the ladies' room."

His low chuckle sent a rush of pleasure through her. "I hate to break it to you, babe, but this is the men's room."

Penny's heart jumped to her throat. She'd been in such a rush to get to the bathroom, could she have gone into the wrong one? Holding her breath, she peered under the divider wall. When she saw a pair of men's loafers worn in the stall next to hers, she had her answer.

Chapter 25

Bones

THE BATHROOM DOOR FLEW OPEN, hitting Bones in the chest. Penny shoved out of the stall and tried to sidestep him, her sapphire eyes spitting fire. He was too big for her to get past him easily, his body too much of a barrier. And there was no way he was moving, not until he was sure she was okay.

Her face was as pale as a puka shell, and she wobbled on her feet. Tears clung to her lashes, and her breath came in short bursts. Bones reached out and steadied her with a hand on her elbow. As soon as he touched her, he felt a physical jolt. If he'd had any doubts about the truth of Hanani's prediction, touching Penny chased them away.

Her blue gaze sliced straight through him, opening him up like a hot laser beam.

"Excuse me." A man walked around them toward the urinals, giving them the stink eye. "This is the men's room."

Penny jerked her elbow away from Bones's grasp. Two bright spots of color burst to life on her high cheeks. "Don't touch me."

"Easy," he said, attempting a smile. "Take it easy, yeah?"

Before the words were out of his mouth, he knew they were a mistake.

Her chin snapped upward, and her eyes scorched a path over his face. "Get out of my way, you big oaf." She slapped a hand to his chest. "Ow! Geez! Are you made of rocks or something?"

He laughed—another false step.

The look Penny gave him made the laugh wither in his throat.

"Penny." Her name was a growl of longing.

"Move!" She shoved him hard, her hand spreading across the center of his chest.

His muscles bunched, and his chest burned. He placed his hand over hers and held her captive. He felt a sizzling heat scorch through him, stirring his desire. "We have some unfinished business, yeah?"

Her eyes widened, and her grin flashed. Lust washed over him like an unexpected wave. He shouldn't be feeling like he wanted to throw her over his shoulder and carry her away Neanderthal style. Not after one touch… and not in the men's room of the airport. He'd planned to seduce her with intimate dinners, sunset walks, and waterfall hikes.

He cinched his fingers around her wrist and tugged her toward the exit. "Let's get outta here."

Penny struggled free of his grasp. "The bathroom is the perfect place to discuss our business," she said, her eyes wild as she tossed her hair. She jabbed her finger at his chest, poking him hard enough to leave a bruise. "Because you are so full of shit."

There was a cackle from the man at the sink, and Bones shot him a glare.

Penny took advantage of Bones's distraction and shoved past him. She rushed out of the men's room and was nearly swallowed in the crowd before he caught sight of her again. He hurried to catch her, his mind registering how fantastic she looked in her short skirt. Her legs were better than he'd remembered. She moved gracefully, as if her high heels were an extension of her long, toned legs.

He caught up to her in several strides and snagged her hand before she could disappear into the crowd. He felt the jolt again, but this time it was followed by a slap to his face.

"I said don't touch me." Penny's voice stung more than the slap.

Bones dropped Penny's hand, shock registering in his gut. The look she gave him was full of disgust. He hadn't expected her to hate him, but there it was, written all over her face. There wasn't a trace of the love they'd once shared. Instead, he saw the opposite.

His cheek burned from her slap, and his heart throbbed. He swallowed roughly, meeting her gaze with a scorching look of his own. "We aren't done."

Her eyes blazed and she took a step closer, her voice dangerously calm. "We were done two years ago."

Her words cut him deeply, shook him to the core. For two years, he'd looked forward to the day he saw her again. So far, it was not turning out as he'd planned.

"Penny!" A man's voice rang out over the noise of the airport. "There you are!"

Bones's stomach clenched, and he slowly turned around. He saw a man carrying two suitcases heading straight toward them, a look of concern etched on his features.

"You scared me." The man set down the suitcases and pulled Penny into a hug. "I thought I'd lost you!"

When Penny wrapped her arms around the man's waist, Bones felt like he'd been slapped again. He blinked rapidly, putting the pieces together. Two suitcases. A loving embrace. *I thought I'd lost you.* Bones struggled to breathe, as if he were under water without his regulator.

The man noticed Bones staring and lifted his head. "Can I help you?"

Bones couldn't move. His mouth was so dry, words escaped him.

"Heath, this is Bones," Penny said, taking a step back. "The best man."

After an awkward pause, the man extended his hand. "Heath Lennox. Nice to meet you."

Wealth and privilege dripped from the man's voice. Bones had neither, but he hadn't been raised to be rude. Reaching out, he clasped the man's hand in a crushing grip. "Howzit?"

Heath winced. "That's quite a handshake you've got there. The name is Bones? Is that a nickname, or did your parents hate you?"

Bones glared at Heath, his temper sizzling under his skin.

Penny stepped between them. "It's a nickname." She gave Bones a warning look. "No one calls Bones by his real name. Hardly anyone calls him by it."

Bones and Penny exchanged a look that made hope surge in his chest. *She* knew his name. She'd called him by it once.

Penny's cheeks flushed, and Bones knew she remembered their last time together.

"Any sign of the bride?" Heath asked.

"Not yet." Penny checked her watch. "It's not like her to be late."

"Lou isn't coming," Bones said, grabbing the large pink suitcase that had to be Penny's. "I volunteered to come for you."

Penny's chin lifted, and her blue eyes narrowed. "Why'd you do that?"

"I'm the best man," he said, turning toward the airport exit. "It's my job."

Chapter 26

Penny

AS THEY FOLLOWED Bones out of the airport, Heath bent his head and whispered in Penny's ear, "It's going great so far. He looks mad enough to rip my head off."

Penny cringed at the thought. "Let's just hope he doesn't try."

But Heath was right. If it was revenge she sought, she was on the right path. Bones did look angry. And sick as it might be, it was really turning her on.

Heath shifted closer. "You doing okay?"

She tore her gaze away from Bones's well-formed backside and smiled up at Heath. "I'm fine."

He dipped his head closer to hers, the bristles of his five-o'clock shadow catching in her hair. "Act like you're mad about me. It will drive him crazy."

If Bones wasn't walking in front of her, looking good enough to take a bite out of, it might be easier to imagine herself as Heath's girlfriend.

She forced herself to try. "You're so funny, Heath," she said, flirting outrageously and loudly enough for Bones to hear. "Lou is going to love you."

Bones halted at a red truck parked at the curb and tossed Penny's suitcase in the back. He turned and glared at Heath, his dark eyes disapproving. "Does Lou even know he's coming?"

"Of course." Penny squeezed Heath's bicep, leaning closer to him. "I told Lou all about Heath."

Bones glanced from Heath to Penny, his mouth a thin line, as if he'd bitten into something sour. "She never said nothing."

Penny had mentioned she was dating but hadn't given Lou any details. She wasn't surprised Lou had never told Bones, especially since her best friend had a scheme to get Bones and Penny back together. "She's got a lot going on with the wedding."

With a grunt, Bones picked up Heath's suitcase and tossed it in the back of the truck. He stepped up to the passenger door, his long, powerful strides exactly as Penny remembered. He opened the passenger door for her, then stopped, his big body blocking her.

"I almost forgot." He lifted the lei from around his neck and offered it to her. "This is for you." He hung the lei around her neck and leaned forward but stopped abruptly, before kissing her on both cheeks in the Hawaiian custom of greeting.

Penny stared up at him, their eyes locking in a silent war. Bones probably thought she was going to slap him again if he tried to touch her, but the thought didn't cross her mind. His masculine scent enveloped her, making her feel lightheaded. He was standing so close, she could see the gold flecks in his dark eyes, and it took all her willpower not to reach up and smooth back a lock of hair that had fallen over his cheek.

She reminded herself she hated him. She told herself she absolutely did not want the soft brush of his lips against her skin.

Bones handed her the lei. "Welcome to Hawaii."

Energy crackled between them, and the rest of the world fell away. An intense longing filled Penny. It was too bad she hated him, especially since he was more handsome than ever. She hated his broad shoulders, his bulging biceps, his muscular forearms, and large, square hands.

"How far is the resort?" Heath asked.

Bones stepped back so Penny could climb into his truck. "About an hour."

"That long?" Heath's voice rang with displeasure.

Penny knew he was used to traveling in luxury. He'd never been to Hawaii, and he was in for an eye-opening experience. Unless a lot had changed in two years, traveling in Hawaii was anything but convenient. The roads crisscrossing the island had been hacked out of the sides of mountains and cut from pineapple fields. They were dangerously remote, twisting and turning as they skirted the rugged landscape.

Bones nodded curtly and walked around the front of the truck. Heath settled in on one side of Penny, Bones on the other. She felt trapped between the two men, and her plan to deceive Bones suddenly seemed ridiculous. Bones's hand grazed her thigh when he reached for the gear shift, and Heath put his arm around her shoulder. She'd never felt more miserable.

Bones rolled down his window, letting in a blast of humid air that stirred Penny's hair. Heath gathered the wayward strands in a knot behind her head and winked at her. She managed a smile, but her heart felt like it was exploding in her chest. Being confined in the cab of the truck between two attractive men who couldn't be more different had her stomach in knots.

They rode in silence, the tension thicker than the Hawaiian humidity. Penny couldn't help comparing the men on either side of her. Bones was a giant of a man, larger than life with a stern, powerful presence. He was dressed casually and smelled of surf and salt, a masculine scent that stirred her blood.

Heath was elegantly handsome, dressed for travel in a lightweight suit and a crisp white shirt. He was used to being in charge and giving commands. His quiet strength was a calming presence.

Penny forced herself to stop thinking about the men and focused on the road instead. It seemed endless, and the minutes dragged by in what was proving to be the longest hour of her life.

Heath pulled his gaze away from the landscape and leaned over Penny to look at Bones. "Tell me more about the resort."

Tension filled the cab of the truck as Bones navigated the heavy traffic. "What do you want to know?"

Heath shrugged. "Why is it so far?"

Bones shot him an exasperated look. "I don't know."

"Who owns it?"

"Some rich *haole*."

"What's a howly?"

Penny felt the annoyance building in Bones's body, so she answered for him. "It's what Hawaiians call people from the mainland."

"It means outsider," Bones said. "No one else would develop a resort where a *heiau* once stood. It's a sacred place."

Heath inclined his head. "Development comes at a cost, but it's necessary to enrich lives. How many people does the resort employ?"

Bones's fingers tightened on the steering wheel. "Eh? I look like I work there to you, or what?"

Penny turned toward Heath. "Why are you so curious?"

He shrugged. "I was just making conversation."

They turned onto a smaller road off the highway, and the island transformed. The hills inclined sharply, and green mountains surrounded them.

Penny craned her neck to look out the window as the truck rumbled along the road. Brush-covered mountains filled their view on one side, and on the other, a sheer cliff dropped into the abyss. The temperature in the mountains dropped dramatically, and a chilly breeze blew in through the open windows.

Penny recognized the road. She'd been on it two years ago, when Bones and Keoni had taken her and Lou sightseeing. Keoni had entertained them with a grizzly story about their ancestor, who'd been a great warrior chief hundreds of years ago. The battle had been fought up the side of the mountain. Once the opposing armies had reached the top of the cliffs, the losers had jumped off the cliff rather than be captured by the ruthless warrior.

Keoni had a way with stories. Penny and Lou had hung on his every word. But it had been Bones who'd put a spell on Penny. At first sight, she'd been infatuated by him. He was so different from any man she'd ever known. She had a thing for intensely masculine men, and there was no one who fit that bill more than Bones.

He shot her a curious look before turning his attention back to the road. "I owe you money or what?"

Color filled her cheeks. She hadn't realized she'd been staring. Tearing her gaze away, she looked out the window at the lush mountains.

"Have you seen Henry?" she asked.

"Yeah. All the time. He's my partner."

"What?"

"I own a dive business." Pride rang in his voice. "I take tourists out on excursions."

Penny's entire body tensed. "Henry's your partner?" She imagined all the terrors that could befall her cousin deep under the surface of the ocean.

"Don't worry." Bones glanced away from the road long enough to give her a reassuring look. "Henry's a good diver. He drives cars off cliffs for a living. Diving is much safer."

"Henry's decision-making skills are questionable at best."

Bones shot her a sharp look. "It isn't dangerous. We take tourists out off the coast at Waikiki. Henry never mentioned it?"

Henry knew better than to mention diving or Bones to Penny. It was the quickest way to get Penny to change the subject. A chill ran down her spine. "You don't think his day job is risky enough?"

"Henry is a good diver." Bones's deep voice was edged with anger. "No need to worry."

Penny glared at him. "Bad things happen to good divers."

Color stained his high cheekbones, and his dark eyes glittered dangerously. He was magnificent when angry, like a warrior in battle.

Penny couldn't trace her lineage back to warrior chiefs, but she knew how to fight fire with fire. "Henry has a wife and family to think about. He can't afford to be selfish."

They stopped at a traffic light, and Bones turned to stare at Penny. Anyone else may have been intimidated by his scowl, but Penny held her ground. Their eyes clashed, and neither one of them looked away. If it was a staring match he wanted, she'd give him one. She could stare at him all day.

His eyes smoldered in the afternoon light, radiating anger and frustration. The dark center of his pupil was surrounded by a starburst of rich brown with rings of gold etched around the edges. She could get lost in his eyes.

A horn honked behind them, and Penny jumped.

Bones leaned out his window and gestured at the car behind them. "Chill out, brah! It's Hawaii!"

He ducked back inside the car and pulled off at an unhurried pace, but the air in the car still pulsed with tension.

"Who's Henry?" Heath asked.

Bones flashed a look at Penny, his gaze full of questions. She froze for a moment, then scrambled to cover the tracks of her lies.

"My cousin Henry," she told Heath. "Remember?" She ground the heel of her hand into his thigh, and he flinched. "We're meeting him and his wife for dinner tomorrow."

Heath nodded, catching on quickly and rubbing his thigh. "Oh. That's right."

Penny forced a smile, hoping Bones hadn't noticed their

mistake. She'd mentioned Henry and Claudia to Heath on the long plane ride, but he'd been so busy pouring over papers from his briefcase the entire flight, he probably hadn't been paying attention.

They turned onto a smaller road heading toward the shadow of the mountains. Land stretched out in long parcels on either side. Trees were more plentiful than homes, and colorful signs advertising the resort popped up every few hundred yards.

They came upon an iron gate and a guard house. Bones slowed and waved at a man who allowed them to pass. They drove slowly along the narrow road lined with palm trees.

Night had settled over the island, and the cool air carried the scent of the ocean. Bones slowed the truck and took a sharp turn onto a wide path. A large hotel sat at the end of the road. It looked as if it had been plucked from the mainland and deposited in the middle of the jungle. As they approached the hotel, Penny saw two figures standing on the front porch.

Keoni and Lou were waiting for them.

Heath took her hand, a silent question in his eyes. Penny nodded slightly and took a deep breath, preparing herself for more lies.

Chapter 27

Bones

BONES STOOD BACK as Penny greeted Lou, then introduced
Heath. Every muscle in his body tightened when Heath hugged
Lou and shook hands with Keoni. When he couldn't take it
anymore, he strode through the lobby of the hotel and stepped
outside on the lanai overlooking the beach. He pulled in a deep
breath of the ocean air and felt his anger simmer.

The reunion between him and Penny had been nothing like
he'd imagined. He'd known it wasn't going to be all rainbows
and sunshine, but he hadn't expected it to be a thunderstorm.
He hadn't expected Heath Lennox.

Keoni came up beside him and leaned his forearms on the
railing. "That didn't go as planned, eh?"

Bones snorted. "Not at all." He gripped the railing and
watched the undulating sea. What he wouldn't give to be out on
his boat instead of trapped at the resort. His boat had become
his solace. He was doing well with his dive business, but it wasn't
just a living that his boat provided. He gave Keoni a sharp look.
"Did you know?" he asked.

"Know what?" Keoni tried to play dumb, but Bones knew him too well. He saw right through him.

He frowned out at the sea, unable to look at Keoni for another second. "Why didn't you say something?"

"I didn't know for sure. Lou thought maybe Penny was lying about this mysterious boyfriend. We didn't think he was gonna show."

Bones ground his teeth. "Is she still in the villa next to mine?"

Keoni didn't answer, so Bones tore his gaze away from the ocean to look at his cousin. Keoni finally nodded. "Sorry, cuz. Every villa is full."

Bones gripped the banister, his fingers digging into the wood. "I have to live with the two of them next door to me for a week?"

"Look on the bright side," Keoni said. "They have to live next door to you too."

THE NEXT MORNING, Bones woke up early and went for a swim. He stroked through the water, trying to calm his mind. It had been a trying night, starting with dinner at the hotel for the out-of-towners and the wedding party. He'd had to make nice with Penny's new boyfriend and listen to stories about how they'd met. It was enough to make him lose his appetite. After dinner, he'd gone back to his luxurious one-bedroom villa and lain awake in the king-size bed, trying to not let his imagination run away with thoughts of what was happening next door.

He swam longer and harder than usual, hoping to rid himself of the image of Penny and Heath. Stroking through the water with focused determination, his muscles burned, but his mind was still on the couple next door.

Were they waking up in bed together? Kissing and touching as they woke with the sound of the sea outside their window?

Bones wanted to punch something, but there was nothing available. And he no longer used his fists to solve his problems.

As he exited the water, he couldn't help looking into the backyard of Penny's villa. When he saw the woman of his dreams stretched out on a lawn chair, his heart raced, and blood instantly ran south. He'd never stopped wanting her. No other woman could compare to the memory of Penny.

She stared straight at him, the intensity of her gaze making his blood pump hot and fast. Her expression was filled with longing. Her eyes dipped down his body, taking in his naked chest and the wet shorts clinging to his lower half.

The burn of her gaze told Bones Penny hadn't forgotten the time they'd come together in his bed. Her eyes devoured him, and electricity zinged between them. Their sexual chemistry hadn't dimmed over the last two years; it had grown stronger.

So what if Penny had brought a boyfriend with her all the way from New York? She still wanted him in the most basic way, and Bones wasn't above using that to his advantage.

Hanani had predicted a tragedy if Bones didn't send Penny away to pursue her dreams and said there would be two obstacles in their path before they eventually came together. Bones believed he'd only survived getting lost at sea because he'd sacrificed his relationship with Penny. And Heath must be one of the obstacles.

Bones didn't mind navigating a few roadblocks along the journey to reach paradise.

SHAKING OUT HIS WET HAIR, he considered going up to her, testing the jolt of energy that surged between them. Would she slap him again if he touched her? The risk was worth the reward.

But before he could take another step, the back door to Penny's villa opened, and Heath walked out. His hair was wet and combed back from his face, and he wore a starched white shirt and casual slacks. He sat in the chair next to Penny and said something to her that made her laugh.

The sound carried across the sand, high and lovely, music to his ears. It filled his soul at the same time it twisted his gut. Another man was making her laugh when it should have been him.

And then something worse than the laugh happened. As Bones watched, Heath draped his arm across Penny's shoulders, leaned forward, and kissed her.

It was like watching a car wreck. He didn't want to see the carnage, but he couldn't look away.

The kiss went on forever. As the moments ticked by, Bones felt his gut tighten. Pain lodged in his chest like a fist clenching his heart.

Penny and Heath were so busy making out, they didn't notice him walk by and go into his villa. He fumed under a freezing cold shower, dressed, and left the resort.

Even though he'd told Keoni he would be there to help all week with wedding duties, Bones had a life to live and people who counted on him. He'd promised to help at Makamaka Farms, and they were in need of his labor. Glad for a day of backbreaking farm chores, Bones threw himself into the job. With his mind occupied, he was clumsier than usual. He slammed his hip in the gate and couldn't focus on anything more complicated than splitting wood. At the end of the day, he was covered in sweat and dirt, but he still couldn't shake the image of Penny kissing Heath.

When he got back to the resort, he checked in at the main house and found Keoni, who was stressed about the evening's plans. Lou's parents were arriving, and they were having dinner together.

"You're supposed to be helping around here," he said. "That was the deal, remember?"

"I was needed at the farm," Bones said, his defenses up. "I got a life too."

"You can't just duck out whenever you feel like it because you don't want to face Penny and her boyfriend."

Anger pulsed through Bones as the memory he'd been trying to forget all day came surging back. He rubbed his temples, trying to erase the image of Penny and Heath kissing. It was no use. He'd never forget the way they'd laughed together moments before they'd kissed or how Heath had looked at Penny like he worshipped the ground she walked on.

"Whattaya want from me? Eh?" he growled at Keoni.

Keoni pinched the bridge of his nose between his thumb and first finger and inhaled deeply. "Sorry, brah," he said, letting the breath go.

Bones forced himself to relax. This wedding wasn't about him; it was about his best friend. No matter how much he wanted Penny back, it was his job to support Keoni. "What can I do to help?" he asked.

Keoni shook his head. "Nothing. You can't make Lou's parents like me."

"You're stealing their daughter," Bones said.

"They're gaining a son."

Bones laughed. "I don't guess they see it that way."

Keoni scoffed. "Take a shower. You stink."

"Thanks, eh?" Bones left the main house, heading for his villa on the beach. He couldn't help but glance over at the villa next door and imagine what Penny and Heath were up to. *More kissing*, he thought with a scowl.

He took another ice-cold shower and headed outside where he could see the ocean. His heart ached, and one way he soothed himself was to be near the water. He couldn't imagine living in a city like New York filled with skyscrapers instead of sandy beaches.

Penny didn't seem to mind. From what Lou and Henry had

told him, she was thriving in New York. She and Heath must be pretty serious if he'd traveled halfway across the world to be her wedding date.

No sooner had he sank onto a lawn chair facing the ocean than he heard his name being called from nearby. There was no mistaking the voice. He'd heard it in his dreams for two years.

"Bones?"

He looked into the yard next door and saw Penny rushing to the flowering hedge

that separated their yards. Her brow was creased with concern, and her movements were frantic.

His heart surged to his throat, and he hurried toward her. "What's wrong?"

"I need your help."

He jumped over the bushes and dropped down beside her. Rising in one fluid motion, he scanned the backyard for danger. "What happened?"

She laughed, and the familiar sound sent warmth spreading through his chest. "It's nothing life threatening, but I do appreciate your sense of urgency."

He flushed. His protective instincts had taken over, and he'd definitely blown his cool. He dusted his hands on his pants and tried to save face. "Are you okay?"

"I'm fine." She started across the lawn. "But Lou is wasted."

Bones spotted Lou sprawled on a lawn chair and choked back a laugh.

"She had a little too much to drink at the dress fitting earlier," Penny said.

"I've never seen Lou drunk before. She's usually the responsible one."

"It was Keoni's sisters." Penny's blue eyes went wide. "They're professional partiers. Lou didn't stand a chance in keeping up."

Bones glanced at the villa. "Where's your man?"

Penny frowned. "Heath's out."

"Where'd he go?"

"He had a call from New York he had to tend to." She crossed her arms over her chest. "He's a very important businessman."

An uncomfortable silence settled between them. After a moment, Penny marched to the lawn chair where Lou was slumped. "She has to sober up. Help me get her out of the sun before she burns to a crisp."

"I got her." Bones scooped Lou into his arms and hoisted her against his chest.

Lou stirred and looked up at him. "Bones?"

"That's right."

She giggled and let her head fall against his chest with a thump. "Ouch. You're a horrible pillow."

"Thanks, eh?"

He raised an eyebrow at Penny, and she rolled her eyes, opening the glass door to the villa for Bones.

The villa was set up exactly like his next door. There was a sunken living room with mosaic tile flooring, decorated with low-slung, modern furniture. A shiny wooden bar with rattan-backed stools stood in front of a wall-length mirror where chrome shelves held bottles of liquor, and watercolor paintings of the ocean view lined the walls.

"Where do you want her?" He hoped she wouldn't say the bed. Bones was a kind man, but he wasn't a saint. One look at the bed where Heath and Penny had slept might make him lose his mind.

Penny paused before crossing the room. "Let's get her into the shower."

Bones stiffened, bracing himself for strength as he followed Penny down the hall toward the master suite.

Lou stirred in his arms, tightening her grip around his neck. "Where's Keoni?" she asked.

"He's at the main house," Bones said.

She sighed and squeezed her eyes shut, seeming to sober up. "He's going to kill me for blowing this. We wanted to impress my parents…" She trailed off with a grimace.

Bones knew what it was like to crave his parents' approval and come up short every time. Even though he had his own successful business, it wasn't enough. He didn't have a suitable wife, and he doubted he'd ever live up to his father's expectations.

Bones thought it was ironic that to most Hawaiian parents, Keoni would be the ultimate catch for their daughters, but Lou's parents would never approve of him. Keoni was one of the most beloved people on the island. Famous for his daring ocean rescues, he'd been selected as one of the first lifeguards to serve the dangerous North Shore, and was known as a local hero. But to Lou's parents, he was low class and inferior.

Penny opened the door to the master suite, and Bones marched past her to the bathroom, refusing to glance in the direction of the bed.

"A cold shower will fix you right up," Bones said, hoping for Lou's sake it was true.

Penny brushed by him in the small space and turned on the shower.

Bones set Lou on her feet, and Penny rushed over to help her stay steady.

"I'm fine." Lou plucked at a strand of hair stuck to her damp forehead. "Just let me shower in peace."

Penny looked at Bones and nodded. "Okay. But I'll be right outside the door."

Lou pushed them toward the door. "Go!"

"Where's the gratitude?" Penny teased.

"Thank you. Now get out."

Penny and Bones went into the bedroom, and Lou closed the door.

"Are you sure she's okay?"

"We'll wait right here." Penny leaned against the door, her ear pressed to the wood.

Bones glanced at the door, anywhere but at the bed, where his traitorous gaze wanted to stray. Visions of Penny and Heath together filled his head, and his stomach turned. Suddenly, he couldn't get away quickly enough.

Chapter 28

Penny

"I SHOULD GO." Bones took a step back and stumbled.

His hands shot out, but not in time to catch his fall. He crashed to the floor and groaned when he hit hard.

"I'm so sorry," Penny said. "My stupid suitcase tripped you. Are you okay?" She offered him her hand. "Let me help you."

His gaze was hard and hot, his jaw set. She could feel the pain and frustration in his dark gaze like a brand all over her body.

"You love him or what?"

Heat flushed through her body. "You don't get to ask me those questions." Her chin quivered as she stared down at him. "My life is none of your business."

He flinched as if she'd slapped him again. "I know I don't deserve an answer, but I need to know."

Emotions swelled inside her, so many she couldn't untangle. Anger and frustration simmered with passion and lust. Bones never failed to spark her desire, and seeing him sprawled on the ground, his chest heaving as he panted for breath, ignited a fire in her belly.

When he'd walked out of the ocean that morning like an Olympian, her body had pulsed in response, every nerve coming alive. Then Heath had come out and caught her staring at their neighbor. He'd asked if she still loved Bones, and Penny had laughed it off. When he'd dared her to prove it, she'd let him kiss her.

And Bones had watched.

The kiss had been better than she'd expected. Heath was clearly a skilled lover. But there was a spark missing. It had been like a very efficient business transaction, satisfactory but lacking in fireworks.

Bones was fireworks.

"Just tell me," Bones said, his voice a low growl that made her belly flutter.

"I forgot the question," Penny said. She'd been distracted by his lush mouth and her desire to kiss him.

Bones reached for her wrist, shackling it with his long fingers. He paused as if waiting for her to demand release.

She didn't.

"Do you love him? Because it rips me apart to see you together." His hand stroked up her arm. "I need to know, even if it kills me."

Suddenly, she needed to know if his kiss was as good as she remembered. She couldn't wait any longer to find out. Pushing him to the ground, she crawled on top of him and pressed her lips to his.

For a terrifying moment, Bones was still. Just when Penny thought he would reject her, he sprang into action, returning her kiss with unrestrained passion. His hands gripped her tightly, spreading up her back, as if he might never let her go. His lips were hungry and hot, firmly staking their claim.

Liquid heat scorched through her body until she was on fire with need.

She squirmed closer, and he groaned into her mouth. He was hard for her already; she could feel his thickness pressing against her pelvis. She rocked against him, and he clutched her tighter, grinding their bodies together. His tongue delved into her mouth, tangling with hers in a sultry dance.

The shower cut off, and Penny pulled back abruptly, coming to her senses. She'd nearly lost herself in the kiss, but it was time to get back to reality. She was here for revenge, not a make out session.

Penny rose to her feet. A little wobbly, she braced her hand on the wall for balance.

Bones never took his eyes off her. He narrowed his eyes, watching her like a panther watches its prey. His muscles were coiled and ready to pounce, and she was helpless against him.

"You should go," Penny said.

He rolled to his feet in a fluid motion that sparked a memory deep in Penny's mind. Every move the man made was pure sensuality, pure grace.

"So, you don't love him?" He took her by the waist and pulled her close, nibbling softly at her lips before letting her go. "We definitely aren't done here," he said.

"Just go." Penny straightened her dress, doubt creeping into her mind as Bones turned and left.

His kiss had turned her on like nothing else, but that wasn't anything new. She still hated him for what he'd done to her.

Didn't she?

"I'M HAVING dinner with my parents tonight, and I look like something the cat dragged in." Lou's voice rang with fresh disappointment.

Penny pulled her gaze away from Bones's villa. "You're lucky you have the best maid of honor in the world at your service." Penny dug her makeup case out of her suitcase and waved it with a flourish. "I'll have you looking like your fabulous self in no time."

Lou leaned back and checked the clock on the wall in the bedroom. "You better hurry. I'm supposed to meet them at the restaurant in thirty minutes."

"Plenty of time." Penny dragged a comb through Lou's thick hair and twisted it into a fancy braid. "You don't need much help because you're gorgeous already."

Lou's shoulders slumped. "I think I'm still drunk."

Penny didn't want to say *I told you so*, but she had warned Lou. "You'll have to fake it."

Lou covered her face with her hands. "I'm breaking out in a rash just thinking about seeing my mother again. She hates the idea of me living here, and she hasn't been shy about letting me know it."

Penny tried to think of something nice to say about Lou's mother, but it wasn't easy. Mrs. Hunter wasn't the warm, motherly type. Penny's mother had been more of a mother figure to Lou when they had been in school. "Keoni's family will win her over. Maybe Miri will get her drunk."

Lou groaned into her hands. "How can someone so tiny drink so much?"

Penny laughed. Keoni's sister Miri was barely one hundred pounds, but she'd put away twice as much as Lou without even getting tipsy. Penny pointed at the toilet. "Sit there so I can do your face."

Lou obeyed, turning her face up toward Penny so she could work her magic. Even though Lou was still half drunk, there was no denying her natural beauty. It didn't take much for Penny to take Lou from disaster to gorgeous. Her green-blue eyes, flawless skin, and lush mouth were easy to work with.

When Penny was done, Lou looked in the mirror and managed a half-hearted smile. "This reminds me of old times."

Tears sprang to Penny's eyes. She and Lou had always been

there for each other, no matter what. When they'd thought Bones was dead after he had gone missing at sea, Lou had been the one to keep Penny sane. Even though they'd promised to keep in touch, it hadn't been easy. The four-hour time difference, the expense, and the pace of their busy lives had made a rift in their relationship.

"I wish John were here," Lou said. "Maybe we should have waited."

Penny shared Lou's love for her little brother. Penny didn't have a brother, and John had been the closest thing. The thought of John Hunter, age twenty, being lost or dead somewhere in Vietnam was enough to break her heart.

"Love stinks," she grumbled.

Lou laughed weakly. "You're not supposed to say that to a woman getting married."

"Sorry."

"You're not a very good bridesmaid."

"At least I'm good with makeup." Penny put the final touches on Lou's face and checked her own face in the mirror. "I have to get ready myself. I'm meeting Claudia tonight."

"She's more gorgeous in person than she is on the big screen." Lou wrinkled her nose. "I wish I could hate her, but she's actually nice. And she's head over heels for Henry."

"She better be. I don't care if she's the biggest star in Hollywood, she better treat Henry right."

"What are you gonna do?" Lou asked with a laugh. "Fight a pregnant woman?"

"Of course not." Penny caught a glimpse of herself in the mirror. Her lips were still a little bruised from the way she'd crushed them to Bones's mouth. She touched her bottom lip, reliving the fabulous kiss in her mind.

"Where's your boyfriend?" Lou asked, giving her a knowing look.

Penny grabbed the brush and yanked it through her hair. "He had something with work, a business contact visiting

Hawaii he had to meet with." Guilt tightened Penny's belly. Kissing her ex wasn't part of her plan for revenge.

"Heath's not really your boyfriend, is he?"

Penny dropped the brush and went into the bedroom. She was never good at lying. Fibbing over the phone was one thing, but being in Hawaii with Lou and pretending she was in love with Heath was something different—especially after the way Bones had kissed her. She couldn't stop thinking about how good it felt to be in his arms again. He made her feel safe and protected and, at the same time, more turned on than any man she'd ever known. "Why would you say that?"

"I don't know…" Lou followed Penny into the bedroom. "Maybe the pillow and sheets stacked on the sofa?"

Heath had been a perfect gentleman the night before. He'd volunteered to sleep on the sofa before Penny had even asked, giving her the huge bed all to herself. After a long night with little sleep, she'd been in such a rush to meet Lou and get their dresses fitted, she'd forgotten about putting away the evidence.

"You seem pretty alert for someone who was too drunk to stand not a half hour ago."

Lou gave her a knowing look. "You're gonna spill sooner or later."

A flush spread up Penny's chest. "There's nothing to spill."

Lou doubled down on her penetrating gaze. "Tell me."

Penny felt all the air seep from her lungs as if a balloon had popped. She couldn't keep a secret from Lou to save her life. And she was horrible at lying. She squeezed her eyes shut and let the truth tumble out. "Heath came here with me because I didn't have a date to the wedding."

"Hah! I knew it."

Penny felt the hot burn of shame. Admitting how pathetic she was hurt like hell. "I'm his daughter's dance teacher. He feels sorry for me."

"That's not all he feels for you." Lou adjusted her dress and checked her reflection in the mirror over the dresser. "I saw the way he looked at you. He's in love with you."

It was nice to know their ruse was working. Lou didn't realize Heath was just a good friend and a very good actor. "He's just a friend," Penny insisted.

"Just a friend who happens to be in love with you."

Penny stared at Lou, a sinking feeling hitting the pit of her stomach. She hadn't considered Heath's feelings. Was Lou right? Was he in love with her? Heath could have any woman he wanted. There was no way he wanted her. "You're crazy. Heath has women falling all over him in New York. Half the teachers at Miss Donna's are in love with him."

"But you're not?"

"No!" Her heart was in another man's hands… big, capable hands that made every inch of her body tingle and throb.

"Oh, Penny! What a mess."

A lump formed in Penny's throat, making it hard to swallow. "Don't worry. I won't do anything to ruin your wedding."

Lou's eyebrow arched. "You mean anything like make out with the best man while I'm in the shower, sobering up?"

Penny's mouth fell open. "What?"

Lou locked eyes with her in the mirror. "Don't play dumb."

The slamming of a door echoed through the villa, then footsteps sounded down the hall. "Penny?"

Sweat broke out on Penny's forehead, and her heart raced. "In here," she called in a strained voice.

Lou grabbed Penny's hand and squeezed. "I'll give you some privacy."

Penny nodded. She was on her own with Heath and her guilty conscience.

Heath peeked into the bedroom, carrying a bouquet of tropical flowers. "Ah! The beautiful bride is here. I guess I should have brought two of these." He offered Penny the bouquet. "Forgive me for abandoning you today?"

"Sure."

He gave her a quick kiss on the cheek. "I had no idea Leonardo was here until this morning. Sorry he kept me away all day. I hope you were occupied."

Lou and Penny exchanged a meaningful look. Penny smiled at Heath. "We had the dress fitting," she said. "Lou is going to be the most beautiful bride."

"I have no doubt."

Lou headed to the door. "Have a nice dinner with Henry and Claudia."

When she was gone, Heath wrapped an arm around Penny's waist and pulled her close. His body heat warmed her, and the clean, fresh scent of his cologne invaded her senses. His lips brushed her cheek before he straightened and announced he needed a quick shower.

Maybe Lou was right. Maybe Heath did have feelings for her other than friendship. Then she remembered Bianca's warning. Heath was good at pretending. And he had no shortage of women in love with him. Penny didn't plan on being one of them. She had enough trouble already.

<hr>

Chapter 29

<hr>

Bones

BONES TOOK his place next to Keoni, scanning the crowded yard for a glimpse of Penny. Lights were strewn across the immaculate lawn, and a stage had been erected for the entertainment. The entire wedding party and all of the out-of-town guests were at the celebration, but Penny was nowhere to be found. *Where was she?*

Anger burned in his belly when he thought of her back at her villa with her date. If things were right in the world, Penny would be by his side at the celebration, not cozying up with Heath.

He took a long gulp of pineapple swipe, grimacing when the potent booze seared his throat. "Chee! Uncle made it strong tonight."

Keoni slapped him on the back as he choked. "He brewed it special for the wedding celebration, yeah? Only the best for me and Lou."

Bones forced his thoughts away from Penny and tapped his cup to Keoni's. "Congrats, cuz."

Keoni frowned at the stage. "Why is she here?"

Bones followed Keoni's gaze to the stage and saw Ryla Aikau, stunning in a silver gown that hugged her generous curves, chatting with her band members in preparation for the entertainment.

"Ask Miri and Kaliah. They handled the entertainment." Bones knew because he was part of the entertainment. He was performing the hula at a show the following night. "Ryla's the most talented singer I've ever heard. You're lucky to have her."

Keoni pulled at the collar of his shirt. "I just wanna get this over with, yeah? Auntie Kiki is driving me nuts. She keeps asking me when we're gonna have kids."

Bones grimaced. "Better you than me."

Keoni nodded at a man in a tuxedo across the lawn. The rich businessman who'd offered his resort for Keoni's wedding weekend probably wanted to make sure the groom had everything he needed. "I gotta go make nice with Mr. Rossi."

"Aloha and mahalo." Ryla's voice rang out from center stage. "I know most of the faces in the crowd, but for those who don't know me, I'm Ryla Aikau, and this is my band, 'Ohana." She paused and smiled graciously at the sudden burst of applause from the audience. When the clapping and hooting died down, she spoke into the microphone again. "I'm pleased to sing for you a traditional Hawaiian song to celebrate the bride and groom. I've known Keoni since hanabata days, when he was kind enough to let me tag along with him and the older kids." Her voice was thick with tears. "Keoni was a kindhearted boy, and he has grown into the most incredible man. I wish him all the happiness." Her eyes swept the crowd and settled on Keoni. She flashed a beautiful smile tinged with sadness. "Keoni, this one is for you."

Bones noticed Ryla never mentioned Lou by name. He wasn't surprised, given that Ryla had been in love with Keoni for as long as he could remember.

The band started the song, and Ryla bowed her head. When

she opened her mouth, it was as if the heavens had parted and allowed an angel to come to Earth. A hush fell over the crowd.

Ryla owned the stage. All eyes were trained on her. Even though Bones had heard Ryla sing more times than he could count, he was still moved by her amazing talent. He recognized the traditional Hawaiian song she sang as one normally reserved for more somber ceremonies, such as funerals. A grin curved his lips. Leave it to Ryla to put a twist on her performance.

Keoni was probably fuming, while Lou and the guests from the mainland had no clue what the words meant.

Bones swept his gaze over the crowd and saw Keoni glaring at the stage. Hell, Keoni deserved it. He'd broken Ryla's heart a couple of years ago and had been avoiding her ever since.

Bones drifted his gaze over the faces and skittered to a halt when he spotted Penny. She looked radiant in a gold dress that brought out the copper in her hair. His heart froze, then pounded as if he were swimming in a race. A giddy feeling, which had nothing to do with the strong swipe his uncle had brewed, filled his entire body, and Ryla's melodic voice faded to the background.

Heath stood beside her, his arm draped over her shoulders as if he owned her. Bones drained his cup of swipe, feeling his temperature rise.

He barely registered Ryla wrapping up her song and hurrying off stage to an enthusiastic round of applause. He couldn't take his eyes off Penny. He knew he was looking at the woman he wanted to wake up next to for the rest of his life.

It didn't matter what his family thought. Penny was the one for him.

Their journey to happiness may have taken a detour, but he was determined to get it back on course. Starting as soon as possible.

Heath was an obstacle. But after the way Penny had kissed him earlier, Bones wasn't worried.

He strode across the lawn, dodging nosey aunties and talkative cousins along the way.

Keoni's wedding was a nice distraction for his aunties, who loved to pester Bones about when he was going to settle down. He'd been avoiding the topic of marriage for so long, it was second nature for him to change the subject or walk away when someone brought it up.

He wondered how his family would feel about Penny. It was his father's opinion that Bones really feared.

Growing up, he would have given anything for approval from his pops. He'd done everything he could to please him, but nothing was ever good enough. Not even buying his own boat had made his pops proud. As the only son, Bones was expected to carry on the traditions of the family, including marrying a suitable woman and having sons to carry on the Keakealani name.

Bones's sister was right about one thing: their pops wasn't going to be happy about him marrying a *haole* woman.

"Bones?"

He turned his head and saw Ryla coming toward him. If it were anyone else, Bones would have kept walking toward the love of his life, but he felt compelled to stop for Ryla. He'd been there the day she was born, and she held a special place in his heart.

"I need to talk to you," she said.

Across the lawn, Heath said something to make Penny laugh, and Bones felt his blood boil. "Not now, eh?"

Ryla smacked Bones on the shoulder. "You need to hear me. This is important."

"What?" Bones was distracted by Penny's laugh drifting across the lawn.

Ryla grabbed him by the collar of his shirt and hauled his face down toward hers. "You gotta stop this wedding for me."

His jaw dropped open. "What?"

"I mean it. You gotta stop this wedding before it's too late."

Bones touched his hand to Ryla's forehead like his mom used to do when he was a kid. "You sick or something?"

"It's not right. Keoni can't marry her."

"Why not?"

Ryla darted a glance over her shoulder, and tears filled her eyes. "You have to stop it. Please."

Bones drew Ryla aside, finding a private spot behind a grove of trees where they wouldn't be overheard. It wasn't like Ryla to be anything but cool and collected. She'd been performing since she was a teenager, and she was always calm and reserved, regal even.

"You're talking nonsense, Ryla. There's no way we're stopping this wedding. What are you thinking?"

"She's not right for him. Keoni needs to be with somebody who understands him. Somebody who gets him, you know?"

"Somebody like you?"

Her dark eyes flashed. "Yes. Why not me?"

"It's just a stupid crush. You gotta get over it."

"He loves me too."

"He loves Lou. And he's marrying her."

Ryla hung her head. "I just need another chance with him."

His chest squeezed. He understood better than she knew. All he'd wanted was a second chance with Penny. He cupped Ryla's shoulders and gave her a gentle shake until she looked up at him. Light from the nearby tiki torches sent shadows dancing across her face. Even in the darkness, he could see the pain in her eyes.

"Have you tried talking to him?" he asked.

Tears glistened on her long lashes, and her lips trembled. Under her dramatic makeup, Bones could still see the little girl she'd been. She'd been so cute with her braids and plump cheeks. Ryla and his sister Kaliah had been inseparable growing up. They'd followed him and Keoni around like puppies.

"He won't talk to me. Not since…" She broke eye contact and looked at the ground. The darkness couldn't hide the flush staining her cheeks. "It's been awkward between us since that night when you went missing."

Bones grimaced. He had known Ryla and Keoni had hooked up, but the last thing he wanted to think about was them getting it on. It was like picturing one of his sisters doing it. It wasn't something a sibling wanted to know about.

"That was a mistake," he said.

Ryla's mouth fell open. "You know what happened?"

His jaw clenched. "I know enough," he grumbled. "Keoni felt like shit about it."

"Chee! Thanks, eh?" Tears spilled down her cheeks, making a mess of her makeup.

"Shit!" Bones pulled her into his arms. "Don't start with the waterworks." He held her tightly, wishing there were something he could do to ease her pain. Ryla had been obsessed with Keoni since she was old enough to notice boys. Keoni had never given her a second glance, until that night when Bones had been lost at sea. Keoni had been so messed up, he'd taken her up on her offer. "Keoni's not the one for you. Some other guy is gonna come along and sweep you off your feet. You hear?"

He squeezed her tightly and rubbed her back. She was so tiny, her head barely came to his collarbone. He had to crane his neck to kiss the top of her head in a brotherly gesture. It was hard to think of Ryla being all grown up. Even in her sexy gowns and dramatic makeup, she was still a little kid to him. Everyone in Hawaii knew Ryla as a singing sensation, but to Bones, she was just the girl next door who used to try to keep up with him on his bike.

He gripped her shoulders and leaned back to look at her. "Listen to me, sister. You are Ryla Aikau, a descendant of the beautiful and mighty chieftess Makolea of Kona. You have the voice of an angel and the face of a goddess. You are destined for greatness. There is a man who will give you everything your heart desires."

She gave him a weak smile. "You just want me to quit crying."

He lifted her chin and used the cuff of his shirt to wipe the makeup tracks from her face. "Damn right, I do. Because I need something from you."

Her eyebrows shot upward. "The great and mighty Bones Keakealani is asking for something?"

He wasn't much for depending on others. Bones liked to get things done himself. But in some cases, like winning back the love of his life, he needed a little help. "There's this woman."

"You love her?"

Bones lifted one shoulder, his muscles straining against the fabric of his suit jacket. "Yeah."

Ryla smiled, her perfect pout stretching wide. "Finally. Maybe Kaliah will shut up about you."

Tension filled his neck. "Kaliah needs to mind her own business."

"Yeah." Ryla bit her lip, wiping away the last of her tears. "Look at me. I'm a mess." She laughed at herself. "You really want relationship advice from me?"

"You're the only thing I got."

Ryla rolled her eyes. "Too bad for you, cuz."

Bones gripped the back of his neck, rubbing the sore spot. "I just want you to tell me how to get her back, yeah?"

Ryla nodded knowingly. "You already messed up, eh? What did you do?"

His stomach clenched. He'd sent Penny away in hopes she'd come back, and she had. She'd just brought another man with her. "Nevah mind that. Just tell me what to do. She brought a man with her to the wedding. Some rich haole."

Ryla's eyes widened. "You talking about the tall redhead with legs for days in that amazing yellow dress?"

A frown turned down his mouth. Penny in that dress knocked the breath from his lungs. "Yeah."

"What's your plan so far?" Ryla asked.

"I dunno."

"Well, it's not good if she brought a date. Maybe she isn't interested. Maybe you need to take some of your own advice and let her go."

His heart hammered. "Not a chance."

Ryla pointed her finger at his chest. "You love her."

Bones nodded curtly.

"Stinks to love someone who's in love with someone else, yeah?" Ryla looked off into the distance, her pain stamped on her face.

"I was thinking maybe I could make her jealous so she remembers she wants me."

Ryla turned toward him, jabbing him in the chest. "That's why you asked me to help? You want me to help make her jealous?"

He shrugged. Seeing Heath and Penny kiss had torn Bones up, but it had also made him realize how much he still loved her.

"Men!" Ryla poked his chest. "You are so dumb! You are lucky you have me around, yeah?" She poked him harder. "Dimwit."

"'Kay then." He took a step back before Ryla poked him again, squaring his shoulders. "What am I supposed to do?"

Ryla glared up at him. "You put on this tough act, yeah? But we all know you're a softie. Show her that pile of mush under your armor."

He crossed his arms over his chest. "How am I supposed to do that?"

"You gotta figure that out on your own. I can't do everything for you."

Bones glared at her. "Promise me you won't do anything to ruin this wedding."

Ryla sighed, looking forlorn. "I promise."

Bones put his arm around her shoulder and led her back along the stone path toward the party. "Look at it this way. Your heartache will give you plenty to sing about."

She punched his arm. "That supposed to make me feel more bettah?"

"Yeah."

"Try harder next time."

"Nice choice of songs, by the way. You sang the same one at Uncle Ku's funeral last month."

A wicked gleam came into her eyes. "Yeah? I didn't realize."

They approached the outskirts of the party, and Bones couldn't help but scan the crowd. Now that Ryla was no longer planning to ruin Keoni's wedding, he needed to find Penny.

He shrugged. "You could sing the menu from the Drive Inn and people would love it."

"You're sweet." Ryla reached up and patted his cheek. "Too bad I don't think you're sexy."

Bones bumped her with his hip. "Admit it, you dream about me every night."

She giggled. "In your dreams."

He gave her a squeeze, hoping she could find a way to get over Keoni. When he lifted his gaze, he saw Penny a few feet away, staring straight at them.

Penny's eyes went wide, and her mouth dropped open. She looked from Bones to Ryla and back, then spun on her heel and rushed back to the party.

"Oops," Ryla said.

Bones watched Penny hurry into the crowd. "Should I go after her?"

"Nah. You might as well see if your plan worked."

"I thought you said it was a stupid plan."

Ryla shrugged. "What do I know?"

Bones watched Penny until he couldn't see her anymore.

"Remember what I said." Ryla patted his arm. "Show her the mush."

Chapter 30

Penny

HEATH HADN'T BEEN ready to leave the party yet, but he'd been a good sport when Penny had said she was tired and wanted to go back to their villa. She'd been silent as they walked along the stone path, but Heath had hardly noticed. He was too busy commenting on everything he'd experienced. From the food to the entertainment and the decor, he was thoroughly impressed with the resort.

"Did you see the chandelier in the lobby?"

Penny nodded, her mind on something else she'd seen: Bones and the gorgeous singer sharing a very intimate moment. Her chest ached, and her skin felt clammy. If she didn't know better, she'd think she was coming down with the flu.

"The spread of food was like nothing I've ever seen before. I can't get over how delicious the macaroni salad was." He laughed. "I don't even like macaroni salad."

Penny thought of the way Bones had lifted Ryla off her feet, making her giggle, and she frowned. "Neither do I."

When they got back to their villa, Heath settled himself at

the bar counter with a glass of whiskey and his briefcase. "I guess I should thank you for dragging me away early. I still have a lot of work to do."

"You really don't mind?" Guilt flapped its tiny wings when she breathed. Penny shifted her shoulders, stretching her tight neck muscles. The day had caught up with her, and all she wanted was the firm mattress and soft sheets of her bed.

Heath stacked his papers on the counter, already immersed in his work. "I don't mind." Glancing up at her, he furrowed his brow. "Are you okay?"

Penny felt like her heart was being ripped out of her chest. "I'm just tired."

Heath studied her for a long moment, then got up and crossed the room. He cupped her shoulders and bent to look into her eyes. "Your heart still belongs to him, doesn't it?"

Penny's chest squeezed, and at the same time, her heart swelled. Bones filled every pulse beat, his presence too large to deny. The kiss they'd shared was seared on her soul. She pushed away the memory of his lips on hers, focusing instead on the image of him and Ryla walking along the shadowed path together. Pain sliced through her, and anger hardened the brittle shell around her fragile heart. "I just want to get through this wedding."

Heath's eyebrows drew together. "You didn't answer my question."

His deep voice brought goose bumps to her skin. He was standing close enough to smell the clean, spicy scent of his aftershave.

"I know it's a shot in the dark," Heath said, trailing his hands down her arms to link their fingers. "But I have to take it." He took a breath, chuckling a little at himself. "I'm probably making a fool of myself, but I've wanted you since the first moment I saw you. Those extra lessons weren't just for Bianca. They were an excuse to see more of you."

Lou had been right. Heath wanted more from her. More

than she could give at the moment. "I can't," she said. "You understand?"

To her relief, Heath nodded. He didn't push her. He dropped her hands and turned her toward the bedroom. "Get some sleep. I'll see you in the morning."

Penny took a few steps but turned around to look at Heath. Her breath caught at the cautious optimism in his expression. Unlike Bones, Heath was all in for her. He'd traveled halfway around the world for her. The least he deserved was a chance. "I have a busy day tomorrow running errands with Lou, but maybe we can have an early dinner, just the two of us." The night before with Henry and Claudia had been fun but draining. Pretending she and Heath were a couple was exhausting.

Heath smiled as he set his briefcase on the table. "I'd like that."

"I hope you don't mind filling the day on your own."

He shook his head. "Not at all. I'm dying to try out the golf course on the resort."

Relief spread through her, and her shoulders inched away from her ears. She went to bed feeling determined to put Bones in the past and focus on her future, and she woke feeling more rested than she had in weeks.

The next morning, she showered and dressed. When she came into the kitchen, Heath was fighting with the automatic-drip coffee machine. He was dressed in pin-striped pajama bottoms and no shirt, and his hair was mussed from sleep.

Like most men of his wealth and status, Heath played tennis, golf, and squash. He skied and sailed. Although he spent a great deal of time in an office, he had the toned body of an athlete. His chest was well defined with muscles, and lightly tanned. Sandy-blond hair dusted the top of his chest, narrowing to a thin line that disappeared under the waistband of his pajama pants.

He looked as good without his shirt as he did in his tailored business suits.

"Thank God you're here." He replaced the urn and held his hands up in defeat. "I have no idea how to work this thing, and I can't function without coffee."

Penny laughed. She guessed Heath hadn't brewed his own coffee in years, maybe ever. "Move over. I've got this."

Heath slid past her, running a hand through his messy hair. "You probably think I'm helpless."

"No. I think you're rich and spoiled."

He made a face, and she laughed again.

"No offense."

He grinned. "None taken."

Penny finished the task and pressed the button. "Does Mason make your breakfast every day?"

Heath shook his head, his eyes crinkling as he smiled. "I don't eat breakfast," he confessed.

"That's something we have in common. I can't eat before noon."

Fresh coffee dripped into the urn, filling the kitchen with its rich fragrance.

Penny pulled two mugs from the cupboard and opened the fridge. "Do you take milk?"

"Black is fine."

"I have to load mine up with milk, but luckily, this resort thought of everything." She grabbed the milk, then turned and found Heath staring at her. "What?"

He leaned his hip on the counter and flashed a smile. "You look very pretty today."

Penny smiled. Heath was nothing if not charming. And he didn't look bad himself, barefoot and shirtless. There was a vulnerability to him that wasn't present when he was in his business attire.

She ran a hand through her hair. "You're just saying that because I'm making coffee."

A slow smile spread across his lips. "True. But you're a lot prettier than Mason."

Penny's eyes met Heath's, and her cheeks warmed. Maybe she should give him a chance. There were worse things than having a rich, handsome man pursuing her. If only she could forget the man who'd broken her heart and haunted her dreams, but there was a magnetic pull between her and Bones she couldn't seem to break.

A knock on the door sounded, pulling her attention back to the present. "That will be Lou," Penny said.

"Can she stay for a cup of coffee?" Heath asked.

"I'll check." Penny grabbed her bag and hurried to the door, excited to see Lou and spend the day with her. She pulled the door open, but it wasn't Lou standing under the threshold.

It was Bones. He stood with the tropical garden as his backdrop, wearing a white linen shirt, tan slacks, and dark sunglasses. His hair was secured at the nape of his neck in a ponytail, and his jaw was freshly shaved. Butterflies took flight in her belly as she caught his masculine scent. He smelled just as fantastic as he looked.

"What are you doing here?" she asked.

He pulled off his sunglasses and dug a piece of paper out his breast pocket. "Lou gave me a list of errands and told me to pick you up." His gaze darted over her shoulder and darkened.

Penny turned to see Heath walking up behind her. He placed a hand on the small of her back and offered her a mug of steaming coffee. "Here's your coffee, babe."

She glanced at the coffee in the mug. Heavy on the cream, just the way she liked it. "Thanks."

"You want one?" he asked Bones.

Bones made a grunting noise that passed for a no.

Heath dropped a kiss on Penny's cheek, his stubble a rough caress. "Have a good day. I'll see you for dinner."

Penny watched Heath walk back into the kitchen, her heart beating a mile a minute. When she turned back to look at Bones, he'd replaced his sunglasses, and his mouth was set in a stern frown. His stiff posture radiated disapproval.

"You ready or what?"

Penny took a sip of coffee and watched Bones over the rim. His frown deepened as he waited for her answer.

She gestured toward the kitchen, where Heath was padding around in his bare feet, whistling a tune. "Sure you don't want a cup?"

Bones stuffed the list back in his pocket. "I don't drink coffee," he said. "Remember?"

Penny hadn't forgotten a single thing about Bones Keakealani, but she wasn't about to admit it to him. "Oh! That's right." She followed him out, noting the stiff set of his shoulders and his clenched fists. *Serves him right.*

Penny took another sip of the hot coffee, smirking at Bones's back as he marched toward his truck. Revenge tasted sweet.

Chapter 31

Bones

SEEING the rich haole walking around in his pajamas making Penny's coffee soured Bones's optimistic mood. His scowl deepened when he thought about Penny not remembering he didn't like coffee. It wasn't a good sign. They hadn't spoken a word since they'd started driving. That was not a good sign either.

He took a sharp turn onto the main road, heading south. Penny held her mug printed with the resort's logo up in the air, and some of the coffee sloshed out over the rim.

"Don't spill that, eh?"

"If you weren't driving like a maniac, it might be easier."

He stared straight ahead, his glare so full of frustration, it could burst the windshield. He'd been a fool thinking Penny still cared about him. The intimate scene he'd witnessed told him everything he needed to know. Penny had moved on. Maybe the kiss they'd shared had been more one-sided than he'd thought. She seemed determined to hurt him. And he deserved every blow.

He forced himself to focus on driving. Roads along the

North Shore were narrow and tricky. It was one of the reasons the resort wasn't doing as well as it should. Bones made it no secret that he was glad the luxurious resort wasn't thriving. The sacred lands on which it had been built were part of the island's rich history.

Unfortunately, the Hawaiian family who'd owned the land had fallen on hard times. They'd sold their property to a rich businessman for enough money to live comfortably for the rest of their lives. But to Bones, there wasn't enough money in the world to make it right. A golf course sat where sacred ceremonies had once been held. And that chafed him enough to make it hard to sleep in the beach villa at night.

Keoni was lucky he was Bones's favorite cousin. There was no one else he'd give up a week of his life for. Bones couldn't deny he was happy for Keoni and Lou. Even though they were from completely different backgrounds, they suited each other perfectly.

Their relationship had given Bones hope that things could work between him and Penny. He hadn't counted on the rich haole.

"Where to first?" Penny asked. Her voice was too cheerful for the amount of tension in the cab of the truck. So cheerful, it made Bones suspicious.

He gave her the side eye as he dodged a pothole in the gravel road. Sure enough, her chin was raised, and her jaw was clenched so tightly, it could split wood. She felt the tension as much as he did.

"We'll work backward," he said. "Go to the farm first and pick up the leis, then the graveyard for the swipe." He gripped the steering wheel hard. "If we have time, we'll get the rings."

They hit another bump in the road as Penny attempted a sip of coffee, and more liquid sloshed over the side. With a sigh, she poured the remaining coffee out the window. "I have to be back at five o'clock."

When she crossed her legs, it was all Bones could do to keep from staring. Bones gritted his teeth. "I'll have you back by then."

"You probably have plans tonight as well."

"Yeah." He was dancing in the hula performance for the guests. The last thing Bones wanted to do was dance, but he didn't have a choice. At least he could take his anger and frustration out on stage.

After driving thirty minutes without speaking, they turned onto a smaller dirt road. Clouds of dust blew into the truck, forcing them to roll up the windows and turn on the air conditioner. The cab of the truck filled with enough tension to taste.

"Plans with the singer?" Penny asked.

Bones jerked his gaze away from the road to look at Penny. "What?"

"You know what."

Bones narrowed his eyes at Penny. "Nah, I don't."

Penny crossed and recrossed her legs. "I know what I saw."

"You don't know what you're talking about." There was nothing between him and Ryla and there never would be, but Penny didn't need to know that. "You got a lotta nerve, kissing me one minute, then kissing that haole the next."

"If you weren't driving, I'd slap you."

He glared at the road ahead. "Nah. You know I'm right."

"That kiss between us meant nothing. As far as I'm concerned, it didn't even happen."

Bones inched his shoulders up closer to his ears. "It happened, and you liked it."

"In your dreams." Penny turned and stared out the window.

The blush creeping up to her cheeks told Bones he was right. He curved his lips into a smug smile. Whatever her rich boyfriend was doing in the bedroom, it wasn't enough. Penny still responded to Bones. She might hate him, but she wanted him. It wasn't much to work with, but it was something.

"Are those llamas?" Penny asked, breaking the silence.

Bones glanced at the cluster of furry animals standing together under an enormous tree. "Alpacas."

"They're so cute!"

He chuckled drily. "They look cute now, eh? They don't look so cute when you're holding 'em down to shear 'em."

Penny's eyes went wide. "Poor things!"

He followed her horrified gaze to the animals beyond the fence. "It doesn't hurt them."

"It sounds terrible."

"It hurts them more if you don't trim them. Their hair gets too long and matted."

Penny narrowed her eyes at him. "How do you know so much about alpacas?"

"I work here sometimes. When they need muscle."

Her gaze lowered to his arms, and he felt her checking out his biceps. They passed a fenced-in area with horses grazing under the canopy of a giant koa tree.

King palms lined the lane, and wild orchids bloomed under the shade of their swaying fronds. The only sound was the quiet hush of the wind and the song of birds.

The peaceful abundance of Makamaka Farms soothed Bones's soul. He'd thought about moving to one of the *hales* on the farm and living there full time. Logistically, it made sense for him to live at the farm. He was there three times a week, picking up picnic baskets for his dive excursions. The thought of living in a traditional thatched hut like his ancestors appealed to him, but he'd never give up his home on the sea. He needed water to survive. After a few days away from the ocean, he started to feel hollow inside.

He stopped the truck at one of the long houses. Horses grazed right up to the wooden fence, and a cat lazed in the sun.

A dozen people sat at long, low tables, weaving leis, while others stood at counter-height tables, sorting and cutting leaves. Music, laughter, and lively conversation drifted from the open bays, and a sense of community filled the air.

"What is this place?" Penny asked.

"It's where we make the leis."

Penny studied the shelter. "Do you work here too?"

Bones shrugged. "I do whatever they need. But no, I don't make a lot of leis. They mostly need me for labor." He got out of the truck and jogged around to Penny's side.

She glared at his hand when he offered to help her down. "I can open a door myself."

He pointed at a mud puddle on the ground. "I know, but you don't want to step in that."

Penny followed his gaze. With a huff, she took his hand and let him lift her over the puddle. "Thanks."

He held her for a moment after she was on the ground, unable to make himself let go. She felt slim but strong, her body toned from years of dancing. In her flat canvas sneakers, she was still taller than most women in high heels. The top of her head came to just under his jaw. He dropped his chin and breathed her in. The scent of her fruity shampoo brought a tidal wave of emotions crashing over him.

"Penny." Her name tore from his mouth. Suddenly it wasn't enough to hold her and breathe in her familiar scent. He wanted more. It killed him to think of her in another man's arms. "I'm sorry."

Her hands fluttered against his chest as if she couldn't decide whether to yank him closer or push him away. Finally, her palms flattened against his chest, and she tilted her face back to look up at him. "For what? For making me fall in love with you and then telling me to leave?" Her hands balled into fists and beat lightly against his chest. "For not calling me after you were rescued?" Her voice broke, and she hit his chest harder.

Bones grabbed her wrists and steadied her fists. "For all of it."

Her eyes fired flames. "You broke my heart."

"It was for a good reason." He drew her closer. It had nearly destroyed him to lose her.

She shook her head. "I was just another tourist to you. One of the many."

He flinched. His relationships with tourists fell into two categories: before Penny and after Penny. Before Penny, there had been many, many tourists. After Penny, there had been none.

He framed her face in his hands, his thumbs lightly caressing her cheeks. "Come back to me, and there will be no one but us."

Her eyes widened. "You can't be serious. You expect me to drop everything and come running back to you."

"You loved it here," he said. *She'd loved him.*

"I've done that once before, and it left me with nothing."

"It will be different this time. I promise."

She pressed her lips together and shook her head. "What about your family? Will they accept me now?"

Frustration gnawed at his belly. "I don't care what my family says." He nodded at the shelter where a buzz of conversation and laughter drifted toward them. "These people are my family too. They accept me for who I am and will welcome anyone I love." *And I love you.*

A bitter laugh escaped her mouth. "What about your pretty singer?"

Bones shifted his hands to cup her neck, threading his fingers through her soft hair. "Ryla is my friend."

"It looked like a lot more."

A smile stirred his soul. Maybe his plan wasn't so bad. "You're jealous."

"So are you."

A flash of Heath coming out of the kitchen shirtless made his shoulders stiffen. "Yeah."

A smug smile played on her lips, and Bones had the wicked urge to wipe it away with a punishing kiss. He lowered his head a few inches, then stopped abruptly.

The next move was Penny's. She needed to be the one to kiss him.

Their gazes locked, battling for dominance. Penny moistened her lips with the tip of her tongue, clearly anticipating Bones's kiss.

He slid his nose along hers and heard her breath catch. "Come meet my family." He took a step back and led the way to the shelter, where the buzz of conversation and music welcomed them.

By the end of the day, she was going to change her mind. He planned to pull out all the stops, revealing his mushy insides, even if it killed him.

Chapter 32

Penny

THEY SPENT the better part of the morning at Makamaka Farms, where Bones taught Penny how to make a lei from maile leaves and orchids. They stayed for lunch, eating poi and chicken long rice in the main house on the farm with some of the others.

Penny wasn't surprised to find out everyone adored Bones, and when they found out she was Henry Longchamp's cousin, they welcomed her with open arms.

Everyone knew Henry as the fearless stuntman on *A Long Road Home.* Henry had been helping out on the farm with the horses, and he also collected picnic baskets for the dive excursions on the days Bones couldn't.

"Henry is your partner?" Penny asked as they drove away from the farm.

"Nah. I don't have a partner."

"But he leads dive excursions, picks up the picnic baskets, and helps out on the farm."

"Yeah." Bones turned onto a winding road that led into the lush green mountains. "But he's not my partner. I'm the only owner of *A Hui Hou*."

Penny transferred her gaze from the green landscape rolling by to Bones's profile. "*A Hui Hou*. What does that mean?"

Bones turned to look at her. "It means 'until we meet again.'"

A shiver ran down Penny's spine. He'd named his boat for her. It was subtle, but it was definitely for her. Determined to fight her growing attraction to him, she tore her gaze away from Bones and stared out the window.

The temperature in the mountains dropped dramatically as the truck climbed toward the sky. A chilly breeze blew in through the open windows, whipping Penny's hair in her face.

She'd been on the road before. She recognized Punchbowl Crater, a volcano tuft where military veterans were buried.

Two years ago, Bones had taken Penny and Lou to Keoni's childhood home in the graveyard.

"Are we going to Keoni's?"

"Yeah," Bones said, turning onto a narrow road. He gave her an appreciative look. "You recognize it?"

"Of course. I never knew anyone who grew up in a cemetery before."

Keoni's family were the caretakers of a Chinese cemetery in a lush forest with a high peak overlooking the city of Honolulu. Penny craned her neck out the window to get a better look. It was exactly as she remembered. The road descended into a valley surrounded by thick jungle before it climbed into the hills deeper into the forest.

"Abbott and Costello!" Penny cried, waving at the ominous duo of stone lions guarding the cemetery entrance.

Bones saluted the lions and drove through the entrance. "Snobs," he said. "They never wave back."

Penny shifted her gaze from the scenery to Bones's strong profile, noting the slight smile lifting the corner of his mouth.

His hair was loose around his face, and he leaned one forearm on the windowsill. His powerful masculinity pulled her in like a magnet.

It was as if no time had passed between them. He made her pulse quicken and her blood hum. A giddy feeling spread through her chest. He'd promised her she would fall in love with him by the end of the day, but he'd been wrong. The day was only half over, and she was already there. The man sitting beside her had a firm grip on her heart.

She had to figure out how to survive the next few days and learn to forget him again.

She forced her gaze back to the scenery. It hurt too much to look at him. "What are we doing here?"

"Gotta pick up some more swipe."

Penny shuddered. "That stuff is dangerous." She wasn't much of a drinker, and a few sips of swipe was all it took to make her tongue loose. When she was drunk, she always said things she regretted.

"I've seen grown men pass out in their plates from too much swipe." Bones's low chuckle filled the cab of the truck. "Probably see a few more of them tonight."

They drove up the winding road and stopped at the caretaker's house. Bones got out and jogged around to her door. "Wanna take a walk for old time's sake?" He reached for her hand and helped her down from the truck. "I wanna show you something."

Her hand was small in his, and he towered over her. The sheer size of him was overwhelming, invading her senses and flooding away her better judgment. "Yeah, I could stretch my legs a bit."

He nodded solemnly and offered his arm. She linked elbows with him and allowed him to draw her close. The path narrowed and wound between groves of trees, toward a wooden shed at the top of a hill.

"I always thought Keoni would get married here," Bones said, casting his gaze around the peaceful scenery.

"What's wrong with the resort?"

Bones stiffened. "Everything."

"You must be joking. It's beautiful. We have villas on the ocean front."

Bones lifted his shoulders. "I live right next to the ocean. Remember?"

Penny squinted at him. "Did you finish your boat yet?"

"Would you like to come over and find out?" His voice deepened to a sexy growl.

Her belly fluttered, and she questioned her sanity. She should have shut the door in Bones's face that morning instead of going off with him, risking everything.

His footsteps slowed as they approached the wooden shed perched on top of the hill. "You asked me once how I got my nickname." His brown eyes were serious, and his lips were set in a stern line. "I'm gonna tell you."

A rush of anticipation tingled through Penny's body. She'd often wondered about Bones's nickname. Not even Lou knew its origin.

"This is a Chinese cemetery," Bones explained. "The Chinese have different traditions for their departed than mainlanders or Hawaiians."

Penny shivered, remembering they were in a graveyard. It was easy to forget with so much beauty all around them.

Bones gestured at the windowless shed behind them. "This is where the skeletons of dead Chinese immigrants are stored and dried while waiting to be sent back home for a proper burial."

Penny stared at the wooden house, imagining it full of bones.

"When I was growing up, I spent a lot of time at the graveyard with Keoni's family. Being the only boy in a family of sisters, my pops was hard on me. I was punished for the smallest mistakes."

He shrugged as if it was nothing out of the ordinary, but Penny had a feeling his father's wrath had been severe. "What kind of punishments?"

"Never mind that. This is a different story." He lifted his head and cast his gaze down the hill they'd just climbed, where a green carpet of grass rolled over the land dotted with tombstones. "I felt more at home here than I did with my own family. But Keoni and his brothers were pranksters. We were always trying to pull one over on each other."

Having spent her early childhood on a family farm with many cousins, Penny knew the trouble kids could get into. "Henry and I were like that, always finding something to get into."

"Yeah? Henry's awright."

"I've missed him so much."

"You'll see him again tomorrow."

"No," she said. "Probably not until the wedding."

"Aren't you coming on the dive excursion?"

Penny's gut clenched. The thought of diving made her feel nauseous. "What dive excursion?"

"We're taking all the out-of-town guests on a dive. Didn't you know?"

Fear coiled in her belly. "Do I have to go?"

He cleared his throat and glanced down at the dirt path. "Not if you don't want to."

"I don't want to," she said on an exhaled breath.

Bones bent his knees and lowered himself to her eye level. Tipping her chin with two strong fingers, he raised her face until their eyes locked. "It's okay," he said. "You don't have to do anything you don't want to do."

Penny took a few shallow breaths, picturing Bones lost at sea, adrift in the middle of the ocean while Henry searched the waters nearly a mile away. She shivered as if she'd just been dunked in an ice bath. Every time she looked at the ocean, she felt a sense of dread. It was beautiful, but deadly. It had stolen so many lives.

No, she couldn't dive. But nor could she admit her fears. It was a tough place to be. So, Penny changed the subject. She broke eye contact. "Tell me the rest of the story, please."

All day he'd been going out of his way to charm her. He'd shown her the best of what Hawaii had to offer, and piece by piece revealed a side of himself she'd never known. He was trying to wear her down, win her over. As if his very powerful presence and delicious scent wasn't enough to make her swoon, he had to go and be vulnerable too. It was getting to her. She wanted to weave her arms around his neck, trace the smooth line of his jaw with her kiss.

Bones took her hand and drew her closer to the house of bones. "My cousin Tau was the oldest and came up with the best pranks," Bones said. "I was a scrawny kid."

Penny let her gaze drop over his body, which was sculpted with muscle under every inch of bronzed skin. "I don't believe that." She was breathy, dammit. Her words came out on a soft pant.

His energy spilled into her personal space, made her feel as if she'd inhaled too big a breath of air.

"One time, when we were sleepin' in the backyard, my cousins carried my sleeping bag into the bone house and locked the door." His voice dropped low. "They smothered Vaseline over my eyes while I was asleep, so when I woke up and opened my eyes, I couldn't see nothin'. I thought I was going blind, but then I saw the skeletons everywhere and I knew I was dead."

"That's terrible." Penny glared at the bone house, feeling the horror Bones must have experienced. "Poor thing."

"They started calling me Bones after that, and it stuck 'cause I was so skinny." He drew her close, his hand wrapping around her wrist. "No one knows the real story except Keoni and his brothers. Not even my family."

Stunned by his confession, Penny rested her head on his chest and held on. "No one else knows?"

She felt him shake his head.

"Not even Kaliah?" It was huge if his nosy sister didn't know.

"Nah. Not even Kaliah."

Chapter 33

Bones

HE HAD one last stop before the day was over. One more chance to make Penny realize she was still in love with him. So far, things had been going great. She'd started warming up to him at Makamaka Farms. And at the cemetery, his confession had gone a long way.

The jewelry store was gonna be exactly what he needed to top the day off. Women loved jewelry.

Bones opened the door to No'ono'o Jewels for Penny and watched her eyes go wide as she took in the magnificent display of glittering jewels.

He wandered to the display of engagement rings and surveyed the case. When he saw the unique marquis-cut diamond set in the filigree band still in the case, his gaze fixed on it.

"Back so soon?"

Bones lifted his head and saw the same clerk who'd shown him the ring the first time. His throat constricted, and he shot a quick glance at Penny. Luckily, she was bent over a case at the opposite end of the store, out of earshot.

"This is the one, right?" The clerk's hand hovered over the selection of rings before he dropped it to pluck up the one Bones had been eyeing. "You want to see it again?"

Bones stole another quick glance at Penny, his heart thumping wildly in his chest. "Nah. I'm picking up the rings for Keoni Makai's wedding. That's all."

The clerk pulled his hand away and closed the door. His sympathetic smile made Bones's jaw clench. "I'll go check on that for you."

Bones nodded curtly, then crossed the store to Penny's side. He bent and looked at the selection of jewelry she was inspecting. A row of pearl bracelets in different sizes caught his eye. They would look magnificent against her creamy skin. He wanted to buy her everything her heart desired, and then strip her clothes off until she was down to only the jewels.

"See anything you like?"

She stepped a few feet to the right and tapped a case containing black coral bracelets. "Those are beautiful."

Pride surged through him. "Those are made from black coral."

Penny straightened, her eyes finding his. "This is what almost killed you?"

He dipped his chin, keeping his voice low. "I'm fine."

She bit her lip, and her eyes filled with tears.

Bones touched her elbow, trying to pull her close, but she brushed by him and shoved the door open. Bones followed her onto the sidewalk where they stood speechless as Penny dragged in harsh breaths.

Bones took her shoulders and squeezed. He recognized panic when he saw it. He'd seen enough divers suffer from it. Added to the panic was the underlying thread of anger. When Penny glared up at him, tears filling her sapphire eyes, he felt the fury of her anger.

Before she could speak, he cut her off. "I want to tell you why I asked you to leave."

"Now you want to tell me? After all this time?" She turned her back. "I don't know if I want to hear it."

Bones stepped up behind her and turned her into his arms. He was surprised when she didn't fight him, but instead melted into his arms as if surrender was inevitable.

"I went to see an old friend of mine, and she told me I was right about you." He stroked a hand over her hair. "You were the woman I was meant to love."

Penny gasped against his chest and buried her face against his shirt. He could feel the sobs wracking her body.

"Why did you send me away?" she asked. "I would have given up everything for you."

Bones pulled her tighter against him, feeling the soft pliancy of her body against his. It was as if they'd been cut from the same cloth, meant to fit together. "That's just it. I didn't want you to give up anything for me." He stroked a hand down her hair. "I wanted you to choose me. To choose Hawaii."

Penny clutched his shirt, pressing her face against him. "I chose you." She sobbed. "I always chose you."

Regret swelled inside him. He'd blindly listened to Hanani, thinking it was the only way. But what if she'd been wrong? What if they'd lost all that time for nothing? It felt strange being vulnerable, letting someone in. He preferred to keep the fragile parts of himself hidden. It was physically painful to reveal his weakness. Except, Penny was his weakness. She could bring him to his knees.

He stroked her soft cheek, tracing the path of the tear to the corner of her mouth. "It rips me up to see you cry."

"Good," she said. "You deserve the pain for the way you treated me." Her voice broke with fresh tears.

He let the last of his guard down. "Can you forgive me?"

"Why should I?" She pushed against his chest, fighting him with surprising strength.

Bones captured her hands and forced her to be still. Unspoken words throbbed between them as he searched for the right thing to say. There was only one thing to say: the truth. "Because I love you, that's why."

The fight visibly drained out of Penny, and she sagged against him. "You can't do this to me."

He pressed her firmly against his chest, his hands molding her body to his. "I love you, Penny. Please forgive me. I know I'm stupid."

A small laugh escaped her mouth. "I would have given anything to hear you say that two years ago."

"It's not too late."

She was quiet for a long moment. "We had our chance."

He bent his head, whispering in her ear. "Give me another one."

Her head lifted, and their foreheads touched. He rubbed his nose against hers. She stretched up on her toes so their lips met softly.

His heart whooshed, and his hands fisted in her shirt to yank her close. Her breath puffed against his lips and then he felt the silky slide of her mouth against his. A bolt of tenderness shot through him. His hands spread against her back, and he bent his knees. Stooping down, he wrapped his arms around her waist and lifted her against him.

Their bodies fit perfectly together. Her willow softness melted against his steel.

The kiss was slow and deliberate, a meeting of lips on equal territory. He was sorry. She was forgiving. They met halfway.

Her fingers slid into his hair. He slanted his head, tracing the seam of her lips with his tongue. She opened for him, and their tongues met in a sweeping caress.

Her taste flooded his mouth. That familiar spice and sweetness he'd been missing for two years was finally his again.

He'd never been one for public displays of affection, but he didn't care who was watching. He deepened the kiss, cinching her tightly to his chest.

When they parted, she clutched the hair at the nape of his neck and held him close. "I can't lose you again."

Joy filled his heart, and he trailed kisses along her cheeks, tasting the salt of her tears. "You won't."

"That was the worst day of my life." She blinked up at him, more tears filling her eyes. "I thought you were dead."

Pain tore through him as he imagined what he'd put her through. "I'm here now."

Her eyes pierced his in a blaze of sapphire blue. "You're still diving for coral. You keep risking your life? Why?"

"You don't need to worry." His shoulders stiffened, and a pain crept into the back of his neck. "I can handle it."

"Is it the money? Do you need the money that badly?"

Diving for black coral wasn't only about the money. It was about the thrill. But when Penny looked at him with such devastation stamped on her face, the thrill was gone.

He cupped her cheek, his thumb swiping the tear that trailed down to the corner of her mouth. "I don't need the money."

"Then why? Why risk yourself?"

It hit him that he didn't have a reason anymore. At first it had been the money. That kind of money was hard to turn away from. But diving for coral had become something else. An addiction.

His heart thudded loudly, echoing in his head loud enough to drown out his thoughts. "I don't know."

"I want you to stop." Her fingers tightened in his hair, pulling hard enough to send a shock of pain through him. "I want you safe."

A smile lifted the corner of his mouth. "I want you mine."

She yanked his face toward her and crushed her mouth to his. Her kiss was fiercely possessive, her tongue pushing past his lips to claim him, leaving no doubts in his mind.

She was his. He was hers. Their time was now.

He didn't care if he never dived for black coral again. As long as Penny gave him another chance, he had everything he needed.

Chapter 34

Penny

THE RESORT HAD FOUR RESTAURANTS. Heath chose the fine dining restaurant with outdoor seating under the canopy of the resort's expansive roofline. The oceanfront tables were set with pristine white tablecloths and candles, and romantic music drifted across the sand.

The hostess seated Penny and Heath at a table for two nestled under the sweeping branches of a giant mangrove tree, then disappeared quietly.

Penny shifted in her seat, staring out at the sparkling sand. The sun was a bright orange ball, hovering on the horizon. The canopy of the mangrove tree cast the table in shadow, providing privacy and shade.

"Compliments of Mr. Rossi." The hostess was back, presenting a bottle of wine.

Heath smiled and lifted his chin at the bar, nodding at someone. Penny turned and saw a handsome man in his fifties, with jet-black hair beginning to gray at the temples. The man nodded back and leaned his elbow on the bar to talk to the bartender.

"That's Mr. Rossi? The owner?"

"Yes." Heath inspected the bottle of wine and raised an eyebrow. "Chianti Classico. A very good year."

The hostess opened the bottle and poured them each a glass, telling them briefly about the menu selections.

Penny tuned out the server's melodic voice. Her appetite was gone. She watched Heath from across the table as he sipped his wine and smiled at the server. Shadows danced across his face, highlighting the angles of his cheekbones and jaw. The low lighting made the contrast between his tanned neck and white shirt as crisp as a black-and-white photo.

When the server left, Heath lifted his glass to hers. "What should we toast to?"

Penny toyed with the stem of her glass. Her shoulders were so tense, she felt them creeping up toward her ears. She forced herself to meet Heath's gaze across the table. "To paradise?"

Heath's smile grew. "I like that."

Guilt gnawed at her chest as she clinked glasses with Heath and downed a large sip of wine. She felt like she was living a double life, in love with one man and having dinner with another.

The server brought an appetizer of sweet potato roasted and charred in banana leaf with mango dressing. Penny took a tentative bite, her stomach clenching as she chewed.

Heath made small talk, describing his day at the pool and how he'd met the owner of the resort at happy hour in the main lobby.

Penny pushed her food around her plate. "I thought you were playing golf with your friend."

"He had to reschedule for tomorrow. Would you like to join us?"

Penny put her fork down and pushed away the plate. "I'm not much for golf. Plus there's a dive excursion planned for the wedding party." She hadn't decided she was going on the dive until that moment. Even though she was terrified, she had to see Bones's boat for herself. She needed to know he wasn't taking risks with his life on a daily basis.

Heath ran a hand through his hair. "More plans with the wedding party?"

Penny's jaw flexed. "It is why I'm here."

The server collected the plates and dropped off the next course. Heath waited until she was gone and leaned across the table to take Penny's hand. "I'm sorry, I didn't ask about your day. How did it go? Was he decent?"

Penny dropped her gaze to the tablecloth. Her heart hammered as she remembered the key moments of her day with Bones. Everything about it had been special. She felt like she'd gotten to know Bones more in one afternoon than she had the entire time she'd been in Hawaii before.

"Fine."

"What happened?"

Penny pulled her hand free and reached for her wineglass. She took a fortifying sip, then locked eyes with Heath. "I'm still in love with him."

Heath's smile slipped, and some of the brightness dimmed from his eyes. "I'm sure it feels that way. Love can be confusing."

Confused didn't begin to describe how Penny felt about Bones. Every one of her senses was overloaded with him. A blush crept up her neck to her cheeks as she relived the kiss they'd shared at the jewelry store.

Heath narrowed his eyes at her. "Are you telling me after everything he's done, you want to give him another chance?"

Bones had destroyed her heart, but she still wanted him. She wanted a chance at the love she knew they could have. "I appreciate everything you've done for me, but I can't pretend with you anymore."

"What happened to hating him? To wanting revenge?"

"The revenge plan is over."

Heath covered her hand with his. "I think you're making a huge mistake. Think about your life in New York. There are so many opportunities waiting for you. You're on your way, Penny. My mother plans to make all your dreams come true."

Penny bit softly on her bottom lip and thought of the way Bones had carried her over the puddle, how he had shared with her something about himself no one else knew. "Not all of them," she said.

Heath leaned forward, his blue-gray eyes piercing hers with fierce intensity. "Just promise me you'll think things through before rushing into anything."

A headache built behind her temples. She'd been impulsive once before when it came to Bones and it hadn't turned out well. Thinking things through wasn't her strongest attribute. She was impulsive and led with her heart. But Heath was right. She had a life in New York, one that promised her fame and wealth if she took a chance with Hilary. "I promise."

Heath lifted her hand to his mouth and brushed her knuckles with a kiss. "I'm here for you. I'm not going anywhere. I'll be here to pick you up when he breaks your heart again."

Heath was trying to be nice, but the tiny kernel of fear he planted grew inside Penny for the rest of the meal. When it was time to join the rest of the wedding party for the evening's entertainment, she was nervous to see Bones again. What if she was setting herself up for heartbreak again?

And what about Heath? She'd tried to tell him what was in her heart, but it was like talking to a wall. He wasn't listening.

After dinner, they joined the rest of the wedding party on the main lawn, where a stage had been set up for the evening's entertainment. Penny searched the crowd for Bones but didn't see him. She spotted Lou and Keoni standing with the rest of the bridal party, but Bones was absent. Her heart raced at the thought of seeing him again. She needed to see him more than she needed to breathe.

A hush fell over the crowd as a man carrying a drum crossed the wooden stage and sat cross-legged in the back corner. Next, Ryla strolled onto the stage. Wearing a long silver gown, she looked more beautiful than ever.

Her voice rang out without the need of a microphone. "I'm pleased to bring you a very Hawaiian experience. We welcome you to the island in the spirit of aloha with this hula performance."

The drumbeat began again, and Ryla chanted a verse in Hawaiian. A harmonious male response echoed from the shadows. Ryla sang another verse, and the chanting response was accompanied by a rhythmic rattle, as three tall, bronze-skinned male dancers marched onto the stage wearing traditional grass skirts over loincloths. Bracelets of shells rattled around their wrists and ankles.

Ryla moved aside as the men strode across the stage to take their positions. Penny's breath caught when she recognized Bones commanding center stage. His naked chest glistened under the torchlights, and his ebony hair flowed across his muscled shoulders. Dark slashes painted across his broad cheeks enhanced his bold features and intensified his fierce stare.

The chant ended with a final stomp and rattle of the shells, and a haunting silence settled over the yard. When the drum started again, the dance began.

And what a dance it was. Penny's heart leaped into her throat as the men dominated the stage. They stomped in unison, first going left, then quickly turning right. Their outstretched arms reached and pulled as if they held an invisible rope. Turning to face the audience, the men set their hands on their hips and crept forward, their knees tapping the floor with each step in an incredible display of strength and agility. A gasp filled the crowd when they rose with a slow, sensual hip roll back to standing.

It was nothing like the flowing, feminine hula dances Penny had seen in movies. There was a raw sexuality in the story they told with their bodies as they stomped and strode across the stage.

Her temperature rose as she watched Bones perform. His passion came through in every move he made. Years of practice had gone into perfecting the steps of the dance. He was mesmerizing, seducing her with each flick of his wrist and roll of his hips.

She couldn't take her eyes off him.

When the dance was over, the audience went wild. Thunderous clapping sounded over the boom of the drum and the rattle of their anklets as they left the stage.

Penny felt like she'd been put in a trance. She watched Bones until he disappeared behind the stage.

"That was incredible," Heath said.

Penny snapped out of her stupor. "I'll be right back. I have to find Lou."

She found Keoni instead. Tugging him aside, she demanded to know where she could find Bones. "I have to see him." Her voice broke. "Now."

Keoni's brow creased in concern, but he didn't question her. He led Penny to the hotel, and they rode the elevator to the third floor. He walked down the hall and stopped in front of a room, where the muffled sounds of men's voices could be heard inside, and rapped his knuckles on the door.

"Yeah?"

"Eh? Yous decent or what?" Keoni asked.

A grunt of confirmation came from behind the closed door, and it opened. Keoni raised his brow at Penny. "Take it easy," he said, before turning to leave.

Penny slipped into the hotel room and came face-to-face with three nearly naked, broad-chested Hawaiian men.

Bones met her gaze and told the others to scram. They grumbled in disapproval but didn't hesitate to obey. Gathering their belongings, they quickly left and shut the door behind them.

When they were gone, the room seemed to shrink.

The hotel room that had contained three burly males was barely big enough to contain the energy pulsating between Penny and Bones.

A blush of color rode high across his cheeks, and sweat glistened on his bare chest. His black hair spilled over his muscular shoulders, and his dark eyes blazed with emotion.

Penny swallowed roughly, overcome with the need to touch him. Stepping forward, she placed a hand on his chest. The stark contrast of her pale, narrow hand against the breadth of his bronzed chest brought a flood of emotions crashing through her.

He closed one hand over hers, trapping it against the wild pulse of his heart. His other hand wrapped around the back of her neck, and he tugged her closer. She fell forward against the hard wall of his chest and tilted her chin upward to meet the brilliant onyx of his gaze.

He lowered his head and covered her mouth with his. He kissed her slowly, sensually, like the beginning of a dance. His tongue slicked over hers, and his fingers curled at the nape of her neck. She let him take charge of the kiss. Her resistance melted, and her body hummed in anticipation of his touch.

No one kissed like Bones. No one compared to him in any department.

She trailed her hand down his chest, enjoying the feel of his muscles flexing against her fingers. She skimmed her nails along his sweat-glistening pecs and grazed the tiny pebble of his nipple. He sucked in a breath and deepened the kiss.

He tasted of musk and sweat, a heady combination that made her knees weak. He pulled back slightly, his heavy-lidded gaze finding hers.

"Do you know the story of the wedding hula dance?" he asked.

"No, but it was amazing. One of the best performances I've ever seen."

"Thanks, eh?" He offered her a tight smile. "I've performed that dance dozens of times at ceremonies, but it never hit home like it did tonight. The story tells of a search, high and low, for the most delicious seaweed. A man tries all the seaweed, wanting to find the one that tastes the best." He rubbed her jaw with the calloused pad of his thumb. "Hawaiians are mischievous in their traditions. The underlying meaning is the search for the perfect lover. The dance is performed at weddings to symbolize that the perfect seaweed you want to eat for the rest of your life has been found."

"The dance meant all that?"

He kissed her softly, his lips lingering. "You're my perfect seaweed."

Her chest tightened, and she searched his gaze. His words weren't traditional in any sense, but they were exactly what she'd needed to hear.

But Heath was at the party, probably wondering where she'd gone. "I have to get back to the party."

The dark slashes of his brows pinched together. "To him?"

"It isn't like that between us, but I owe him."

"You don't owe him shit, Penny."

Penny pushed out of his embrace. "He came all the way to Hawaii for me."

Bones reached for the waistband of his costume. "If you think he did that for you, you're a fool."

Her eyes tracked his movements as he stripped out of the grass skirt and reached for the knot on the loincloth. "I guess I'm a fool."

He let the cloth drop to the floor and reached for a pair of long pants. "He did it for himself." His voice was gruff as he pulled on his pants. "You can't go back to the villa with him. Not now."

"I don't have a choice."

"You always have a choice, Penny." His response was gruff.

She swallowed the lump in her throat. "Nothing is going on between us. We are just friends."

"Nah," he said. "He wants more. I can see it in the way he looks at you."

"I don't want more with him." Penny crossed her arms over her chest and stared at Bones. "Do you trust me?"

He pulled on a shirt and slipped into his shoes, then replaced the lei around his neck. It was made of the same glossy leaves they'd worked with earlier that day at the farm. She remembered how much care each lei had required, and how much the people at the farm loved Bones and had welcomed her as part of the family. Her heart beat wildly against her ribs as she waited for his answer.

Finally he looked down at her, his mouth a stern frown. "Yeah, I trust you."

She linked her arms around his neck and pulled him close, crushing the lei between them. "Good. Because I'm coming on the dive excursion tomorrow."

A smile curved his mouth. "You are?"

She nodded.

He sat on the edge of the bed and pulled her onto his lap, then buried his head against her shoulder. "Thanks, eh?"

His words were casual, but Penny could feel how much it meant to him. She threaded her fingers through his thick hair and tugged until he lifted his face. "You're welcome." Her heart swelled in her chest when she saw the tears shining in his eyes. "I don't know how I'm gonna handle it. I might lose my mind."

"I've got you. Nothing will happen as long as you're with me. You're safe with me. You know that."

A thick lump formed in her throat. "I'm not sure what happens next," she said.

His mouth turned down. "What do you mean?"

She combed her fingers through his luxurious hair, loving the way the silky strands felt against her fingertips. His lap was solid and safe. In his arms, she felt protected, loved, and cherished. If only she could stay like this forever, but the world wasn't a hotel room. "I have a life in New York. I have a job, friends…"

Bones cut her off with a kiss. "We'll figure things out, yeah?" He traced her bottom lip with his calloused thumb. "It will be different this time."

Penny closed her eyes and sank into his kiss. When he touched her, she felt like nothing else mattered. Not all the fame and fortune in the world equaled what she felt for Bones.

"I trust you," he said. "Now you gotta trust me. Everything is gonna be okay."

Penny hoped this time he was right.

Chapter 35

Bones

ON HIS WAY to the marina the next morning, Bones made two stops, one at Makamaka Farms and the other at No'ono'o Jewels.

At the farm, he picked up the prepared lunch for the diving excursion: sandwiches made on homemade bread, macaroni salad, and poi. At the jewelry store, he bought Penny a ring. Not just any ring, the one he'd had his eye on. It was the most beautiful ring in the store, and also one of the most expensive.

He paid for it with the money he'd made on his last dive.

His diving business was profitable, but it didn't bring in the money diving for coral did. He'd promised Penny he wouldn't dive anymore, but in order make his plan work, he needed an influx of cash. There was one sure way to get quick cash: diving for rare coral.

He parked at the marina and was getting out of his truck when Henry's Mustang GT squealed around the corner and skidded to a stop beside his truck. Henry was just the man Bones was looking for.

He leaned out his open window and yelled over the blaring music. "You think pregnant chicks are contagious?"

Bones stared at Henry, rethinking his earlier idea to involve him in his plan. "You want me to explain the birds and the bees or what?"

"Nah," Henry said, cutting the engine. "I got that down pretty good."

He climbed out of his car, and Bones saw he was in full cowboy getup from head to toe. The horsey smell coming off him was so pungent, Bones moved aside to stand upwind. "You come from the stables?"

"Yeah. I got a new horse last week. He's giving me some problems."

"Why didn't you change first?"

"No time." Henry tossed his hat in the trunk and scrubbed a towel against his face, taking off a layer of dirt. "Claudia tears up every time this sad cat food commercial comes on," he said, stripping off his shirt. "You know the one?"

"The one with the kid with the broken leg?"

"That's the one. She cries every time. And then I wanna cry." He pulled on a T-shirt. "This pregnancy thing is hard on a man."

Bones snorted. "Better not say anything like that to Claudia."

Henry wrapped a towel around his waist and changed into shorts. "I learned my lesson already."

"What did you do?"

"I said her belly was cute."

"Not smart, eh?"

"But it's the cutest thing I ever saw." He made the shape of a small belly with his cupped hand, and a sappy smile transformed his face.

"Get a grip, brah." Bones lifted the heavy bag and settled it on his shoulder with a grunt. "I gotta talk to you about something before everyone gets here. I need your help."

Henry tossed the towel into the trunk and slammed it shut. "Penny, right?"

Bones wiped his sweaty palms on his shorts and grabbed the basket of food. "How'd you guess?"

"Doesn't take a genius, big guy. Penny's here. You need to talk to me about something." He bumped his fists together. "I put two and two together. Makes five, right?"

Bones rolled his eyes. Henry drove him crazy, but he needed him. He'd turned out to be a pretty good dive partner. Plus, he was Penny's cousin. Bones knew Henry would help him out, if only for Penny's sake. He'd apologized to Henry and explained as best he could about Hanani's advice, and Henry had reluctantly forgiven him. They'd somehow become friends, despite everything.

Henry spared him a glance as he started toward the docks. "Spill it."

Sharing his feelings didn't come easy to Bones. He'd been raised by a stern, traditional father, who believed feelings were for women and babies. "I need a favor, brah." Bones cleared his throat. "Another coral dive."

Henry's eyes lit up. "I'm in."

"Claudia won't mind?"

"I crash cars and jump off buildings for a living. Claudia's used to it." Henry paused and glanced sharply at Bones. "If you need money, you can just ask."

Bones took a deep breath. He hated feeling vulnerable, but Henry was the only one who could help. "It's not just money I need from you."

Henry stopped and looked at him, his expression serious for once. "What is it?"

Bones kicked off his shoes and stepped onto the deck of his boat. "I'm thinking about taking some time away."

"Leaving Hawaii?" Henry's voice rose dramatically. "You can't do that."

Bones turned and glared at him. "Who says?"

"I mean, whatever turns you on, man." Henry shrugged. "I just can't picture you leaving, you know?"

"Yeah," he grunted. "I know. But I need your help to pull it off. Can you take over for a few weeks if I'm gone?"

A strange look came over Henry's face. "This is for Penny, right? To go visit her in New York?"

Bones grunted an answer and turned away.

Henry grabbed him by the arm, and Bones spun around. But he didn't raise his arm to fight. He deserved whatever Henry dished out.

"I knew the minute I met Heath they weren't a real couple. She's still in love with you. And you're still in love with her. Don't hurt her again." Henry's jaw tightened "If you do, I'll kill you."

Bones nodded. "You can try."

He shrugged off Henry's grip and started his pre-dive check-list with single-minded determination. He checked the oxygen tanks three times and made sure all the safety equipment was in place. Every few minutes, he glanced up toward the parking lot, eager to see Penny walk down the dock.

Despite the heat of the day, chills raced across his skin. His stomach felt queasy and sweat ran down his temples. He slicked his hair back from his face and tied a bandanna around his forehead.

Filled with familiar faces and boats of all shapes and sizes, the marina had been part of his life for as long as he could remember. The gentle waves lapping the dock were a part of him. The water may as well have been running through his veins.

His family. His friends. His boat.

A drum beat in his head, thumping louder with each heart-beat. What would he be without Hawaii? He didn't belong in the city with concrete and steel. He might die without the ocean nearby.

"Relax, brother," Henry said, nudging his shoulder. "You're making me nervous."

Bones mopped the sweat from his brow and shoved the rag down the back of his waistband. Henry's curious eyes on him did nothing for his shaky nerves.

"Make yourself useful, eh?" He darted a gaze around the boat, looking for a chore to keep Henry busy. "Clean the masks."

Henry frowned. "I already did that."

"Clean 'em again," Bones snapped.

Henry gave him a mock salute, then started on the task with a cheerful whistle.

A glance at the clock told Bones it was past time for the bridal party to arrive. They should've been on deck five minutes ago. He rubbed the coral beads on the necklace he wore for luck. He never dived without them, insisting they brought him good luck.

When Penny and the rest of the bridal party walked onto the deck, a gentle hum filled his body. The air felt cleaner. The sun brighter.

His mouth spread into a smile. She was everything. He would give up his world to wake up next to her.

He strode across the boat, waiting to help her on board. When she saw him, her smile beamed and she picked up her pace. She walked straight into his arms, linking her hands around his neck and burying her fingers in his hair.

He cinched his arms around her waist and lifted her off the dock. The smell of her shampoo invaded his senses. He breathed her in before dropping a kiss to the place where her neck and shoulder met. "Shoes off," he said.

"Oh!" She laughed and toed off her canvas sneakers. "I'm not much of a boater."

Bones smiled. "Don't worry. I'll teach you everything you need to know." He set her on her feet on the polished wood of his boat. "Welcome aboard."

"It's beautiful."

Pride made his chest swell. He glanced around his boat, wondering how he was going to part with it for months at a time.

"Penelope!" Henry scooped Penny off her feet and twirled her in a circle. "It's great to see you again."

A warm feeling spread through his chest as Bones watched their exchange. Penny didn't just have Bones on the island. She had Henry. Lou too. It was enough to ease his guilt over the plan he had in mind.

Chapter 36

Penny

"PICK scuba diving so you can come with me," Bones said in a low whisper.

A cold chill ran down her spine. "I don't know if I can."

Bones framed her face in his hands and bent his knees so they were at eye level. His thumbs stroked her jawline. "Nothing is gonna happen to you as long as you're with me, you hear?"

"I hear."

He lifted the coral necklace from around his neck and slipped it over her head. "Take this. It's my good-luck charm."

She fingered the polished gems strung on the necklace. "Won't you need it?"

Bones grabbed a sun hat from the center console and plopped it on her head. "Nah. I'm all good. Get into the shade," he said, pushing her under the protection of the roof. "And quit worrying about me." He tightened the cord of the hat under her chin. "I'm good at diving. The best. I don't take chances, and neither does anyone on board my boat."

They set anchor just outside a small island, and Bones

explained they were going on a shore dive. Henry and Bones clearly had a system down. They unloaded the equipment on the beach, then explained the important safety details before splitting into groups based on experience.

"Those who want to scuba dive, come with me and Keoni," Bones said, meeting Penny's eyes. "Those who want to snorkel, go with Henry."

Penny was torn. She didn't want to disappoint Bones, but she didn't think she could scuba dive. She couldn't help but remember what had happened to Bones when he was lost at sea. Flashes of the torment she'd experienced, waiting to hear if he was alive, haunted her.

Lou and her parents walked over to stand next to Keoni, but Penny couldn't do it. With a silent apology to Bones, Penny went with Henry.

"Let's switch," Bones said to Henry as he handed out equipment. "I'll go with Penny. Between you and Keoni, you've got the rest."

Henry took the tank, and they helped everyone strap on their gear. When they'd waded into the ocean, Penny and Bones worked together to lay out the picnic under a grove of trees for later.

"I'm sorry." She shook out the blanket, her voice catching. "I know you wanted me to dive. We can still go snorkeling if you want."

"Let's just take it easy." He smiled and reached for her hand. "No pressure."

"I'm not afraid of the water," Penny said.

He squeezed her hand, his brown eyes soft with sympathy. "What are you afraid of?"

"I don't know."

But she did. She just didn't want to tell him. It seemed silly to worry about him diving when it was his job. He'd agreed to stop diving for black coral, which was the real danger, but Penny couldn't shake the fog of fear that had settled on her shoulders like a wet blanket.

"Come on, I'll show you around the island."

They strolled along the shoreline, where the sand was so fine, it felt like powder. The smell of the open sea was in the breeze, and the sky was dotted with puffy clouds that blocked the full power of the bright sun.

"Keoni and I discovered this place as teenagers. We named it ʻAʻohe Wāhine, which means 'no women.'"

The breeze pushed her hair into her face, and she shoved it aside to look up at him. "Uh-oh, does that mean me?"

He winked. "I gave that up a long time ago. This island is perfect for my excursions. There's a sapphire lagoon and a ledge that drops off fifty feet to the ocean floor." He led her away from the beach toward the center of the island. "Back in the day, this was the only place we could get away from our sisters and Ryla. They followed us around like puppies. We spent every free moment here. We even built a treehouse. Wanna see it?"

"Absolutely."

They walked along a well-worn path under the giant trees. "We stole Declan's dad's boat to bring out the materials." Bones parted some low branches blocking the trail and revealed a wooden house perched among the wide branches of a massive mangrove tree. "It was Declan's plan, but we all did the work. You shoulda seen the trouble we got in for all the time we wasted out here—Declan especially, for stealing his dad's boat."

The house was made of gleaming wood with wide windows covered by bamboo shades. It looked like it had been plucked straight from an island fairy tale. The man beside her had been pulled from the same story. On the tiny island, he was in his element. She could imagine a young version of Bones building a house in the treetops.

He led the way to the giant trunk of the tree, holding down the overgrown bushes for Penny. "Don't worry, it's safe. I just came out here a few weeks ago." He stepped up on the first rung of the wooden ladder and turned to grin at her. "It's still the only place I can get away from my sisters."

Torn between envy and annoyance at the mention of Bones's ever-present, disapproving sisters, she followed him up the ladder. "Do you still have family dinners every Sunday?"

Bones propped open the hatch door for Penny to climb through. "Yeah." He reached down to give her a hand. "You wanna come with me next week?"

Penny's heart halted, then skipped back to beat faster than normal. "My flight leaves Monday morning." She had only substituted her dance classes for a week. Tuesday evening, she was expected to be teaching intermediate ballet to young socialites whose parents lived on Fifth Avenue. In another life, she would be waking up in Hawaii. But in reality, she knew she was going to be back in her apartment in New York come time for Sunday dinner.

Bones closed the hatch door and straightened to tower over her. His black hair was held back by a faded bandanna, emphasizing his high cheekbones and strong jaw. His eyes, under the imposing arch of his brows, were dark and inviting, like warm velvet. He took two steps across the polished wooden floor and wrapped his arm around Penny's waist.

"You're not leaving without me this time." He cinched her close to the hard planes of his thighs.

Her heart beat hard enough to explode as he backed her against the wall and pushed aside the neckline of her dress. He kissed her collar bone, more tenderly than she'd expected from the speed and urgency he'd used to press her to the wall. His lips were softer than ever, a mere whisper.

"Ahh." Something inside her melted, and her breath came out in a smoky sigh.

"I mean it, Penny." He spoke against her mouth, pressing kisses to each corner. "I'm not letting you go."

Penny opened her eyes and met his intense gaze. Her gooey center melted even more when she saw the raw vulnerability shining in Bones's expression. His eyes drifted shut, and he took her lips in a possessive kiss that sparked a fire low in her belly.

"Marry me, Penny." His words were a gruff whisper, a demand. He dragged his chin down her jaw to her neck, leaving a burn of arousal in his wake. The steel of his thigh rubbed against the silky fabric between her legs. She spread her thighs in desperate need to get closer, her mind spinning. His lips didn't help with her confusion. His kiss left a hot trail down her neck, across her collar bone, and along the tops of her breasts.

She threaded her fingers through his hair and jerked his head back so their eyes met. "Did you just ask me to marry you right now?"

A small smile lifted the corner of his lips. "Yeah."

Her throat went dry. She searched his eyes, and she saw he was serious. A balloon of joy expanded in her chest. Her smile grew in her heart until it burst across her lips. "What am I supposed to say to that?"

"Say yes."

Penny's heart slammed in her chest. "Yes."

"Yes?"

Her fingers tightened in his hair to draw his face close. "Yes." She kissed his bottom lip, licking the seam of his lips as she pushed against his chest. She gave him a playful shove, loving how his hands wrapped around her waist so eagerly and tugged her closer for more.

He lifted her off the floor and hooked her legs around his thighs, then lowered himself against the wall so she sat straddling his lap. His arms locked her to his chest, but she didn't want to be anywhere else. She would stay with him like this forever—freeze time so she could sit in his lap and kiss his mouth for as long as she wanted.

His tongue pushed into her mouth, and a hot bolt of lust tore through her. The slide of his tongue, a caress and a demand, melted her defenses. Penny had fallen for the same man twice in one lifetime. It probably wasn't smart. No one had ever accused her of being smart. They said she was talented, beautiful, a live wire. Never smart.

If this was dumb, that was what she wanted to be. Penny fisted her hands in the hem of his shirt and yanked impatiently. If she was going to be dumb, she wasn't going to stop now. "Off," she said against his lips, dragging his shirt up his chest.

With a soft grunt, he disentangled himself enough to pull his shirt over his head and toss it aside. Then his hands were on her again, his palms cupping her cheeks. "Look at me." His soft growl stirred her soul. She lifted her gaze from the rounded planes of his bronzed chest to his dark eyes. They shined with so much emotion, she could feel it pouring over her like molten lava.

She'd been going through the motions in New York City, missing Bones and not even knowing it. She pulled in the heat from his gaze. "I'm looking."

His hands spread to cup the nape of her neck. "Where you go, I go."

Her gaze dipped down to his lips. She was mesmerized by his deep, sexy voice. His well-formed lips, shaping to make his words, entranced her. Tracing her fingertip along his bottom lip, she bent to kiss him.

His fingers tightened in her hair, and he tugged her face back so their eyes met again. "I can't come on Monday when you leave. You gotta give me a few days to take care of things here."

Her hands dropped to his chest, and she gave him a gentle push. "What?"

"I can't come on Monday. Maybe Friday."

Her heart skipped. "Come where?"

"To New York City."

She plastered her hand against the smooth wall of his chest. "You're coming to New York?" She must have missed it when he'd said that. She'd been distracted by his mouth. His hands. His masculine scent.

His expression turned serious. "Where you go, I go."

She blinked slowly, her mind whirring as his words sank in. "You don't want me to come here?"

He touched his forehead to hers, running his nose along her nose. "Of course I do. But we are doing things differently this time." His lips touched hers possessively. "I love you."

Her heart melted, and her body went pliant against his. She'd heard him say those words before, but this time it was different. This time he was backing up his words with action.

"Wait, you're gonna leave Hawaii? For me?"

He nodded. "You're stuck with me, yeah?"

She laughed and spread her hands against his glorious chest. "I'm not complaining."

Then his mouth was on hers again, claiming, possessing. When the kiss turned raw and passionate, Bones gently eased away. "Not here." He pushed up to his feet, taking her with him. "Come back to my place."

Penny clung to his shoulders. "Do you have furniture yet?"

His lips twitched in a smile. "You'll find out."

Chapter 37

Bones

HE HAD FURNITURE. A whole house full of it. And he'd been working on his boat. But it might take a while for Penny to see any of it, because he wasn't planning on giving her a tour. Maybe when he was finished exploring every inch of her body, she could see his furniture and the canoe he'd nearly finished.

After securing his boat at the dock, he whisked Penny off to his house. They barely made it in the front door before he took her in his arms and kissed her hard. She responded with a sexy little noise that released the beast inside him. He pushed up her dress and filled his hands with her ass. Her flesh was soft and firm, warm from a day in the sun. She had on a bikini under her dress, but he'd never gotten to see her in it.

He dropped to his knees and pushed her dress up her belly, placing hot kisses on her pale skin. She hooked her leg over his shoulder and arched her back against the door. He licked a path up her ribs, spreading his hands across the small of her back to hold her in place. He couldn't get enough of her taste. She was sunshine and honey, her skin taut as the muscles in her belly quivered under his tongue.

He hadn't forgotten how responsive she was. He had relived every moment they'd ever had together in his dreams.

Penny in his arms was better than any dream he'd ever had. He was going to show her exactly how much he'd missed her. He cinched his arms around her hips to lift her and carried her down the hall toward the bedroom.

Penny wiggled against him, looking over his shoulder. "That sofa is horrible."

Bones paused and turned to look at his living room. His sofa was comfortable, and it was big enough for him to stretch out on. As far as he was concerned, that was enough. "What's wrong with it?"

"The fabric is hideous."

"Oh yeah?" He made a sharp turn and headed for the sofa. Dumping Penny onto the bouncy surface, he leaned down and settled his knee between her thighs. "I think it will do just fine."

He pulled her dress up to her neck and yanked down her swimsuit top. His mouth closed over her pebbled nipple, and she cried out. She buried her fingers in his hair, and she arched her back. His hand spread beneath her, holding her up so he could feast on her for as long as he wanted.

He was going to make her come with just his lips and tongue first, then he'd move on to his fingers, and finally his cock, which was so hard it felt like a weapon in his shorts. He scraped his jaw across her sensitive flesh, making his way to her other nipple. She threw her head back, exposing the pale column of her. He kissed his way up to the hollow of her throat, wishing he could suck hard and brand her with his mouth. Later. When they didn't have to be in front of a hundred people at a wedding, he was going to brand her all over.

He gripped her hip and pulled her up his thigh so she could feel the hard bulge in his pants. Feel what she did to him.

Her hands flew to his chest, then lower. She unbuttoned his

shorts and shoved down the zipper. Her fingers circled his massive erection, and he sucked in a sharp inhale. His breath came in a ragged gulp when she closed her fingers around him and stroked urgently.

The sound of a door slamming made him lift his head. He looked over and saw his eldest sister marching down the front hall.

"What the hell?" He pulled Penny's dress across her chest, covering her.

"I knocked, but you didn't answer." Her eyes widened when she took in the sight of them sprawled on his sofa. "Guess you were busy."

Bones pulled back and zipped up his pants. "What the hell, Alana?" He couldn't think of anything else to say. His head thundered with his raging pulse, and his dick was so hard it ached. Mortification that his sister was seeing him so vulnerable made him more angry than embarrassed.

Penny scrambled up on the sofa, grabbing one of the throw pillows and holding it to her chest. She looked at Bones with wide eyes, her lips plump and swollen from his kiss.

"Penny, this is my sister, Alana." He dragged his gaze away from Penny and back to his sister. "What's the emergency, eh?"

"I'm sorry." She nodded at Penny, then cast her eyes at the floor. "You told me if he came back to let you know."

A real estate developer had been sniffing around for the last few days. Both Kaliah and Alana had called Bones at the resort to complain. The asshole developer was collecting signatures from residents who wanted to cash in on their property.

"He's back?" He swung his legs off the sofa. "Now?"

"Yeah. He's at Uncle Ro's. A bunch of people from the neighborhood are there. He's saying he's gonna make us all rich." She crossed her arms over her chest. "Some of the younger ones are fallin' for it, thinking it's time to sell."

Bones grabbed his shirt and pulled it over his head. "Over

my dead body." He leaned down and gave Penny a firm kiss on the lips. "I'll be back."

She scrambled to her feet. "Oh, no you don't." Grabbing his shoulder, she pulled him around to face her. "Where you go, I go."

Despite the grave circumstances, a smile teased his mouth. "Yeah?"

Penny adjusted her dress and tossed her hair over her shoulder. "Damn straight. Let's go bust some real estate developer ass."

Alana grinned. "I like her."

Bones shoved his feet into his shoes and pushed past Alana. "I don't care."

Alana swatted Bones on the back. "Whatever you say, little brother."

"Shut up. I need a minute to gather my thoughts."

"Don't think. Just get rid of him, okay?" Alana clenched her teeth. "He's as slimy as they come. And now he has a partner. They are promising everybody is gonna get rich. You gotta do something."

Bones grabbed Penny's hand and pulled her close as they left his house and headed down the street to his Uncle Ro's. "This won't take long," he said quietly, his voice a low, frustrated growl. "I wasn't done with you."

Alana coughed into her hand and rolled her eyes.

"It's okay." Penny slid her hand up his arm and pressed close to him. "I like seeing this side of you."

He winked at her. "Yeah?"

"It's a real turn-on."

He almost stopped and went back to his house. It had been two years since he'd been with the woman he loved.

"Hurry." Alana tugged his free hand. "He might be getting more signatures."

Bones set aside his desire for Penny. He'd waited this long to have her underneath him, screaming his name. He wouldn't rush things now. He picked up his pace and cut through Uncle Ro's yard. People from the neighborhood spilled out onto the porch, and a glimpse through the window showed a full house.

"Where's Pops?" Bones asked. His father would want to be there for this. Pops was a pillar in the community. Everyone respected him and listened to him.

"He's fishing. Went out with Taki and Kai this morning and won't be back until late."

Bones puffed up his chest. If his pops was gone, it was up to him to lead. His veins pumped with the blood of warriors. He was ready. "And Mom?"

"She's on her way."

Bones marched up the steps and threw open the door to Ro's house. When he entered the living room, a hush fell over the crowd, and every eye turned toward him. He swept his gaze around the room, nodding at some of his cousins and friends. His gaze caught on an unfamiliar face. A dark-haired man wearing a suit and tie, looking as out of place as a cloud over Waikiki Beach, nodded at him and offered a tentative smile.

Bones glared, his blood already boiling. His fists flexed, and he took a deep breath to keep his head on straight. A movement next to the stranger caught his eye, and he flicked his glance to the right. What he saw punched him in the gut and took his breath away.

It was Heath.

Penny's date stepped forward and offered his hand. "It's nice to see a familiar face."

Bones stared at Heath, and the puzzle pieces clicked into place.

Heath was the haole asshole trying to steal his family legacy. Bones turned and glared at Penny.

And she was part of it.

Chapter 38

Penny

AN ICY BLAST raced down Penny's spine. Heath Lennox was the last person she'd expected to see in Bones's remote neighborhood. But there he was, standing in the middle of the crowded living room with a clipboard in his hand.

Heath's gaze lit on Bones, and his mouth thinned for a fraction of a second before his expression cleared. He stepped forward, smile fully in place, and extended his hand toward Bones. A hush settled over the crowd as Bones declined to shake Heath's hand and turned his head to look at Penny.

Her temperature rose, and a flush spread through her cheeks. She tore her eyes from Bones and looked at Heath. She knew what he was seeing. What everyone in the room was seeing as well. If her disheveled hair and wrinkled dress weren't dead giveaways, there were also her bee-stung lips and rosy cheeks. She looked like a woman who had just moments ago been getting hot and heavy with an equally rumpled-looking Bones.

Heath's gaze swept over her, and his frown deepened. "Penny, I didn't expect to see you here."

The quiet audacity in Heath's voice shook Penny to the core. Her chin jerked upward, and she tossed her hair over her shoulder. "I could say the same about you."

Tension pulsed in the small room. Penny felt every eye on her, and her cheeks flamed redder than her hair.

"You know this guy?" Alana nudged herself between Bones and Penny.

"Yes." Penny wrung her hands together. "He's my date for the wedding."

Alana's eyebrows rose. "You brought him here?"

Bones pinned Penny with his intense stare. "Did you know about this?"

"No." She reached for him, but he flinched away. "I swear, I had no idea."

Kaliah came to stand on the other side of Bones. Flanked by his sisters, Bones was an immoveable force.

"You don't belong here," Kaliah said, looking down her nose at Penny.

"Wait." Heath cleared his throat, attracting the attention of the crowd. "This is an incredible offer you don't want to refuse."

The dark-haired man stepped forward with a practiced smile. "At least take a look at what we're suggesting." He had a cultured European accent, and his clothes were the kind of expensive tailored pieces that screamed wealth and elite status. "Everything is detailed in these pamphlets. The numbers don't lie."

A murmur broke out through the crowd as people expressed their opinions. It grew louder, with some shouts and insults hurled around the room. *I'll show you numbers! Let me see those numbers!*

Heath opened one of the pamphlets, showing a full-color rendering of a high-rise hotel tucked under the secluded cliffs on the sparkling beach. A lush golf course spread out in the valley. "This could be a luxurious resort offering the best of what

Hawaii has to offer. It will bring new life and jobs to the area, as well as make every one of you rich."

Protests rang out, but some of the people jostled to grab a pamphlet. Arguments rose above the buzz of excited conversation.

Bones's deep voice boomed over the noise. "Our blood, sweat, and tears are part of this land," he said. "We will sell when the tide stops washing up the shore and the sun quits shining." He stepped forward and grabbed the pamphlets from Heath, then tossed them to the floor. "We will sell when the wind stops blowing and the sky turns black." His foot landed on the stack of pamphlets. "We will never sell."

Applause rang out, and several others piped up. The room exploded with angry voices and shouts of protest.

"Anyone want a pamphlet?" Bones swept his gaze around the room, and a chorus of noes rang out. He nodded once and strode to the door. Wrenching it open, he planted his feet wide and flexed his fists. His dark gaze landed on Heath. "You wanna leave on your own? Or you want me to help you out?"

The dark-haired man set the rest of his pamphlets on the coffee table on his way to the door. "We don't want any trouble."

Heath stopped at the door and extended his hand toward Bones. "Think about this offer. It's for the best."

Bones's nostrils flared as he glared at Heath's hand. "You should go now." He lifted his chin and nodded at Penny. "You too."

Tears filled Penny's eyes. "You don't mean that."

"Get out." Kaliah pointed toward the open door. "If he won't throw you out, I will."

"Kaliah, hush. I can handle this." Bones crossed his arms over his chest and nodded behind Penny's shoulder at the door. "It's best you go."

The quiet growl of his voice broke Penny's heart. His stern expression showed nothing of the emotion he'd shown her earlier. His eyes were cold and angry, unforgiving. Penny felt like the stupidest woman on Earth. She'd assumed everything was going to be okay because Bones had said he loved her.

She should have known it wouldn't be that easy. With a final glance around at all the hostile faces staring at her, Penny turned and left.

The door closed behind her, shutting her out of Bones's life.

Penny dragged in a deep breath. The smell of salt and sea filled her nose. She held in her breath and stood utterly still on the front porch for a long moment. The look Bones had given her flashed in her mind over and over. He hadn't even given her a chance to explain. And his sisters were just as bad as Penny remembered.

"Hey, Pen. You okay?" Heath bent his knees to look into her eyes.

Fire spit in Penny's chest, stirring up so much anger that when she raised her eyes to Heath, she was surprised he didn't spontaneously combust. "What the hell is going on?" She brushed by him, marching onto the patchy lawn strewn with surfboards. "What was that?"

Heath attempted a smile, throwing a look at the tiny bungalow where Bones's entire block was gathered. "Rough crowd if I ever saw one. I think I'd rather face down a herd of female teenagers."

Penny's hair stood up on her arms. She'd never felt more like an outsider in her life. And she was a nearly-six-foot-tall redhead. She was used to being different. "Tell me what that was all about."

"We should probably get out of here." He hurried across the lawn toward the street. "They weren't kidding when they said the natives on this side of the island weren't friendly."

The natives? Penny's jaw clenched. "What did you expect?"

Heath gestured at the dark-haired man, who was leaning on the hood of a red sports car. "This is my partner, Leonardo Siebezzi."

Leonardo strode forward and greeted Penny with a kiss on both cheeks. "Ciao, bellissima." He smelled of cigar smoke and hair pomade. His cheek was cleanly shaven and velvety soft against hers. "It's my pleasure to meet you."

Penny's shoulders stiffened as she pulled away. "You're Leonardo?" She felt dizzy with confusion. "I thought you were a friend of Heath's, someone he plays golf with."

Leonardo grinned. "Heath is very good at golf. He beats me every time we play. Of course, I'm much better at tennis."

A modest smile curved Heath's lips. "He's very good at tennis."

Penny's blood heated. "This isn't a game." She pointed at the house, where the love of her life had just told her to leave for the second time in their short history together. "Those people live here."

Leonardo nodded, his eyes gleaming with earnest intensity. "They will never see half the amount of money we are offering in their entire lives. They could retire tomorrow and never work again."

Heath reached for the door of the Rolls-Royce idling at the curb. "We are trying to help these people."

A shiver ran down Penny's spine. "You're trying to help yourselves."

"It's business," he said. "Not personal." Opening the door, Heath gestured for her to get inside the car. "We can talk more on the way back to the resort."

Leonardo told Heath he'd be in touch, then got behind the wheel of the red sports car and took off down the street. Penny watched the dust fly up in the wake of Leonardo's car and felt like her whole world was shifting. Heath hadn't been playing golf and lounging at the pool as he'd said. He'd been trying to buy up property. She'd been a fool.

Penny tried to control her breath, but alarm was setting in. She scanned the street, noticing the brightly painted houses on small well-kept lots. Flowers bloomed from pots, and porch swings swung in the breeze. Salt and sea filled the air, and the sound of laughter drifted from the beach. There were surfboards leaning against palm trees, and towels hanging from clotheslines. She couldn't imagine it all gone, replaced by a hotel and golf course.

Penny swallowed hard, holding back a rush of emotion. "You didn't come here for me at all, did you?"

Heath sighed heavily. "It's not all black and white. I would be stupid to let an opportunity like this pass by."

Penny laughed harshly. "You planned this from the beginning."

Heath placed his hand on the small of her back and urged her toward the back seat. "I'm not the bad guy here." His eyes narrowed. "If anything, you've been using me this whole trip."

Penny shot him a scalding gaze. "You didn't seem to mind."

He inclined his head, his eyes searching hers. "No, I didn't. I told you before, I'm here for you. When he uses you up and throws you away, it's me who's going to be there to pick you up and take you home." He stepped closer, crowding her. "If you'll let me."

Penny slid into the back seat. She would let him take her home, because otherwise she would be stuck in the middle of nowhere with no way to get back to the resort. But as soon as they were back, Penny never wanted to see Heath Lennox again.

Chapter 39

Bones

THE SMELL of flowers assaulted his nose. As the best man, Bones had been draped in so many leis, he could hardly see over the pile of them. Keoni was stumbling drunk, mumbling about missing his baby brother and worrying that he couldn't get married without him. Bones did his duty and kept Keoni upright as toast after toast demanded the groom drink.

"Try some water, eh?" Bones shoved the glass under Keoni's nose and forced him to drink.

"It's bad luck," Keoni said. "Gotta toast or it won't take."

Bones slammed the glass on the table, his anger seeping out of the neat box he'd shoved it into. His own views on love and happiness had taken a beating over the last twenty-four hours. "Bullshit."

"Come on, dance with me." Ryla grabbed his arm and pulled him up from the table.

Bones tried to shove her off, but she was insistent. He unfolded himself from the table and caught Penny's eye as Ryla led him out to the wooden floor. She looked away quickly and inclined her head at one of the bridesmaids next to her.

Bones couldn't help but notice the haole asshole she'd brought as her date was nowhere to be seen. Probably off trying to score more land off unsuspecting islanders…

"Stop staring at her." Ryla lifted her hands and placed them on Bones's shoulders. "It's creepy. You're scary enough as it is, you big oaf."

Bones rested his hands on Ryla's hips and swayed gently to the music. "You're not scared of me."

"I've known you since the day I was born." She tugged on his shirt collar to get him to make eye contact. "You didn't take my advice, did you?"

His lips thinned. "I did exactly as you said, and look where it got me."

"Staring at your woman from across the dance floor." Ryla twirled in his arms, smiling playfully as she spun to face him. "You're pathetic."

Bones gritted his teeth and cast another glance in Penny's direction. When he'd come out into the yard after settling everyone down, she'd been gone. She'd left with *him*.

"Ouch." Ryla slapped his chest. "Watch it."

Bones mumbled an apology, his eyes straying back toward Penny. Did she have to wear that dress tonight? It was his favorite color on her: bold, bright pink. It set off her skin and made her eyes so intensely blue, he could see them blazing from across the room.

He wasn't the only one staring. She was watching his every move as well. Lifting his arm, he twirled Ryla in a circle and pulled her close. Penny's eyes narrowed, all but directing a bright-blue laser straight at him.

Bones's chest tightened. Had they gone back to hating each other so quickly? Just like that?

He didn't hate Penny, far from it. He wanted to know the

truth behind why she'd invited Heath Lennox as her date. Were they really in it together?

She knew how special the land was. The pristine beaches and lofty cliffs were his legacy.

He watched as Penny and Lou left the party together. Anger spiked his temperature, and sweat broke out on his brow. The room was suddenly too hot, and he needed some air. When the song ended, he stepped away from Ryla.

"You're on your own." He dragged a hand over his hair. It had been slicked back in a neat ponytail at the beginning of the night but was beginning to come undone.

She tossed a glance over her shoulder. "I doubt I'll have trouble finding a more capable partner."

Bones took one of the leis from around his neck and hung it over Ryla's head. "Sorry about your foot."

Ryla's gaze shifted over his shoulder, and her eyes narrowed. "Keoni's not looking so good. Maybe I should go comfort him."

"Forget about it." Bones stormed across the dance floor and stopped at the table where Keoni was slumped over his plate. He grabbed him by the back of the neck. "Time to go, brother."

Keoni got up without a fuss. He wobbled on his feet and let Bones lead him from the party. The remaining guests cheered as Keoni made his exit.

As soon as they got to the lobby, Keoni headed for the door. "Wrong way, cuz." Bones steered him toward the elevator.

Keoni struggled to get free. "I'm going to see Lou."

"The hell you are." Bones pushed Keoni into the elevator and hit the button for his floor. "It's your wedding night. You don't want bad luck."

Keoni leaned against the mirrored walls. "We're shacking up. Who cares if we spend the night before our wedding together?"

"Nah, nah, nah." Bones dragged Keoni out of the elevator. "It's my job to keep you straight. You're going to your room like a good little groom."

"All I want is to see her. I need to tell her I love her."

Bones stopped in front of Keoni's room and held his hand out for the key. "Not gonna happen. Lou wouldn't want you to ruin things. You know that."

Keoni fit his key in the lock and pushed the door open. "I just want to see her."

"You'll see her tomorrow at the wedding and not a moment before."

"You're an ass."

"I'm the best ass, and I'm gonna make sure you don't do anything stupid." Bones crossed the room and opened the night-stand. He plucked out a trio of condoms. "Really, brah? You can't go a few days?"

"Shut up. I don't make enough money to have a family yet. Better safe than sorry."

Bones pushed aside a Bible and found what he was looking for. He tossed the notepad to Keoni. "Write her a letter. Pour your heart out, and I'll take it to her."

Keoni took the pen Bones offered and sank onto the bed. "That's not a bad idea."

"It's why you picked me, eh?" Bones went to stand at the window and pushed aside the curtain. The view of the tide gently kissing the shore reminded him of what he'd told Heath. He would sell when the waves stopped lapping the sand.

He turned his back on the peaceful view. His chest burned with frustration, and a pounding ache drummed in his head. His very way of life had been seriously threatened, and he couldn't easily forget it was Penny who'd had brought danger to his doorstep.

Generations of his family had lived there before him. He'd learned to ride the wild waves on a homemade surfboard before he'd learned to ride a bike on the dusty, dead-end road.

Keoni ripped the paper off the notepad and folded it in half. "Don't read it. It's private."

Bones dutifully tucked the note into the front pocket of his shirt. "You want me to stay?"

"Nah. I think I'll play for a little while." He got up and grabbed his guitar, which was leaning against the wall. "I'm working on a song for Lou. It's not quite right."

When Keoni started strumming, Bones made his way to the door. "I'll see you in the morning at eight."

Keoni nodded. "Thanks, eh?"

"Yeah." Bones glanced over his shoulder and saw Keoni was already absorbed in his music, pausing his strumming to scribble something on a notepad. "Whatever. See ya tomorrow."

Something made his gut clench, and he realized this was Keoni's last night as a single man. Even though Keoni and Lou lived together, they weren't married. As of tomorrow, it was different.

He'd known Keoni for as long as he could remember. They'd been kids learning to surf and sail together, teenagers picking up girls, and grown men who'd saved each other's asses more than a few times.

"Heh," Bones called sharply.

Keoni lifted his head. Sometimes he looked just like the kid Bones had first met when Keoni's family moved from Maui to the graveyard. His eyes hadn't changed at all. He was still the curious boy, that kid who was always there for him. They were cousins, but more importantly, they were best friends.

"I'm proud of you, brother." Bones nodded his chin at Keoni.

Keoni nodded back. "Thanks."

They held each other's gazes for a long moment, and Bones wondered if he would ever be as close with Keoni as they had been growing up. After tomorrow, Keoni would have a wife to share his life with. He wouldn't need Bones as much.

But Bones still needed him. "Heh, you think you'd be up for one more dive?"

Keoni's eyes narrowed. "Maybe."

"Are you around Monday?"

Keoni's brows rose. "This Monday? The day after my wedding?"

Bones realized Keoni would be gone for a short honeymoon to Maui. Things were changing, and he had to get used to it.

Bones left the hotel and walked along the beach to Lou's villa, which was in the opposite direction from his. He tried to put Penny out of his mind, but his thoughts kept circling back to her. Enough time had passed that he could look at the situation with a clearer head. His gut told him to trust Penny. Even through the hurt and betrayal, he still loved her.

He arrived at Lou's villa and walked around to the front door. After knocking, he pulled the note from his pocket and waited patiently for her to open the door. He was standing with his hands clasped in front of him, his mind straying once again to Penny and the way she'd looked at him earlier. Anger and confusion had distorted her expression, but underneath it all, he thought he'd caught a glimmer of something else too. Something that looked a lot like what he felt for her. Something like love.

The door swung open, and Bones felt the air seep out of his lungs. It wasn't Lou standing in the threshold under the bright overhead light. It was Penny.

Chapter 40

Penny

HER FIRST THOUGHT when she saw Bones standing at the door was that he smelled fantastic. How was it that Bones always smelled good?

The light from the foyer cast his form in shadows, and he looked like a mountain of a man. He stood in his classic power pose, with his feet slightly apart and his hands clasped in front of him. Even though he held himself completely still, energy radiated off his body.

Penny's knees threatened to buckle, and her hand shot out to grab the doorway. Although he was mostly in shadows, the light spilling from the foyer of the villa, she could see his eyes gleaming through the darkness.

Intense was a word that was scared of Bones Keakealani. His gaze could melt a rock. It certainly melted her heart.

She'd been frozen inside since everything had gone down at Bones's neighbor's house. She'd demanded Heath take her to Lou's villa, and she'd been there ever since. She had no idea where Heath was, nor did she care. As long as he didn't show his face, it was all right by her.

Her blood hummed, and her heart pounded. She'd been rehearsing all the things she wanted to say to Bones in her head for the last twenty-four hours, but now that he was standing in front of her, looking positively gorgeous in his white, buttoned shirt and dark pants and his hair pulled back from his face in a low ponytail, her words dried up.

God, he smelled good. Like sun-dried linen and citrus. Inhaling him was like pulling an ocean breeze into her lungs.

"Penny." He stepped closer, and light flooded his face. He looked confused, as if maybe he were imagining her.

She cleared her throat and cast around for something to say. The obvious wouldn't do. How could she begin to apologize for what had happened with Heath? On second thought, why should she apologize? It wasn't her fault. She was a victim here, the one who'd been fooled twice in one swoop. Heath had lied to her, and Bones had dismissed her. For the second time.

She found her voice and lifted her chin. Anger bubbled up inside her and flowed out before she could stop it. "What are you doing here?"

Bones stiffened and glanced over her shoulder into the villa. "I'm here for Lou."

Frustration burst through her chest. Of course he wasn't looking for her. This was Lou's villa, and it was in the opposite direction from Penny's. "She isn't here."

His mouth thinned to a stern line. "Are you sure?"

"Of course I'm sure."

Bones shot a glance over Penny's shoulder as if he expected to see Lou hiding in the living room.

"I'm not lying," she said. "I'm alone. Do you want to come in and check?"

His gaze returned to her, his eyes darkly serious. "Are you inviting me in?"

Penny's knees went weak again. Not only did he look good

and smell good enough to eat, but his voice alone was enough to put her into a lust coma. His deep timbre and melodic accent made her blood hum with lust. Damn the chemistry between them. It wasn't going away, no matter how mad she got at him.

"Fine." She tossed her hair over her shoulder. "Come in." Stepping back from the door, she gestured for Bones to enter. "We always seem to have unfinished business, don't we?"

Bones strode through the door but stopped short before he made it to the living room and doubled back to tower over Penny. "Tell me you didn't know," he growled.

Her throat worked as she formed an answer. The denial was on the tip of her tongue, but his nearness made her heart flutter and her senses charge into overdrive. Tension radiated off his wide shoulders, and a muscle flexed in his jaw. Penny could imagine what it must have been like to see a man like Bones on the other end of a spear, defending his chief. Nostrils flaring, eyes flashing—he was a sight to behold.

"I…" Penny swallowed hard. His masculine presence was like a drug. She breathed it in. "I didn't know."

His shoulders sagged, and he hung his head. Penny's heart went out to him. He looked devastated and relieved at the same time. She reached out and touched his shoulder, her hand molding to the rounded bulge of his muscle. A frisson of electricity passed through them when they touched. Bones's eyes jerked up toward hers and locked. "You didn't know." His words rushed out on a sigh.

Penny stepped closer. "I would never do anything to hurt you."

"Except flaunt another man in my face."

Penny wrinkled her nose. "You deserved that."

"Yeah?"

Her hand shifted up from his shoulder to cup the nape of his neck. "Yeah. But I'm sorry about the rest." It hurt her heart to think about how she'd been used. "I didn't know Heath was planning that."

Bones flinched, his muscles bunching under her fingers. "When I told you to go yesterday, I didn't think you'd listen. I thought you would fight for me."

Penny raised her eyes to his, blinking in confusion. "But you didn't say a word to me all night tonight. You just kept looking at me with daggers in your eyes. I thought you hated me."

His hand wrapped around her waist, and he pulled her close. "My sweet Penny. I could never hate you. These past two years, I've been waiting for you to come back to me. I pushed you away so you could find yourself then come back to me."

Tears threatened to fall, but she held them back. Bones lowered his head to hers and pressed his forehead against her brow. They stayed like that for a long moment, breathing the same breath, sharing the same space.

"I'm sorry. I didn't handle it well. Sometimes it takes me too long to think about something before I act. I guess it's because I used to have a bad temper and get in a lot of fights. I never thought, only acted. Now, I think too much."

It was more than Bones had ever told Penny about his emotions. It was a lot to take in. "I'm sorry too," she said. "I should have demanded you talk to me at the rehearsal dinner. But I didn't want to ruin Lou's night."

"Where is Lou now?"

Penny pulled in a sharp breath. Bones's proximity had her nerves firing. It wasn't easy to focus on conversation when all she wanted was to kiss him. "She went to stay with her parents."

"Good." He took her in his arms and lowered his mouth to hers. He kissed her long and deep, his tongue licking into her mouth as his hands spread up her back.

Penny trailed her hands down his back, delighting in the ripple of muscles under her fingers. She tugged his shirt from his pants and slid her hand up his chest. His skin was smooth and warm, and his muscles were so hard, it was like touching a statue come to life.

He pulled in a sharp breath as her hands shifted up his back.

"Where's the bedroom? We're not taking any chances on getting interrupted again."

Penny took his hand and led him down the hall. When they got to the bedroom, Bones closed the door and locked it behind him. "Take off your clothes."

Her heart almost burst in her chest. His words, uttered in his deep growly voice, were enough to make her comply, but combined with the way he was looking at her, she was helpless to obey. She shimmied out of her camisole and shorts. Standing naked before him, Penny should have felt vulnerable, but the look in his eyes made her feel like the most beautiful woman in the world. Or at least the most desired.

"Get on the bed." His command sent chills up her spine. She backed up until her knees hit the bed, and sank onto the mattress.

A shiver spread along her skin. Bones hadn't been like this before. It had been her leading the way in everything they did. He'd let her take control. This was a side of him she'd never seen before. She licked her lips in anticipation.

"Get back on the bed."

When she did as he commanded, his eyes blazed, then dropped over her, making every inch of her body come alive as if he were already touching her.

"We're gonna finish what we started." He arched an eyebrow at her, waiting for her response. When she nodded, a wicked glimmer shined in his eyes. "Close your eyes."

She did, but when she heard the door open, she opened them again. Her eyebrows pulled together in confusion when she saw him leaving. "Where are you going?"

He put a finger to his lips, then pointed at the bed. "Lie back and wait for me."

His stern tone left no room for argument. Penny sank back onto the mattress. It felt odd to be lying naked on the bed alone, but also extremely naughty. Penny felt wickedly turned on. She'd never lain naked on top of a bed anticipating what a man was going to do to her. How he was going to make her feel.

If her memory served her correctly, Bones knew exactly how to make her feel good. Nobody compared to him.

Her skin tingled, and heat burned low in her belly. She closed her eyes, imagining his hands on her body. Footsteps sounded down the hall, then the door opened and closed. Penny opened her eyes and saw Bones coming toward the foot of the bed, a trio of condoms in his hand.

"Where did you get those?"

He tossed them onto the bed and knelt on the mattress between her thighs. "Lou's bedroom."

Tracing a path from her ankle to her calf, he ran his hand up her leg. His fingers were rough with callouses, his palms wide and strong. They were capable hands—hands that made a living on a boat and knew exactly how to touch a woman. The thought of Bones touching another woman made her tense up for a moment.

"Cold?" He trailed his hand up her hip and along her ribcage, teasing the outside of her breast.

Her nipples hardened to tight buds, but she wasn't cold. The windows were open to the balmy breeze, and it was pleasantly warm in the room.

Bones pressed his lips to her belly, making it quiver. He kissed up her belly, his mouth growing more demanding with each nip and suck. His tongue soothed after his teeth nipped, as if he was savoring the taste of her.

His hand went to her inner thigh, and he pushed her legs apart. His hot, rough fingers traced her sensitive skin, trailing higher until she felt the need to squirm closer. He kissed the underside of her breast and then closed his mouth over her nipple and pulled deep. At the same time, his fingers went to the apex of her thighs, and she cried out with the shock of pleasure.

Her hands went to either side of his head, and she held him close as his mouth and fingers made her senses reel. He remembered exactly how to touch her. She worked her fingers into his luxurious hair, loosening it until it tumbled free over his shoulders. He lifted his head and looked at her, his eyes scorching with hunger.

Somehow, he was still fully clothed, wearing his dress shirt and pants, while she was completely naked and spread out before him like a feast. His tongue flicked her nipple, and his fingers stroked up her wet seam. Pleasure stormed through her. His dark hair spilling over his stark-white shirt when he bent his head to her breast was one of the most seductive sights she'd ever seen.

She squirmed against his hand, suddenly needing more. He read her body like an open book and plunged a finger deep inside. He kissed a path up her chest and neck, suckling and biting as his fingers worked magic between her thighs.

When he finally claimed her mouth, she was so ready for his kiss, she came apart as soon as his tongue stroked into her mouth. Bones slid another finger inside just as she tightened and clenched around him.

She'd been craving his touch for so long, it hadn't taken much to drive her wild. As Bones rolled off the bed, Penny felt embarrassed by how quickly she'd come undone. But then she saw him unbuttoning his shirt, and desire rushed in again, crowding out any shame she felt for her embarrassingly quick response.

He slowly undid his belt and unzipped the fly of his dress pants. Her attention was riveted to his body. She was starved for a glimpse of the man she'd dreamed about for years. When he stood naked before her, he was more impressive than she remembered. Every inch of his body was toned muscle, and his heavy erection made her squirm in anticipation.

She remembered what it had been like to have him inside her. No man could compare to Bones. He was the best she'd ever had, and she was going to have him again. And again.

His eyes blazed over her. She'd never felt more desired in her life. He continued to watch her as he came to stand at the foot of the bed and circled his fingers around her ankles. Tugging her to the edge, he used his body to widen her thighs. He rolled a condom over his impressive erection, grimacing at the tight fit.

She shivered at the intensity she saw in his dark gaze. He slowly teased the thick head of his cock back and forth against her sensitive flesh, and an aftershock of her orgasm buzzed through her body. She wanted to take control, to lift her hips and take him deep, but his gaze commanded her to hold still. He was in control this time.

When he pushed the head of his thick cock inside her, she gasped and bucked to get closer. He clamped a hand on her hip and held her down. Pinned to the bed, she was at his mercy.

But they both wanted the same thing. He didn't make her wait as he sank into her inch by inch, slowly filling her up. She'd never felt so needy in her life as when he was fully seated but unmoving. His hands gripped her hips, keeping her from moving when she tried to buck off the mattress.

His dark eyes collided with hers, and she knew it was taking all his strength to not lose control.

He guided her legs higher and wrapped them around his hips as he settled more fully on top of her. She felt him even deeper, stretching to fit his massive size. He kissed her lips, his mouth so soft, it mesmerized her. Bracing his hands on either side of her shoulders, he moved, sliding in and out of her wet heat. Every time he stroked deeper, she thought she was going to lose her mind. He felt so good. So right. He filled her up, taking control of her body and pumping into her with perfectly timed thrusts.

She locked her legs around his hips, and he drove deeper. He was rougher than he'd been before, pounding into her in a way that she knew would make her deliciously sore tomorrow. It was as if he was claiming her. He spread kisses along her neck and chest, sucked her nipple, and laved his tongue over the sensitive peak.

Small, animalistic sounds escaped her mouth, and she clung to his wide shoulders, holding on as he had his way with her. He buried himself inside her over and over, driving her closer to orgasm with every thrust.

The bed creaked and moaned beneath them, and the room heated with their passion. Sweat slicked their bodies, making each thrust slide home deeper. Penny clutched his back, digging her fingers into the firm columns of muscles around his spine. She arched her back, feeling herself spiral out of control as his mouth took hers again in a long, hot kiss.

Her orgasm built in the tips of her toes and raged through her body like a thunderstorm. A tingle spread along her skin, and she felt more alive than ever—more aware of every sound, every scent, and every slide of his hard cock hitting her in the perfect spot.

She clenched and spasmed around him, her body milking his cock like a tight fist. He thrust deep one last time and dropped his head to her shoulder, crying out as he spent his release.

Chapter 41

Bones

EVERYTHING WAS perfect for the wedding. The weather was seventy degrees and balmy, the sky was clear, and the chapel was filled with Keoni's and Lou's friends and family.

"Last chance to jump ship," Bones told Keoni.

"Nah. I'm all good."

They stood at the front of the chapel in their white tuxedos and leis made from ti leaves, ready for the bridal procession to start. It had always been the two of them against the world, but now their world was getting bigger. Keoni had Lou, and Bones had Penny. After last night, sleeping next to her and waking up in her arms, there was no way he was letting her go.

Keoni slid a finger under the tight collar of his shirt. "Is it hot in here or what?"

Bones choked back a laugh. "A little."

Keoni patted his pocket, then looked at Bones with wild eyes. "You got the ring, yeah?"

Bones thumped a hand to his chest where the ring was in his breast pocket. He had two rings in there. One for Lou, and one for later. He was going to propose to Penny again before she had to leave in the morning. He just wasn't sure how he was gonna do it yet.

The music started, and Keoni blew out a breath, turning his attention to the doors. Keoni's parents came out first, looking handsome and beautiful in their formal wear. Bones wasn't used to seeing them in anything more dressed up than shorts and T-shirts or a muumuu, and the change made them almost unrecognizable. They looked proud enough to burst as they took their seats in the front row.

Next came Lou's mother, escorted by one of the ushers. She gave Keoni a frosty smile and sat stiffly on the bench on the other side of the church from Keoni's parents. It was easy to see where Lou had gotten her good looks, but thank God she hadn't inherited her mother's stick-in-the-mud personality.

Tau, Keoni's older brother, strolled down the aisle next. Flashing a grin and the shaka sign, he took his place beside Bones and faced the doors. The only other bridesmaid was Keoni's sister Myra. She was older than Bones and Keoni by a few years and was always bossing everyone around. She beamed at Bones, then narrowed her eyes at Keoni, gesturing for him to straighten his tie.

Bones looked at Keoni's tie. It was a little crooked. "I got you, cuz." He had reached over to fix it when he caught a glimpse of Penny and froze.

She swept into the chapel through the double doors like a breath of fresh air. The beam of light shining through the windows turned her hair to burnished copper and sparkled against her creamy skin. She glided down the aisle with a dancer's grace, her head held high.

When their eyes connected, her smile bloomed. Bones felt something shift inside him. Last night had been more than sex. It had been a sharing of souls.

A loud clang sounded between his ears, and his vision swam.

"Holy shit," he muttered.

Keoni flicked his fingers against Bones's leg. "Shh."

Bones wobbled a little, blinking at Penny as if he couldn't believe his eyes. His heart pounded so loudly in his ears, it drowned out every rational thought. Sweat popped up on his brow, and he felt like he was going to throw up. His knees went weak, and he leaned against Keoni.

Keoni stiffened and shook Bones off with a slight shrug. "What's up with you, brah?"

Bones blinked, trying to clear his vision. His gaze passed over the wedding guests seated in the chairs. Everyone was looking at him with puzzled expressions. His mom's mouth was open in an O, and Pops scowled at him from under thick brows. Kaliah gave him a haughty smirk, and Ryla's eyes were huge in her pixie face.

Bones tried to focus, but all he could see was Penny leaving on a plane in the morning without knowing exactly what their future held.

He stumbled forward, and a gasp went up from the crowd.

"Bones, what's wrong with you, cuz?"

Keoni grabbed Bones from one side, and Tau took the other. They supported him between them, holding him up when he couldn't stand.

He tried to do what he did on a dive—calm his heart, slow his breathing, settle into his panic—but his usual techniques didn't work. All he could think about was losing Penny. When she got on that plane in the morning, she might be gone forever. He had to stop her.

"Chee! Bones!" Tau hissed in his ear. "No act, brah. Get your shit together."

Bones found enough strength to shake them off. "You weren't lying." He fanned his heated face. "It's hot as hell in here."

Keoni muttered under his breath. "You awright? What happened?"

Bones whispered back. "I gotta tell Penny something."

"Now?"

"Yeah."

"Fuck."

"Sorry, brah."

"Make it quick."

Bones straightened his shoulders, took a deep breath, and strode down the aisle toward Penny.

A hush fell over the crowd, and the processional music paused. Penny gasped and stopped walking when Bones marched up to her.

"What are you doing?" She glanced around at the crowd, a confused smile on her face.

"I have to tell you something."

"Now?" She glanced behind her at the double doors, where Lou was due to walk through any second. "Bones," she whispered fiercely, as if every eye wasn't already on them. "What's wrong with you?"

"There's a lot wrong with me. You'll see that if you stick around. First off..." He paused, blinking back tears. He was really doing this, making an ass of himself in front of his family and friends. He was never going to hear the end of it, especially from Kaliah.

"Quicker," Keoni said, urging him from the front of the church.

Bones dropped down on one knee.

A collective gasp went up from the audience. A few people cheered. Keoni whistled.

Penny teetered in her high heels and clutched his shoulders for support. Her eyes filled with tears.

"Will you forgive me for everything?" he asked.

An impatient *boo* came up from the crowd. That wasn't the question they'd wanted to hear. Bones glared at them to settle down and gazed back up at Penny, who was staring at him as if he'd lost his mind—but also smiling.

She squeezed his shoulders and gave a quick nod. "If you forgive me."

His throat felt too thick to speak, so he nodded mutely. He got lost in her gaze and dove deep into her soul, where all the best treasures lay hidden from the rest of the world.

"Will you marry me?"

Her knees buckled, and he stood to gather her in his arms.

"Where's the ring?" someone shouted.

Bones shifted Penny in his arms, took the ring out of his breast pocket, and slipped it on her finger.

"She said yes," he told the crowd.

A loud cheer went up from the audience, and the double doors burst open. Lou rushed down the aisle, her long veil flying behind her in a sparkle of mesh ivory, and threw her arms around Penny.

"Congratulations!" Lou reached for Bones, enveloping him in a sweetly fragrant hug as her flowers were crushed between them.

The guests clapped, and the pianist started a jaunty beat.

Tau whistled loudly from the front of the church, grabbing everyone's attention. When the crowd settled down, he clapped his hands. "You think we can get this show on the road?"

Lou squeezed Bones and kissed Penny on the cheek, then fixed the crown on her head and hurried back to the exit. When the doors closed behind her, Keoni called, "You look beautiful, Nani!"

Lou's laugh sounded from the other side of the door. "Thanks!"

"I can't wait to marry you!" he said.

A chorus of hoots and hollers went up through the chapel. Even Ryla looked humbled by their obvious affection. Everyone was pulling for them except Pops, who had a scowl on his face. Bones was too happy to care. He'd deal with his father later.

He escorted Penny to her place and bent to kiss her cheek before taking his spot beside Keoni.

"I'm gonna need that ring back, brah," Keoni said.

Bones's mouth flew open. "Shit." He patted his pocket and pulled out the other ring. Penny's ring. "One second," he told the crowd and rushed to Penny. "I need that ring back."

Penny's face paled as she twisted off the ring and placed it in his hand.

Bones slipped the other ring on her finger, the one with the huge diamond that he'd spent all his money on from the last coral dive. The light caught the sparkling diamond, making it dance to life.

Penny gasped, holding out her hand to stare at the gorgeous ring. Then, she threw her arms around his neck and kissed him, with tongue, in front of everyone in the chapel.

Keoni cleared his throat and nudged Bones. "Come on, cuz. Enough already."

"Sorry." Bones took a step back, smiling hugely at his new fiancée.

The bridal procession started on the piano. As the guests stood, the doors opened to reveal Lou on the arm of her father. Her gaze was fixed on Keoni, and every person in the chapel felt the connection between them. Even Mrs. Hunter had a stiff smile on her lips.

Lou looked fresh and modern, striding down the aisle in her short dress. Her smile shined with confidence, and Bones couldn't imagine a more beautiful bride.

Except, maybe he could.

He looked at Penny, who clutched her flowers to her chest and smiled at Lou with happy tears in her eyes. Her face in profile was prettier than an angel's. She turned to look at him, and her smile grew. At that moment, it was easy for Bones to picture trading places with Keoni and Lou... that it was Penny's long stride closing the distance between them. Forever.

Chapter 42

Penny

SHE MISSED HIM ALREADY.

It had only been a few hours since Penny had said good-bye to Bones, but she already felt his absence like a chunk of her heart had been torn off.

She would have to hand in her notice at Miss Donna's and find someone to take over her lease until it was up in December, but she'd be back to Hawaii as soon as she could afford a ticket.

Penny swept her gaze around the crowded airport, hoping to be back soon. Part of her wished she didn't have to leave, but she needed to tie up her life in New York. She couldn't leave Miss Donna in the lurch, and all her possessions were at her apartment. She only had the clothes in her suitcase.

"Penny. How are you?"

Penny glanced up at the sound of Heath's voice. Dressed in a navy suit with a crisp white shirt and striped tie, he looked tanned and rested. His eyes crinkled in the corners when he smiled, and he cocked his head to the side, looking as if he were bracing himself for her reaction.

Penny hadn't seen Heath since she'd told his driver to let her off at Lou's villa at the resort. She'd told him he better not show his face at the wedding, and he hadn't. She'd assumed he'd gone back to New York. She squinted up at him under the bright florescent lights. Maybe he hadn't left because he'd had business to finish with his Italian friend.

Her eyes narrowed to laser points, and Heath winced. "I really am sorry about the way everything happened. I should have told you."

Penny lifted her eyebrows at him. "You shouldn't have done it."

Heath indicated the plastic blue seat next to her, asking for permission to sit.

Penny shrugged. "It's a free country."

Heath hitched up his pants and sat in the seat, sighing as if he was taking a load off. "I'm a businessman," he said. "It wasn't personal. I saw a way to give people some money in their pocket and make a chunk of my own. I'm not the bad guy."

Penny crossed her legs and turned away from him. "You should have gone home." The thought of sitting next to him on the plane made her skin crawl.

"Is that what I think it is?" He was staring at the ring on her finger.

Despite her anger at Heath, a small smile lifted her lips. The ring was hard to miss—a marquis cut in an elegant setting. She'd guess it was at least three carats. It was the most beautiful engagement ring she'd ever seen.

"Bones asked me to marry him."

"And you said yes?"

Penny stared at her ring, admiring the way the light caught the cuts in the diamond. "Obviously."

"Are you kidding me?" Heath's high-pitched voice caused heads to turn. "You used me, Penny."

Penny's lips parted in surprise. "How do you figure that?"

"All this about hating him was just a lie. You wanted him back this whole time."

She could see his hackles rise, and it occurred to her that she'd never seen Heath show emotion. Even when he had been telling her how much he cared for her, it had been dry and crisp, delivered elegantly like fine wine.

Had she used him? She'd wanted to make Bones jealous, and she hadn't given Heath's feelings much consideration. Guilt spread through her, a dark stain on her innocence. An apology formed on her tongue.

Heath took her left hand and examined the ring. "How did a guy like him afford a ring like this?"

Penny pulled her hand from his grasp, the apology ignored. "That's none of your concern."

Heath fixed his blue eyes on hers. "You are going somewhere. Your modeling career is ready for you. You're in the prime of your life." He leaned forward, bracing his hands on his knees. "You mean to tell me that you're giving it all up to move to the middle of nowhere to be with a man who has a horrible track record of breaking your heart?"

Her pulse clamored in her throat, a hard thump that made her lose her breath. Suddenly everything seemed clear. She had nothing to give up. Nothing waiting for her. Miss Donna could find another teacher with a snap of her fingers, and there wasn't a thing in her apartment she couldn't live without. Everything she cared about was here. She had Lou, Henry, and most importantly, Bones.

She rose to her feet and grabbed her suitcase. "That's exactly what I'm going to do."

Penny left the airport and took a taxi straight to the marina to find Bones.

His truck was in the parking lot, but *A Hui Hou* wasn't. Penny stared at the empty boat slip as if she could will it into appearance.

"That doesn't work. I tried it."

Penny looked up and saw Claudia coming toward her. She wore a long dress in a sunny yellow, with a high waist that showed off the plump roundness of her belly. Her skin glowed with health, and her sun-kissed hair fell in a cascade of waves over her shoulders.

Claudia was effortlessly beautiful. Without a stitch of makeup on her face, she still looked like the movie star she was. She had a radiance about her, making it hard to not stare. No wonder she was famous.

"You know what does work?" Claudia flashed a conspiratorial smile. "Walking down the beach to get a shave ice."

Penny swept her gaze over the open ocean, willing Bones's boat to come into sight. There was nothing in the horizon except a few sailboats and gentle waves. "All right. I guess a walk down the beach wouldn't hurt."

Claudia nodded approvingly and led the way. "It will be easier without those." She pointed at Penny's knee-high boots, which were perfect for September in New York but maybe not so suited for a walk on sand. "I hardly wear shoes at all these days." She placed her hand on her belly and sighed. "Nothing fits me anymore. Not even my shoes."

Penny unzipped her boots and peeled off her knee-high stockings. She stepped barefoot onto the sand, feeling more confident with her decision to stay in Hawaii by the minute. Even her toes were happier not being confined in tight boots.

"That is the most gorgeous ring I've ever seen." Claudia picked up Penny's left hand for a closer inspection of her engagement ring. "And the proposal was wild." Claudia laughed heartily. "I thought Lou's mom's eyes were going to pop out of her head when Bones dropped to one knee in the middle of the aisle."

Penny laughed, her heart warming at the memory of Bones looking up at her from his kneeling position. He'd been so handsome in his white tuxedo. "It was wild, all right. But Lou's mom was probably more upset about her daughter's wedding dress than my engagement."

"I thought that dress was all the rage. If I had it to do over again, I would have a small ceremony with just me and Henry here on the island. My agent thought it was best to put on a show for the press."

Penny hadn't been able to come to the wedding. She had just moved to New York and couldn't afford a trip all the way across the country to Malibu. "I'm sorry I missed it."

"It's okay. It was mostly for show. Henry and I don't need all that to know what we have." She placed one hand on her belly and smiled sweetly.

A fizzle of excitement for Claudia and Henry filled Penny's chest. It was also a little for herself. She was going to be around for the birth of Henry's baby. "I'm going to shower that baby with everything a little Longchamp could want."

"You'll have to get in line." Claudia laughed. "I never knew a man with more friends than Henry. He just collects people. Everyone on the island adores him."

Henry was pretty easy to love. He'd give someone the shirt off his back. Actually, he had given Penny his shirt one time, when they'd been chased by a swarm of bees. She'd had to take off hers because bees were covering it, and Henry had given her his so she wouldn't have to walk up to the house in her Playtex bra.

They came upon the busy section of Waikiki in front of The Royal Hawaiian, where tourists sprawled on the sand, sipping cocktails with pink umbrellas. Swimmers dotted the blue ocean, and surfers sailed over the gently breaking waves. It was a typical day at Waikiki. The sun was bright, the sky was clear, and a salty breeze stirred the balmy air.

Some of the world's most beautiful people were strolling the beach or wading in the ocean, but Claudia still drew attention. At six months pregnant, she looked like a goddess.

"If you have any sway with Henry at all, please tell him we can't call the baby Gene."

Penny grinned. "That was our grandfather's name," she said. "But I get it. What if it's a girl?"

Claudia wrinkled her nose. "He wants Agatha."

Penny wasn't aware of a relative on her side named Agatha. "Where did that come from?"

"He says he's never dated an Agatha," Claudia said as they entered the busy section of Waikiki, "and he can't call his daughter by the name of a woman he's dated."

Penny burst with laughter. They approached a man with a cart selling flavored shave ice and got in line.

"He's got mango, coconut, and pineapple. What's your flavor?" Claudia asked, eyeing Penny as if the answer were going to determine the future of their friendship.

"I like mango."

"Good choice."

Claudia's approval made Penny glow. She was excited to get to know her newest family member. She'd seen Claudia on television and in the movies for years, and she couldn't help being a little starstruck. But Claudia was just a regular person, a regular person who liked mango.

"Do you think they'll be back soon?" Penny asked as they walked back to the marina. A thrill ran through her at the thought of seeing him again so much sooner than she'd planned. Once he saw her, he would know what she'd done. She could almost see the smile on his stern mouth. They would go back to his place and this time, they'd be sure to lock the door.

"Probably in the next few hours."

Penny's brow creased. She licked her spoon thoughtfully, letting the mango-flavored ice fill her mouth. "I thought their tours were half days," she said.

"They are." As they approached the marina, Claudia excused herself for a moment to take a picture with one of her fans.

While Claudia posed with the tourist, Penny's blood ran cold. A sense of dread settled over her. If the tours were half days, then Bones and Henry should have been back by the time Claudia and Penny had returned to the marina. It was almost two o'clock.

"Why won't they be back for a few more hours?" Penny stared at Claudia. "Why so late?"

"They aren't on an excursion." Claudia smiled and waved at the tourists with their cameras raised. "They went on a coral dive."

A flood of emotions burst inside Penny's chest. She felt rage, disappointment, and fear in one giant wave. Her throat constricted, and her head drummed with her heartbeat.

"Are you okay?" Claudia took Penny's elbow and steadied her. "You look like you've seen a ghost."

Two years ago, Bones had nearly died on a coral dive, and now that day was happening all over again. A cold splash of ice hit her foot, and she looked down to see she'd dropped her shave ice. Mango-colored ice seeped over the sun-bleached wood of the dock, reminding her eerily of blood.

She squeezed her eyes shut as her vision swam. "He said…" Her words trailed off as she tried to breathe. "He said he'd never… He promised." Her legs wobbled, and she sank to her knees.

"Put your head between your knees and breathe." Claudia lifted the heavy curtain of Penny's hair and held it back from her face. "That's it. Deep inhale. Long exhale." She fanned the back of Penny's neck. "How far along are you?"

Penny snapped out of her trance. "I'm not pregnant."

"Well, what the heck is wrong with you? You started babbling something, and you looked like you were gonna pass out." She jabbed a finger at the orange stain on the dock. "And you dropped your shave ice."

"They could die." Penny glared at Claudia. "Don't you care that they're in danger?"

Claudia stretched her legs out in front of her with a sigh. "You do know what your cousin does for a living, right?"

Penny rolled her eyes. "That's different."

"Look, I don't know what to tell you to make you feel better. Do I worry about Henry? Of course I do. He jumps out of speeding cars." A pained expression crossed Claudia's face, and she stared out at the open sea for a long moment.

Penny felt guilty for raising alarm with a pregnant woman. She was so selfish sometimes. "I'm sorry. I didn't mean for you to worry."

"Too late for that." She sighed again and rubbed her belly. "It comes with the territory of loving a man like Henry." Her face relaxed, and she smiled faintly. "But his fearlessness is one of the reasons I love him so much. He wouldn't be Henry without his passion for adventure." She fixed Penny with a pointed stare. "And Bones wouldn't be Bones without the ocean."

Penny focused her gaze on the turquoise water. What had she been thinking, expecting Bones to come to New York? He would stand out like a six-foot-five sore thumb.

"And why do you think he's on a coral dive now, when he hasn't been on one in months?" Claudia raised her brows at Penny, waiting for realization to set in.

She felt like she'd been hit over the head with a hammer. "He's getting money for New York?"

"Nice one, Sherlock." Claudia softened her words with a smile. "He's gonna be okay. Have a little faith."

Silence stretched between them. The only sounds were the call of seabirds and the rumble of boat engines. Claudia took Penny's hand and gave it a gentle squeeze. The knot of fear in her chest unraveled just enough to allow her to take a deep breath. She stared out at the boats approaching the marina, willing the next one to be *A Hui Hou,* knowing she couldn't relax until she saw it coast into the marina with Bones at the helm.

Chapter 43

Bones

THE HEAVY DOWNPOUR started as soon as they reached the channel between Oahu and Maui. Waves rocked the side of the boat as the ocean churned beneath them, and the sky above darkened.

"Do you want to turn back?" Kai had to shout over the splattering rain.

Bones shook his head and guided the boat through the strong current. "I think we'll be through the worst of it in a minute."

By the time they set anchor, the sky was still overcast and spitting rain. The waves were strong enough to rock the boat and splash over the sides. Bones was starting to think he'd been wrong. The worst seemed yet to come.

"You sure this is a good idea?" Henry eyed the waves with a furrowed brow. "Looks a bit rough."

Bones clenched his jaw. He didn't have a choice. He was booked up the rest of the week, and they were already out there. If he didn't dive now, he wouldn't have another chance until next week. The danger wasn't in the water; it was above. If they drifted away from the boat, it was going to be hard to swim in the strong waves.

But Henry was strong and fit, and Bones was experienced at swimming in rough conditions. He dismissed his worry.

"If you're scared, you can stay here with Kai."

Henry grinned and pushed his wet hair off his eyes. "Who said anything about being scared?" He reached for his fins and grabbed his mask. "I've never done this in the rain before. What's it like?"

Bones set his watch and glanced into the rain. The sea was a stormy gray, matching the sky. "You'll see."

They entered the water with a gentle *plop* and slowly drifted down the anchor line. As they got closer to the bottom of the ocean, the churning waves settled into calm, silent waters. The thump of his steady pulse and the hiss of their air tanks were the only sounds.

Schools of fish flashed by in a blur of bright colors, and clusters of seaweed fluttered in the waves. Everything was distorted under water. The colors were more vivid. The sounds were muffled versions of themselves. And his movements were slower, even though his mind was racing. Diving deep was an experience like no other—an experience he was going to miss like a hole in his heart.

Although his thoughts were under the influence of a chemical cocktail of nitrogen and oxygen, he was still sharp enough to remember why he was sacrificing diving.

He was doing it for Penny. And she was worth it. They were worth it.

At the bottom of the ocean, Henry gave him a thumbs-up sign, and they moved in opposite directions. Bones noted the time and moved toward an undulating coral mound in the distance.

He worked quickly and efficiently, focusing intently on his task. When his time was up, he was pleased with his haul. He spotted Henry and noted he'd done just as well. Multiple coral trees bobbed from his float bag line.

A sense of pride and satisfaction filled Bones. He didn't celebrate his accomplishments, but maybe it was time to change that. Everything he ever wanted was his to grasp.

Henry gestured at him, waving his hand to get Bones's attention. They were rising to the surface, stopping to decompress, and Henry always used this time to act out charades.

Usually it annoyed Bones, and he made rude gestures in response to Henry's antics, but he was feeling generous. With an unusual surge of patience, he attempted to decipher what the hell Henry was trying to convey.

Henry was one of a kind. And he was as good as family.

Bones watched Henry's elaborate movements, laughing at the way his bright hair danced in the current. He mimed filming a camera.

"Movie." The word was garbled around Bones's mouthpiece, but Henry nodded in understanding.

Miming getting down on one knee, Henry clasped his hands together in prayer.

Bones shrugged, trying to think of a movie with an engagement in the title. He spotted a rock pile looming behind Henry and pointed for him to watch out. Henry must have thought Bones was trying to guess the second word because he waved his arms dramatically.

His arm hit the rock pile and dislodged a cluster of sea urchins. Henry recoiled, a sound of pain tearing from his throat. A sea urchin was stuck to his wetsuit. One of its spikes had penetrated the suit, and a trail of blood flowed from the wound.

Henry plucked the urchin off his arm and tossed it into the current, but the damage was done. He'd been stung. Bones grabbed Henry's arm and tugged him closer. Although he was bleeding, it didn't look too bad. Bones knew firsthand how a sea urchin's venom felt pulsing though his veins. It was ten times worse than getting stung by a hornet, but it wasn't deadly.

He looked up from the wound to tell Henry everything was okay, but he saw everything wasn't okay. Henry's eyes rolled back, and his body went limp.

Bones grabbed Henry and kicked hard for the surface. He was forced to skip the last decompression stop to save time. He broke through the waves and saw, to his frustration, that the storm hadn't let up, and the boat had drifted. Tucking Henry's chin under his arm, Bones powered through the angry waves. He swam with a desperate sense of urgency. His best guess was Henry was having a reaction to the sea urchin's venom. If he could get him to the boat in time, he knew could save him, but each second that ticked by was a second Henry could die.

When he got close, he yelled for Kai to help him, and together they dragged Henry's unconscious body onto the boat. There wasn't time to dwell on regret; Bones raced into action. He pushed away Henry's wetsuit and felt for a pulse. It was weak and erratic, but it was better than being gone. Surrounding the urchin sting was a rash of red hives. He was definitely having an allergic reaction.

"What happened?" Kai hovered over him.

"Get the first aid kit. Hurry." Bones pushed away his panic and looked Henry in the eye. "It's gonna be okay. You hear me?" He slapped Henry's face. "Stay with me. I got you."

Henry's eyes drifted shut, but he nodded faintly.

Kai came back with the first aid kit and opened it. "What do you need?"

Bones pulled out a small vial and a syringe. He popped the cap off, inserted the needle into the vial, and drew up a small amount of liquid.

Kai sat back on his heels and watched with wide eyes. The rain had let up a bit, but it was still pouring down his face, plastering his hair to his forehead. "Have you ever done this before?"

"Not yet, but I took a class at the hospital."

"You took a class?" Kai's voice was high-pitched and strained.

Bones readied the needle and didn't hesitate any further before stabbing it through the thigh of Henry's wetsuit and depressing the plunger. Time stood still as he waited for Henry to react. Each moment stretched to the next, dragging his heart along with it.

Henry's face was colorless, except for the blue tinge to his lips. Not a good sign. In the first aid class, they'd made it seem easy, but they hadn't accounted for feelings attached to the victim. If Henry died, his child would be born fatherless. Claudia would be a young widow, and Penny would never forgive Bones.

He loomed over Henry, yelling in his face, "Don't you dare die! You hear me?"

When Henry didn't respond, Bones leaned over him and felt for a pulse. Nothing. His heart leaped to his throat, and he tipped Henry's head back, preparing to perform CPR. He fit his mouth over Henry's, and just as he was about to administer a life-saving breath, Henry shoved him hard.

"Why you kissing me, man?"

Bones fell back, fighting a wave of dizziness. "You're okay."

"I feel like I'm gonna throw up, but that's probably because you had your mouth on mine." He made a show of wiping his mouth with the back of his uninjured arm. "Blech."

"Fuck you. I just saved your life." Bones grabbed Henry by the back of his neck and pulled him into a crushing hug. "I'll kiss you if I want to."

Henry struggled against him. "Don't even think about it." When Bones didn't let go, Henry thumped him on the back with a heavy sigh. "Thanks, man."

"You're a tough one to kill," Bones said, finally letting Henry go.

The rain came to a halt, and the clouds parted, revealing the sun.

Kai stared down at them with his hands on his hips. "If you guys are done making out, can I get some help?"

Bones got to his feet and helped Kai prepare to set sail. "Don't get up for a while. I just gave you a shot of adrenaline. You need to rest."

Henry sprawled out on the deck, his arms and legs like a starfish. "Fine with me."

By the time they got within sight of the marina, Henry was back on his feet. "Do me a favor and don't mention any of this to Claudia. I don't want her worried. It's not good for the baby."

Bones nodded, glad to never bring it up again. He'd promised Penny he wouldn't dive, and this was why. If she found out her cousin had nearly died on a dive with him, she would be irate. He planned to never tell her about the dive.

But his plans were shot to hell. The minute they pulled close to the marina, he made out two figures standing near his boat slip. One was clearly a pregnant woman, and the other was a tall redhead.

His heart soared at the sight of Penny. She was the last person he'd expected to see, and after the tragedy averted with Henry, he wanted nothing more than to take comfort in the warmth of her embrace.

He pulled the boat to a stop and hurried through securing it, his gaze straying toward her every few seconds as if he thought she might disappear. When the boat was tied off, he hopped off and ran to her, stopping short of yanking her into his arms.

She threw herself at him, wrapping her arms around his waist and burying her face against his chest. Her slim body, warmed by the sun, pressed tightly to his, her curves fitting snuggly to all his angles. The soft satin of her hair brushed his bare chest, and he felt the wetness from her tears against his skin. He could hardly believe she was here, but the flowery scent of her shampoo tickled his nose, and the sound of her deep inhales as she breathed him in proved she was.

"What are you doing here?"

She pressed a kiss to the top of his chest, her lips warm and wet with her tears. "Waiting for you."

A lump formed in his throat, and he cleared it roughly. "I thought you'd be halfway to New York by now."

She shook her head, tightening her arms around his waist. "I decided not to go back."

His chest swelled, and he stroked a hand down her back, molding her tighter against him. "Does this mean I can cancel my trip to New York?" he asked.

She laughed softly, lifting her face to his. "Yes."

"Thank God," he said, crushing his mouth to hers. She tasted like mango and home. It looked like Hanani's prediction had finally come true.

Epilogue

Bones went out of his way to make every day more romantic than the last. He brought Penny flowers and skeins of alpaca yarn for her newly discovered knitting hobby, and every time he found a penny, he added it to a glass jar in the living room. He said the pennies reminded him of her. The jar was almost full, and so was her heart.

She'd never dreamed she could be so happy. Lou lived twenty minutes away, in the small town of Hale'iwa, and she could see Henry any time she wanted. Baby Agatha had been born a few months ago with a full head of strawberry-blonde hair and chubby cheeks. She looked a lot like Henry's baby pictures and was such a sweet baby, she made Penny wish for one of her own. Someday.

In the meantime, Penny enjoyed her extended honeymoon with Bones. They fell asleep in each other's arms and woke to the gorgeous sunrises. They were blissfully happy.

Except for one thing.

Bones's family still didn't welcome Penny with open arms. They considered her an outsider. At family gatherings, they spoke in Hawaiian Pidgin, which she could hardly understand,

and regarded her with sidelong looks that were less than friendly.

Alana was on her side, but Bones's other sisters would barely speak to her. His mother was decent, but his father stared at her with open hostility. She knew she wasn't what they would have chosen for their only son, but it didn't matter. Bones had chosen her.

Family dinners on Sunday evenings were often strained as conversation flowed over Penny's head without her participation. Dishes were passed with tittering comments about how she might not like the traditional food, and inside jokes were numerous. Penny tried her best to ignore their lack of enthusiasm toward her, but every week the dinners became more of a chore.

One Sunday evening as they were leaving Bones's parents' house, he announced he wanted to change things up. He and Penny would host the family at their house instead. Everyone was invited, but he would understand if they couldn't make it.

Penny had been shocked, and then incredibly nervous as the date of their gathering drew closer. She didn't know what to serve or where they would all fit. Bones's furniture barely accommodated the two of them. It certainly wouldn't do for a large party. And her cooking skills were nothing to write home about.

Bones had assured her not to worry. He would handle everything, including the cooking and the seating arrangements.

A large table had been borrowed, fish had been plucked from the ocean, and side dishes were prepared and frozen during the week leading up to the dinner. Penny had procured the wine and baked brownies—it was all Bones had allowed her to do.

He'd invited Lou and Keoni and Henry's little family, and they'd shoved the living room furniture to one wall to make room for the table borrowed from Makamaka Farm. Bones set the long table with a runner of ti leaves and seashells.

By the time all the guests arrived, Penny was a nervous wreck.

Bones pulled her into the kitchen and trapped her against the counter by placing his hands on either side of her hips. He nuzzled her neck, and she felt a spark of desire shoot through her entire body despite her worry. She tried to swat him away, but it was a half-hearted attempt, and they both knew it.

"Quit!" She gave him a shove. "Your mother is going to walk in on us."

He nipped her jaw, kissing his way to her ear. "Not likely. She's not about to give up holding little Agatha."

"Penny slipped out of his embrace. "One of your sisters, then," she said, glancing toward the hall. Bones's sisters came through his house as if it had a revolving door.

Penny was right, and he couldn't deny it. Kaliah had walked in on them more than once. They'd taken to locking his bedroom door so they didn't get interrupted.

"After everyone leaves, you're all mine," he growled.

"Fine with me." She rose on tiptoe to kiss his cheek as he marched past. They'd been married for six months, but she couldn't keep her hands off him. She wished the dinner was already over and they were in the oasis of his bedroom with the door securely locked.

She watched him walk out of the kitchen with a suppressed sigh. He'd meant well inviting everyone over, and he'd handled all the preparations, but she still wished he hadn't done it. She was so stressed out, it was a wonder she hadn't broken out in a rash.

Claudia came into the kitchen and leaned against the counter. "Can I get a refill?" she asked, holding out her wine glass.

"Sure." Penny pulled a bottle out of the fridge and held it out to Claudia.

She smiled and cocked her head. "Have you got anything stronger?"

Penny rummaged in the cabinet and came up with a bottle of whiskey. She poured Claudia a healthy serving.

"Join me?" Claudia asked.

Penny shrugged and got a glass down from the shelf. "Why not?"

They drank in silence, listening to the low hum of conversation coming from the living room. Laughter and music drifted down the hall. Keoni had brought his guitar, and someone must have talked Bones into playing his ukulele.

Claudia closed her eyes and sipped her whiskey with a contented smile. "I haven't had a moment to myself in months," she said.

"Agatha is a sweetheart."

Claudia nodded. "Luckily she takes after her father." She sipped again. "Henry's already trying to talk me into another baby."

"So soon?" They'd moved to a bigger home on the east side of the island with three bedrooms, and Henry had confided to Penny he wanted to fill it up.

Claudia rolled her eyes, then laughed. "I wouldn't mind a sister for Aggie. But Henry will have a hard time coming up with a name. He's ruled almost all of them out."

"Maybe you'll have a boy." Her voice came out a little sad. She couldn't imagine what it would be like when she and Bones had children. Would his family finally accept her? Or would their children be outsiders as well?

Claudia eyed Penny thoughtfully. "I know it's not easy being all the way out here away from your family." She raised her glass to Penny. "Just know you aren't alone. You've got me and Henry and Aggie. We're your family."

She felt tears coming, and she blinked them back furiously.

"Penny?" Lou's voice sounded from down the hall.

She cleared her throat. "In here."

"Bones sent me to get you. He's pulling the fish off the grill right now." She glanced between Claudia and Penny. "Every-thing okay?"

Penny nodded. "We were just talking about family."

Lou reached for Penny's hand. They were like sisters, and it was good to be close again. After a moment's hesitation, Lou took Claudia's hand as well. The two of them had never been friendly, but Penny had brought them together over the last few months. A truce had been formed, and they'd developed a tentative friendship.

Penny took Claudia's hand and closed the circle.

Acknowledgments

About the Author

Jill Brashear is an author who believes in love at first sight and the existence of soulmates. In her books, you'll find compelling characters, sexy settings, and plenty of happily-ever-afters. She can't imagine a world without dirty martinis (straight-up with blue-cheese olives), hot yoga, and romance.

She loves connecting with her fans! Reach out on any of the social media platforms, and she promises to write you back.

Also by Jill Brashear

The Aloha Series

Try Easy

Try Me

Try Right

The Blue Ridge Book Club Series

Love, Lacey Donovan

XOXO, Valentina